ANGEL 2

Anthony Fields

Lock Down Publications and Ca$h
Presents
ANGEL 2
A Novel by *Anthony Fields*

Angel 2

Lock Down Publications
P.O. Box 944
Stockbridge, Ga 30281

Visit our website @
www.lockdownpublications.com

Copyright 2020 Anthony Fields
ANGEL 2

This is a work of fiction. Names, characters, places, and incidents either are products of the author's imagination or are used fictitiously. Any similarity to actual events or locales or persons, living or dead, is entirely coincidental.

Lock Down Publications
Like our page on Facebook: Lock Down Publications @
www.facebook.com/lockdownpublications.ldp
Cover design and layout by: **Dynasty Cover Me**
Book interior design by: **Shawn Walker**
Editor: **Lashonda Johnson**

Anthony Fields

Stay Connected with Us!

Text **LOCKDOWN** to 22828 to stay up-to-date
with new releases, sneak peaks, contests and more…
Thank you.

Submission Guideline.

Submit the first three chapters of your completed manuscript to ldpsubmissions@gmail.com, subject line: Your book's title. The manuscript must be in a .doc file and sent as an attachment. Document should be in Times New Roman, double spaced and in size 12 font. Also, provide your synopsis and full contact information. If sending multiple submissions, they must each be in a separate email.

Have a story but no way to send it electronically? You can still submit to LDP/Ca$h Presents. Send in the first three chapters, written or typed, of your completed manuscript to:

LDP: Submissions Dept
P.O. Box 944
Stockbridge, Ga 30281

DO NOT send original manuscript. Must be a duplicate.

Provide your synopsis and a cover letter containing your full contact information.

Thanks for considering LDP and Ca$h Presents.

Anthony Fields

Chapter 1

Angel

"Angel, as always, you look great."

"So, do you, James. So, do you," I replied and meant it.

"Sit please and order some food. This is under the radar, but they have the best Mexican food in the DMV. Try either the enchilada Verdes, a tightly rolled tortilla with fresh salad, and grilled chicken sauteed with roasted corn. Or you can try the quesadillas filled with kabob meat, bell peppers, cilantro, onions, ropy lengths of fresh Oaxacan cheese, and your choice of chicken, beef or fish."

"I'm good on the food, James. I'll just have something to drink, then you can stop wasting my time and just give it to me straight. How much money are we losing?"

James smiled. "Still haven't changed, I see. Ten years of doing business with you and you still haven't changed."

Is that a bad thing?"

"Depends on how you want to approach the question. What are you drinking?"

I picked up the beverages menu and read it. "I'll take a Sangria, Virgin."

"Coming right up." James signaled the waiter and ordered that drink and his food. Once the waiter had left, he said, "Your beauty parlors are cash cows that need to be jettisoned. Fast! The hair you're purchasing in bulk from overseas along with all other hair care products are getting more expensive every quarter. You don't charge enough booth rent in any of the salons to recoup the money that you're putting into them. I know the B and B Palaces are your babies, Angel, but they must go. If they don't make dollars, they don't make sense and you know them better than I do. Top of the Line Fashions are holding its own, but it's time to expand and grow."

I thought about what James said and knew that every word of it was true. Money was always good to make. But sometimes loyalty superseded money. "The salon on Queens Chapel Road is operated by the woman that saved my life. Without her quick response and action, I wouldn't be here. The salon feeds her and her children, I couldn't bear to take that away from her. I don't care if that location never makes money. I owe her. Closing the salon on Queens Chapel is out of the question. We can close the other two shops. No problem. Top Of The Line stays close. What's next?

"The communications outlet, Apple, Google, Amazon, and Samsung have become behemoths entities they care nothing for the little guys. They swallow small businesses up whole. Circuit City has gone out of business it is said that Radio Shack is next. Best Buy is soon to follow. Your outlet is not going to survive another year. Cut your losses and sell them. Take all the money made from others' businesses and invest that in real estate. The resurgence of job growth in the US is powering a rebound in the housing market. Home sales in the DMV area are at their highest levels since 2006. Prices have increased from bottoming out three years ago. Government data shows that the economy added twenty thousand jobs last month alone. I have a friend at the National Association of Realtors, she advised me to get into the game now. A healthy job market means that those who buy a house now are less likely to fall behind on their mortgages. More people are able to save for a down payment. Working families—"

The waiter returned with a tray of steaming, hot quesadillas, and the drinks. I sipped my drink as I watched James bite into his quesadilla, chew, and swallow.

He sipped his drink. "Mexican food is a great lunch. Sure, you don't want any?"

"I'm positive. Listen, I'm feeling you on real estate ventures. Put something together and run it by me in a week or two, I'm in. What about the space I wanna lease at the newly opened Center City DC mall? Are they fucking with me?"

James devoured another quesadilla before answering. "Of course, they are. As long as we can pay all the expenses and leasing fees, which we can. I'm waiting on them to give us a date to move in. But there is another thought, Ang."

"What's that?"

"You can't do business at Center City as One of the Line fashions. This mall is upscale. Rodeo Drive upscale. Versace, Alexander Wang, Diane Von Furstenberg and Hermes, all have stores there. You gotta change the name of this one and I have an idea what the name should be."

"Come on with it," I replied as I continued to sip my sangria.

"Modern Vivendi, it's new, it's chic, and it's fresh. It's Latin and it sounds expensive."

"What does it mean?"

"It means. *A way of life*. Clothes should not only be fashionable but represent your way of life. That's the marketing scheme that I've been thinking about. It sounds urban, yet foreign, we bring in student designers trying to break into the game to make our clothes. But we will still feature all the other big names designer lines. That is if we can get them to agree to distribute to us. What do you think?"

As always, James impressed me with his business acumen. The ton of money that they made me legally over the years was undeniable. I walked into the bistro knowing that I would acquiesce to anything James offered. Anything but closing the palace on Queens Chapel road. "I like it. Anything but closing the palace on Queens Chapel road. I like it. As a matter of fact. I love it. Get the paperwork done and then fax it to me for my signature. Take care of the selling of the two salons and get back at me when it's done. I hate to drink and run but I got a prior engagement that I can't miss."

James wiped food off his face with a napkin and then wiped his hands. He stood and we embraced. "I'm glad that you trust me, Ang. I appreciate it."

"Don't mention it, James. In ten years, you have never steered me wrong. Keep it that way and I won't have to kill you."

The color visibly drained from James' face. He opened his mouth to speak but no words came out.

I laughed to break the tension. "Just kidding, James. Damn you didn't think I was serious, did you?"

"I, uh—"

"Stop taking me so seriously. I was joking, I'm out. Call me in a few days." I reached into my purse, pulled out a fifty-dollar bill, and tossed it on the table. "Enjoy the rest of your lunch, it's on me."

I wheeled my Porsche truck through the streets of DC taking notice of all the construction taking place in the city, what James had said about the real estate boom was accurate. I made a mental note to invest in a construction company and purchase some construction equipment to rent out to contractors. I rode through the streets and remembered when they were mine. I remember when I controlled over eight percent of the drug flow in the city. The quintessential queen pen, coronated by none other than the man who controlled everything. Pulling into a parking space in front of the Whitman Walker Clinic, I killed the engine, hopped out of the truck and went inside the building. Ten minutes later, I was walking into my mother's office area.

Her receptionist, Valeria looked up in front of a call and waved, then she moved the phone and said, "Go ahead back, Angel. Your mom is in her office."

I did as I was told and walked into my mother's office.

My mother walked around her desk and embraced me. "Assalaamu Alaikum, baby."

"Wa laikum Assalam. What's up, Ma? How is the non-profit life treating you?"

"Everything is good, Marsha Allah. What brings you to Northwest today?"

"You forgot about our lunch date, didn't you?"

My mother smacked her forehead. "You're right, baby. I forgot all about our mother-daughter luncheon for today. Where are you trying to go? And what are you trying to eat?"

"Anything but Mexican," I told her with a grin.

"I'm not even dressed for a power lunch."

"Cut it out, Ma. You look great and you know it. Stop fishing for compliments."

Nairmah El-Amin gave herself the once over. "I do look okay, don't I? Especially for a fifty-year-old widower Muslim."

My mother was right. For a woman who'd witnessed as much death as she had, her skin remained flawless and her appearance seemed forever young. Her figure was better than mine and only her naturally curly hair betrayed her by showing hints of grey. That grey now converter by a multicolored hijab that matched her Red Bottom heels that I'd gotten her a few months ago.

"Ma, you're a widower because you choose to be and not because you have to be."

"Child, I have no time for anything else. You, my grandbaby, and this foundation take up enough of my time. I'm good. I'm married to this life I'm living, right now. Keeping Adirah's memory alive is my life's work. Speaking of chic, sit down and let me finish watching this graduation. Howard University. We have seen young ladies from the worst neighborhoods in DC that we give scholarships to graduating today. A 100 percent graduation rate and I am so proud of you baby. I was gonna attend the ceremony but changed my mind at the last minute. It's not about time or us as a foundation, it's about them. Wait—here's Michelle Obama."

Michelle Obama spoke for about twenty-five minutes and I hung onto her every word. In all their radiant splendor, the most powerful black woman in the free world gave Howard's commencement speech like a seasoned vet. She encouraged, admonished, advised, and captivated her audience. She was the epitome of the baddest bitch in the world and I respect her. I stared into the faces of all the young women sitting in the audience and remembered when I was them. Young, hungry, and wanting to rule the world. Back then, the only person that believed in me was Fatima Muhammad. My best friend that later betrayed me and snitched on me to the cops. The best friend that I ordered to be killed.

Thunderous applause broke my reverie. Michelle Obama was now replaced by Howard's female president. The matronly woman spoke for a few minutes and then announced the graduating class. I briefly looked at the screen of my phone and checked my messages, then the name I heard next stopped me in my tracks. Slowly, I raised my head to look at the TV screen. I couldn't believe my eyes. My cell phone dropped from my hand. The name, her face. I couldn't believe it was him. Anger rose in my chest and constricted my breathing. "He lied to me! He lied to me! He fucking lied to me!"

My mother's head spun around as if on a swivel. Her eyes bore into me. "Who lied to you? And lower your voice in here. Cursing and carrying on. What the hell is wrong with you? Who lied?"

"My brother? Which one?"

"Uncle Samir, he lied to me about her." I emphatically stated and pointed at the TV.

Confusion etched in my mother's face. "Angel, what the heck are you talking about? Who are you talking about that Samir lied about?"

I stood up and walked closer to the TV. "I'm talking about her, Ma." She had grown a lot and her hair was a different color under her graduation cap, but her features were unmistakable. Riveted to my spot in front of the TV, suddenly I was in another place, in another time years ago—

The Beauty and barber Palace was empty except for a few stylists preparing to leave. All the barbers had left already. After everyone finally left, I was about to turn off all the lights and head for my office when I heard the knock at the door. I peered out the door to see who was knocking. I assumed it was the homebody who had left something, so I saw the girl and opened the door. She had been in the salon earlier.

"What's up, baby? Did you forget something?"

"Can I come in and talk to you? I need some help."

I opened the door wide enough for the girl to enter the shop. "Sit down. What help do you need?"

"I'ma a little thirsty. Can I have something to drink?"

"Sure. I have some Aquafina waters in the fridge. I'll be right back." I left and got two bottles of water. When I came back into the room, she was holding a gun and it was pointed straight at me. Then I saw the tears that ran down her face right before the explosion and gun blast knocked me up against a wall. I could see the young girl's body buck from the force of the gun in her hands. She shot me again and again until I slid down the wall and hit the floor, I could feel the burning sensation shoot through me. My entire body

warmed up instantly but all I could think about was my child. The baby growing inside me was going to die with me. Tears fell from my own eyes. As I forced my eyes wide open, I stared at the girl who now stood over me.

The last words I heard were, "That's for my father!"

"Angel! You're not making sense. Who is the *her* you're referring to? Who did Samir lie about?"

"Her, Ma," I said again and pointed at the TV screen. "The girl talking at the podium, right now. That's her, the one that I told you about years ago. She's Tony's daughter—"

"That's the little girl that shot you that night?"

I nodded my head. "They said I died that night."

"I know, baby, I was there. Remember?"

"And the paramedics fought to save my life, I remember seeing Phylicia, one of my stylists sitting in the ambulance holding my hand. Then things sorta faded to black. I hovered somewhere between life and death and I had a vision. All the people that I killed surrounded me. They spoke to me, but I could not hear what they were saying. When I woke the next morning, Uncle Samir was at my bedside. His face was a mask of pain.

His voice was strained as he asked, *"Who did this to you?"*

"Tears fell down my eyes as I asked about the baby."

"She's alive and well. A little premature, but unharmed. Alhamdulillah! The baby's in an incubator down the hall in the nursery. Your mother is there with her. She's been at her side since they ripped her from your womb. Listen, Angel, I was in Larton when your sick, perverted father did what he did to you and Adriah. Once I learned of his sins, he was already dead. May Allah roast his old skins and give him new ones to roast and roast them, too. I couldn't protect y'all then and I'm doing a poor job of it now—"

"Uncle Samir—"

"Who did this to you? Let me ensure that they never live to tell about it. Do you know who shot you?"

"I do," I mumbled. *"I know who it was."*

"Who was it? Tell me so that I can kill them."

"Her name is Honesty. Honesty Phillips."

"Her? The person who shot you was a woman?"

Shaking my head, I swallowed the saliva in my mouth. "A little girl. A young girl. She has to be at least fourteen."

"Angel are you high on pain medicine? Are you delusional?"

"No, she thinks I killed her father. I was charged with his murder but I beat it."

"Where am I to find this girl?"

I told my uncle everything I knew about Honesty Phillips and her mother Tina.

"Don't worry yourself. You just get better, the girl is as good as dead.

"With that said, I went back to sleep, comfortable in the fact that the girl wouldn't get away with what she did to me. I believed Uncle Samir when he said he'd kill her. After that night, I can't be sure how many days passed but Uncle Samir was at my bedside again. He told me that it was done. That he had killed the little girl. I believed him, I had no reason not to. But now I know he lied. Your brother, my uncle, he lied."

"Angel, are you sure it's her?"

I stared at the TV at the beautiful face that filled the screen. There was no mistaking who she was. "I'm positive it's her, ma. She's all grown up but it's her. And I can't believe it. I can't believe she's still alive. After all, she did to me and almost killed my daughter. I can't believe Uncle Samir would put my life in jeopardy like that. Here, I've been walking around everywhere and living my life not thinking one of my biggest enemies is still amongst us? How could I have seen it coming? Eight years. Eight whole years and I could've been ambushed and killed I'd have been dead because my lying ass uncle—"

"Angel, your mouth. You will respect—"

"I respect you, Ma. It's your brother I don't respect. He couldn't kill the teenage girl and that's all he had to say. I would have respected and accepted that then hunted her ass down and killed her once I was all the way healthy."

14

Angel 2

Like the sun setting in the West, my mother's face darkened. "Samir couldn't kill a teenage girl, but you could? You could do that, couldn't you?"

"I could and I would have. But that's neither here nor there because that teenager has grown up. She has to be at least twenty-two-years old now. I can definitely kill a twenty-two-year-old. She was never supposed to see twenty-two. That's why you never send a man to do a woman's job. That's what I always say."

"Angel please leave that woman alone. She just graduated from college, her life is different now. Let it go!"

"I can't let it go, Ma. I can never forget the look on her face as she stood over me and shot me. Then she spit on me. She spit in my face. She started this beef and I gotta finish it. I can't sit around and wait for her to decide that she wants to finish the job. I can't take the chance that something might happen to you or Aniyah."

"Sometimes I can barely recognize the child I raised. What makes you so vindictive, Angel? Why must you see so much reinventing? How did you become so ruthless and vicious? What gives you the desire to kill?"

"When I was a little girl I was repeatedly raped by my father. Is that answer enough for you?"

A single tear rolled down my mother's cheek. "Your father's spirit haunts us still. All I can do is pray for you. Ask Allah to change your heart. What about the risks? What about the life you've established since she shot you? Your business? What about Aniyah? Have you no understanding? We need you. What if that girl kills you this time? How can I tell Aniyah that her mother is gone? What if you get caught and go to jail?"

"Ma, I hear you. Trust me, I do but nothing you say will dissuade me from the path that I must take. Let the pieces fall where they may. But that girl has gotta go, she's on TV graduating college. She's forgotten all about me."

"Let him, handle it," her mother pleaded.

"Allah has enough stuff to do already, I'll handle Honesty."

My mother's face showed defeat. "Bring me my grandbaby. If something happens to you, she'll be safe. And I'm gonna have to decline lunch. Suddenly, I've lost my appetite."

Chapter 2

Angel

I couldn't get Honesty's face out of my head. I saw her as both a young girl and a woman. A woman who appeared to be harmless, but was in fact, a natural-born killer, just like me. After being told by my uncle that he had taken care of my problem called Honesty. I never gave her another thought. Just like I did all the other people who had crossed my path and died. But now, knowing that she's alive made me wonder whether or not she knew I was alive? She had to have followed up on the news or something and saw that she had failed to kill me.

Maybe she was waiting for me to surface so that she could try again. Maybe she thought I was dead. Maybe. Maybe never sat well with me. The only definitive way to ensure that Honesty never came for me again was to put her six feet in the ground. Even though I haven't killed anybody in almost nine years, it didn't matter. Killing was like driving a car, you never forget how to do it. I have not been in the streets for years physically, but I still always kept my ears to the ground.

I knew who was moving and shaking, who was in jail, and who had met their demise in the hoods. I knew that the whole drug scene in D.C. had changed literally overnight. There was little to no street corner hustling anymore. Drug dealing had evolved and almost all business was conducted by phone. From the big boys, all the way down to the small-time hustlers. If a crackhead wanted a dime rock, they called the dealer, met somewhere, and transacted the sale. Although the method of drug dealing in D.C. had changed the game was still controlled by the same people.

Carlos Trinidad's organization was still at the top and the dudes I dealt with back in the day were either dead or locked up, only a selected few remained. I drove through the streets of Southeast in search of one of them now. I called out a number and told the voice to activate the system inside my truck to call it. Seconds later, the phone rang inside my speakers.

"Hello?"

"Nome?"

"Yeah, what up? Who dis, Angel?"

"How did you now?" I asked.

"I know your voice. The way it sounds is unique."

"And how exactly does my voice sound, Nomoe?"

"Unique and angelic. But we both know how deceptive that can be. What's good, boo? I ain't heard nothing from you in years."

"What can I say? I was busy."

"I can dig that. So, what's up? Because whenever you call a nigga out of the clear blue, it's either you got something for me, or I got something you need. What is it?"

"You've always been really perceptive. You possibly have something I need. I'm tryna come through and holla at you. Are you still around Condon Terrace?"

"Naw we are on Sixth Street now, Sixth and Chesapeake."

"Are you there, right now?"

"Naww, but I can be there in about ten minutes."

"Good, because I'll be there in about eleven or twelve minutes. I'll see you there, I'm in a red Porsche truck."

"Red Porsche truck. I got you. See you in a minute, I'm gone."

"Disconnect," I said aloud and the system ended the call.

Nome had grown a lot thicker in the few years that I hadn't seen him, but it was good to see that he was still getting money. He leaned on a silver Mercedes S600, dressed in a Louis Vuitton T-shirt. He spotted me as I pulled down Sixth Street and came to a stop in front of him. Nome walked to the truck and hopped in, I pulled off and drove around.

"What's good, Kareemah? You look good."

"So, do you, Nome. I see you put on a few pounds?"

"I know, huh?" Nome said and rubbed his stomach. "It's the lifestyle. Clubbing, fucking, and eating too much. That's all hustlers do nowadays, but enough about that. You didn't come all this way to the hood to chit chat. You said I might possibly have something that you need. What's that?"

"Some shit from the past has resurfaced and I need to take care of it, but I need some guns. Do you still have access to that connection you used to have.?"

"Not the old one, but I gotta get a new one. To survive in these streets, a good man gotta keep a line on major weapons. I gotta military nigga. A white boy strung out on coke that's stationed at Bolling Air Force base. Whenever I need him, he can get what I need?"

"No big shit. Just some handguns. About three or four of them, brand new in the box. No cheap shit like Larkins, High points, or Stats. I'd prefer Rugers if he can get them. And I need at least one of 'em fitted for a silencer. I need a couple of silencers and boxes of bullets. Hydra Shocks if he can get 'em. I got ten-grand for you if you can make it happen."

"Ten racks for that little bit of shit? You damn right I'ma make it happen. When do you need all of it?"

"Yesterday," I told Nome emphatically.

"Drop me off at my cat and I'm on it, right now. I'ma call the number on my phone later today and let you know what's good. That's cool?"

"Of course, that's cool. I'll be waiting and give my regards to Pepper."

"No doubt."

"Oh? And one more thing. Did Wop ever come home off that beef from years ago?"

Nome looked at me quizzically, "What Wop? Kenilworth Wop?"

"Naw, Lil Wop from Congress Park. Used to be in the circle."

"Oh, that Wop. Yeah, shorty came home. He's up the *Pearl* getting money."

"Okay. I have to go and holla at him soon. Call me."

Nome hopped out of the truck and went to his car. I pulled off and headed to get my daughter.

"Assalamu Alaikum, Sister El-Amin," Jamilla Akbar, the principal of the Islamic Village Learning Center, greeted me as I walked through the entrance of the school.

"Wa-Alaikum, As-Salaam," I replied in response.

19

"Your daughter is a really bright student, sister. Just wanted you to know that."

"All praise is due to Allah, but then what's left goes to you and your staff here."

"Marsh' Allah. Let me go and get Aniyah for you."

A few minutes later, my daughter burst into the room. "Mommy!" she called out excitedly.

My heart melted every time I laid eyes on Aniyah. It had only been about eight hours since I'd seen her last, but it felt like weeks. Dressed in a tan shirt, navy skirt, and Ugg boots, Aniyah leaped into my arms. A navy hijab struggled to contain all her thick, unruly curls.

"Hey, baby. I missed you."

"Me too, Mommy. I learned a third of the Quran today, Mommy. All in one surah. Wanna hear it?"

"Of course, I do, baby. Let me hear it."

"It's surah ikhlas and it goes—Qulhu-Allahu ahad—Allahu Samad-lam-yalid, was lam yu lad, wa lam ya kullahu, kufu wanahad."

"That's great, baby. You recite it well. I'm so proud of you."

"Proud enough to eat Chick-Fil-A for dinner?" Aniyah asked and smiled.

I lowered my daughter to the ground. She was growing up so fast and she was getting heavy. I returned her smile and said, "Proud enough to let you eat Chick-Fil-A for dinner."

"Thank you, Mommy. But you can't tell grandma."

"I won't if you don't. Come on, let's go."

***

I sat in the booth inside the Chick-Fil-A restaurant and watched my eight-year-old daughter devour a spicy, chicken, ranch sandwich, potato wedges, and juice. I couldn't help but laugh at her. "You were really hungry, baby."

"I know, it's because I skipped lunch," Aniyah said.

"And why did you skip lunch?"

"Because Anya, Halimah, and Samiyah are supposed to be my friends and all they do is talk about their fathers around me. Anya' father is an assistant Imam at Masjid Al-Nur in Glenarden, Halimah's father is a manager for an IT company in Virginia and Samiyah's dad owns his own restaurants in D.C. and Maryland. They've talked about it so much that I know everything by heart. They know that I don't have a father—"

"Aniyah, you do have a father, baby. He's just not here for you."

"Like I said, then Mommy, I don't have a father and they know it. I believe they are just trying to make me feel bad because of it and I refuse to do that. So, I skipped lunch."

"But why skip lunch? Why not just stay away from Samiyah and company?"

Aniyah gave me a look that I swear reminded me so much of her father that it scared me. "Mommy, the way our lunch break is set up, all the girls have to eat together. There's no way to avoid them."

"I'm sorry, baby."

"It's okay, Mommy."

"No, it's not okay Aniyah. If this situation makes you skip lunch."

"Well, who is my father, Mommy. And what does he do? Why doesn't he want to know me? Does he hate me? If so, why?"

I looked into my daughter's eyes and my heart broke for her.

"Your father's name is Carlos, baby. He's a businessman from Puerto Rico. I met him here and fell in love with him. But before you were born, he had to go back to Puerto Rico. I was pregnant with you and didn't even know. We lost contact with each other and he never knew you existed. But that's my fault, baby. Not his, if he knew about you, I'm sure he would be here with you, for you. I know he would. And no, he doesn't hate you. He just doesn't know that he has a daughter as beautiful and smart as you here, That's all."

"Mommy, where is Puerto Rico?" Aniyah asked me.

"Puerto Rico is an island, baby, a couple of hundred miles off the Florida Coast."

"Can we go and find him one day? Tell him that I'm his daughter?"

"Sure, we can, baby. Sure, we can."

***

"What can I say to you to change your mind?"

I put the last of my daughter's clothes in a rolling carry-cart. "Ma we already discussed this. My mind is made up, the girl was fourteen-years-old when she tried to kill me about her father. If she knows I survived that night and should see me somewhere—out at the grand opening of my new store in Center City, D.C. What if she tries again? Right now, she has to be twenty-two or twenty-three. She has to hate me more today than she did back then. I can't take the chance of letting her live. I just can't."

"And there's no way you can just reach out to her and talk to her? Tell her that you didn't kill her father? Broker a peace between y'all without having to kill that woman?"

"The answer to every one of your questions in no, Ma."

"Aniyah? Come on down here so that we can leave!" My mother shouted.

Seconds later, my daughter ran down the stairs and hugged me tightly. "Don't forget about what you said earlier, Mommy. Me, you, and Puerto Rico."

"I won't, baby. Have fun over Grandma's house."

"What's all this talk about Puerto Rico?" My mother asked.

"Can we go there when you get back?" My daughter asked.

I hugged both my daughter and my mother. "Y'all have a safe trip. Call me when y'all get home."

***

One of the best things ever created was the Internet. In order to kill Honesty, I had to check on and eliminate the one person who would suspect me in her death. The detective that investigated her father's death, Sean Jones. I thought about the last time I'd seen the detective. It was right after I beat all the murder charges that the city tried to convict me of.

"Hello, Ms. Angel."

"Do I know you?" I asked.

"I'm the detective who investigated the murders of Anthony Phillips, Dearaye James, Ronald Fletcher, and Thomas Murphy. You know, all the people you killed. I just want you to know that even though you walked away Scott free on those charges, you'll kill again. Psychopaths like you always do. And I'll be there to catch you. I'll personally see to it that you get the needle for it. I don't care how long it takes, I'm devoting the rest of my career to bringing you down. So, enjoy the fresh oxygen that you're breathing because one day, you'll be breathing recycled air that bounces off the walls of a jail cell. On your way to that chamber where the lethal injections will be waiting for you."

Using my phone, I went to Google and typed in three names, Detective Sean Jones, Tina Brown, and Honesty Phillips. I quickly learned that Sean Jones was still with the P.G. County Police Department, but he was no longer Detective Sean Jones, he was now Captain Sean Jones. I poured over all the info the net had on him, memorizing it. Google linked me to various social media websites for Honesty. She had very active accounts with Facebook, Instagram, Twitter, LinkedIn, Tumblr, and a few others. For the next hour or so, I viewed all her pictures and stole all the comments posted for her on each site.

I copied and paste, and sent everything to my wireless scanner, printer. There was a collage of photos on her Facebook page, Photos of her father and mother, her father and her, and one of all of them together. I felt like a vicious stalker, but I kept them to print. The ones of her father, Tony Bills, especially gave me pause. I had actually forgotten how truly handsome Tony was. I thought back to all the times we'd spent together and then eventually the day that I blew his brains out. Killed him for his cash and his pot in the drug game.

Back when I was young and dreamed of running the world. I saw that Honesty's mother, Tina wasn't on any social media sites but Google search did give me a work and home address for her. I checked the address that I had for Honesty and saw that the address was the same. I then Google Mapped the address and Google earthed in it to see exactly what the house looked like. A Mercedes SUV was parked in the driveway next to the house. I printed all the information I'd found. I laid across my bed and stared at the ceiling. In the blink of an eye, my whole life had changed.

Twenty-four hours ago, all I cared about was starting my new businesses and raising my daughter. Now, my main objective was to kill Honesty Phillips. The old me was slowly coming back. I could feel the thirst for blood taking over me. I could hear the roar of the animal that laid dormant inside me, now awakened. A side of me long suppressed, was surfaced and I didn't know if that was good or bad. Remembering the person that I used to be made me think about all the men in my life. Almost all of them I had killed I thought about Andre Ford breaking me in. I thought about Tony Bills and the Twins Deataye and Deandre. All of them were pretty good in bed. The thought of killing and sex made me horny. Suddenly, I was reminded of the fact that I hadn't had sex in years. Unbuttoning my pants, I reached inside my panties and rubbed my clit. In seconds, my pussy was soaking wet and my clothes felt restricted. I totally undressed and did something else that I hadn't done in years. I played with my pussy until I came hard and loudly.

After I made myself cum one more time. I got up and walked to the dresser. Standing in front of the mirror, I stared at my reflection. At thirty-two-years old, I still looked nineteen. Time had definitely been kind to me. My 5'3 frame still held my one hundred and forty pounds well. My hips and ass were still exactly the same. My breasts were small, but they were still perky, not saggy. Caramel with dark brown nipples that swelled up to the size of tootsie rolls when touched. I traced the scar that ran from my navel to my pelvis, then the ones on my side, shoulder, and chest. Scars from the gunshot wounds that Honesty had put there the night she tried to kill me. Tried and failed. That was good for me and bad for her. Because she'd never get that chance again.

Angel 2

***

Early the next morning I was awakened by my cell phone vibrating on the dresser. I reached it in time to catch the call. It was Nome.

"I got everything that you asked me for!" Nome said.

"That's great. When can I come and get it?"

"The early bird catches the worm. I'm out and about. Call me when you're ready to meet and pick it up."

"Give me about an hour to get myself together and I'll call you when I'm close."

"That's a bet. I'm out." Nome hung up.

I tossed the phone in the bed and walked naked to the shower. It was exactly what I needed.

***

"Nome, do you still ride a motorcycle?"

"Yeah, I gotta get a new joint. The Kawasaki 1900 SR."

"Are you trying to make another quick ten-grand?" I asked.

"Always. Why what's up? What do you need this time?"

"Are you and Wop from the park, friends?"

"Naw, not really. Why?"

"Because he threatened me some years ago and I don't appreciate it."

"I hear you but what does that have to do with me?"

"This is what I need you to do."

***

"You're sure he's outside the rental office?" I asked before putting the helmet over my head and face.

"I'm sure, I just rode through there a few minutes ago. There's a small crowd around him, though. A few dudes I recognized, a few I didn't. The streets have been harassing niggas in every hood. They on some straight-up *stop and frisk shit* like New York. So, I'm thinking maybe them niggas ain't strapped out there. Not on that hot ass corner. But I could be wrong. I think you should work a choppa and just drive by as opposed to you walking up on him, but the choice is yours."

"Doing a drive-by won't ensure his death. And I'm not tryna come back for his head a second time. I'ma do it like I told you. If somebody returns fire, it is what it is. We pull up, I jump off the bike and do me. Then I run back and hop on, you hightail it outta there. Simple as that. You ready?"

Nome nodded and then put his helmet on. He lifted the visor and said, "It's your circus, I'm just a clown performing in it. Let's roll."

I hopped onto the back of Nome's Kawasaki and wrapped my arms around his waist. The Ruger behind my back was hidden by my jacket. Before Nome could start the bike engine, I tapped his back.

"What's up?" He asked.

"You didn't tell me what Wop was wearing. I haven't seen him in years, I wanna make sure I get him."

"I believe he had on jeans. Yeah, blue jeans and a grey Hugo boss shirt, and New Balance."

"Dreads? Plaits? Any hair at all?"

"Naw, he rocking a low haircut."

"Okay, let's do this."

As the motorcycle approached 13th and Congress Street I spotted Wop leaning on the black cast iron gate that encircled the rental office building at the entrance to the circle. He was dressed exactly as Nome had said. In his hand was a dark green bottle that he occasionally switched from every now and again.

"Enjoy your last shot of Remy, Wop."

There was only one dude around Wop now. A tall, dark-skinned dude dressed in similar attire as Wops'. Two pretty, young females were their audience. Nome slowed the bike as I reached behind me and extracted the Ruger. Right in front of Wop, the bike stopped completely. Trying my best to conceal my weapon, I hopped off the bike and approached the sidewalk. By the time it registered in Wop's mind what I was up to, it was too late.

He dropped the bottle just as I swung the gun up and fired simultaneously. The bottle of Remy hit the ground and shattered into pieces as my first bullet found Wop's face. The dude and two females scattered immediately. Wop's head snapped back, but his body was held in place by the gate. I kept firing the Ruger into his chest and neck until he fell forward. Calmly, I walked back to the bike and hopped on. Nome took off down the street and raced the bike to safety miles away.

About thirty minutes later, Nome and I stood beside my truck. "Here's the ten grand I promised you."

Nome accepted the stack of bills and pocketed them. "Man, your shit is wicked. I heard about your gun game and all the muthafuckas that you were supposed to have murked back in the day, but to witness your fine ass in action is truly a work of marvel. I'd hate to be beefing with you."

"Well, never do then and you'll be good," I replied and smiled as if I was joking, but I was literally dead serious. "But listen I got another dude that I need to touch, and I might need you again. Are you down with that? I'm paying the same thing."

"Shid this was the easiest ten stacks I ever made. I can always use another ten to go with this one. So, holla at your boy when you need me."

A'ight. That's a bet. You are cool," I said and got into my truck.

I watched Nome rev up the engine on the Kawasaki and fishtail the back wheels before taking off down the street as if he was shot out of the Ruger now under my leg. Two days later, I made my next move.

***

The Prince George's County Courthouse is alive with activity. The most talked about trial in the state of Maryland was underway and I had a great seat in the gallery along with about one hundred other people. Michael Johnson the man that P.G. Authorities dubbed the *Repairman Killer* was standing trial for the murders of five suburban housewives over a three-day period.

Usually, a story such as that would never have created so much publicity, but race had a way of making a 4x6 picture appear to be an 8x9 blow up in no time. Johnson was black and all his victims were white. According to the newspapers, the DA's Office had an airtight case against Johnson. From my seat, I spotted the man who I had come to find. Captain Sean Jones was the lead detective on the Johnson case and was scheduled to testify in a few minutes. It was amazing what one could learn from the internet. I watched Sean Jones, who looked visibly older. His hair was cut low but peppered with grey. He wore a dark suit and shirt, but his lavender tie stood out in contrast. The more I stared at him, the more I remembered him. I remembered the first time we met after I killed Tony at the apartment and our last encounter, the day he threatened me.

"Let's see if you can investigate your own murder after you die," I said softly to myself.,

An hour and a half later, I called Nome's home. "Be ready to scoop me from in front of the court building in about ten minutes." I disconnected the call and followed Sean Jones out of the court-room.

He took an escalator down to the lower level and headed for the garage. I was on his heels. Just as Sean Jones stepped on the elevator and the doors closed, I stuck my hand between the doors. They opened back up automatically. Once on the elevator, I asked the cop to hit the garage button.

"I already did," he replied. "That's where I'm headed.

The elevator's bell sounded and the doors opened. I let Sean Jones exit the elevator first, then I stepped off. Ducking down beside a car to the left, I retrieved the bag that I'd left there earlier. In it was the Ruger with a silencer attachment screwed onto its barrel. Skulking through the maze of cars, it didn't take me long to catch up to Sean Jones. As he stopped in front of a silver Lincoln SUV and fished inside his pocket. I appeared behind him. Not knowing if he was wearing a vest or not, I aimed at the cop's legs and opened fire. My bullets found their mark and Sean Jones collapsed to the ground. The look on his face was one of pure terror as he grabbed at his legs. He pulled back bloodstained fingers. I inched up closer to him.

"You should've left well enough alone eight years ago, Detective. Oh, my back, I mean Captain."

"Who are you?'" Sean Jones asked meekly. Pain etched across his face, mixed with shock and fear.

"Don't recognize me, huh? Well, it's me, the woman you promised to spend the rest of your career bringing down."

"Kareemah El-Amin," Sean Jones muttered. "Angel"

"That'll be me, Captain Jones. You should've arrested me when you had the chance. Because now you'll never get that chance again."

"You shot me!" Sean Jones hollered suddenly.

"No, captain, I killed you," I replied and shot Sean Jones in the forehead. I walked up on him and made sure that he was dead.

Having already scouted out the garage, I knew there were cameras placed in different areas of the garage. I quickly went to one of the many blind spots and pulled off the black Washington Nationals baseball cap and black nylon wave cap that covered my cornrowed braids. I unzipped the black sweater hood exposing my black sports bra. Next, I kicked off the tan, butter Timberlands boots, and jeans. I dressed quickly in a grey Morris Brown sweatsuit and pulled the throwback Jordans' from the bookbag. Once I was dressed, I threw the Louis Vuitton backpack over my shoulder and walked out of the garage through a side exit. I walked down a side street and bent the corner until I saw Nome's Benz parked at the curb of the entrance to the courthouse. I walked up to it and slipped inside.

"Did you find the dude you were looking for?" Nome asked.

Letting the backpack fall from my shoulder, I leaned back in the seat and said, "I sure did." Then I reached up and started undoing the cornrowed braids in my hair.

Chapter 3

Angel

"Prince George's County residents are in shock tonight as they grieve and mourn one of their own. A decorated twenty-two-year member of the P.G. Police department was brutally gunned down inside the garage of the P.G. County Courthouse earlier today. Authorities were called to the scene of a man found dead inside the garage a little before noon. Upon arriving at the scene, P.G. Police discovered that the deceased man had been shot numerous times in the face, head, and body. It didn't take long before the man's identity was revealed.

"The victim has been identified as Captain Sean Jones, a supervisor in the department's Homicide Division. The decorated officer was forty-two years old. Authorities are investigating the homicide and ask that if anyone has any information about this heinous crime, contact D.C. Crime Stoppers at 202--727-1900—In other news today, outrage over D.C. Mayor's Mary Bowser's anti-crime plan escalates.

"The Mayor's controversial effort to address this year's spike in homicide by allowing law enforcement officials to perform warrantless searches of violent offenders appears likely to die in the D.C. Council. At a hearing today, council members, legal experts, and scores of residents blasted the plan, which would require those serving sentences for violent crimes to consent to speed up searches as a condition of early release. They saw that Bowser's effort to focus on those who police say are most likely to commit new crimes would backfire and further erode trust between law enforcement and residents in the city's most crime-stricken neighborhoods—"

My phone vibrated as I clicked the T.V. off and went to check on my Peruvian Chicken and fries that warmed in the microwave. I scooped up the cellphone as I walked into the kitchen. The caller was Nome.

"What's up, Nome?"

"Did you happen to catch the news?" he asked.

I detected a little panic in Nome's voice, but I could have been wrong. "I caught it. Why? What about it?"

"You didn't say anything about offing no pig, homegirl."

"I have no idea what you're referring to. Who offered a pig?"

"Don't fucking' play me like I'm stupid, Angel. I know—"

"Listen why don't we meet somewhere and talk. These jacks are—well you know what I mean."

"Cool. Do you know where Uncle Julio's Mexican restaurant is in Arlington?"

"I know exactly where it is," I responded.

"Meet me there in one hour. I'll be inside the restaurant waiting for you."

"I'll be there. And Nome—don't forget to take deep breaths, baby boy. It's gonna be a'ight," I joked to lighten the mood.

"One hour, Angel. Uncle Julio's, peace."

I disconnected the call and dropped the phone on the table. All the while shaking my head and thinking that I might have to kill Nome. I grabbed my food out of the microwave, stood beside the kitchen counter, and ate. I could barely taste my food because my mind was elsewhere.

Nome was at the back of the restaurant sitting alone in a booth by the wall. I walked to the booth and scooted into it. After placing my purse on the table, I looked Nome straight in the face and said. "Whew, it's muggy as shit outside and I don't ever remember it being this hot in the evening in the city."

"Global warming," Nome stated. "It's a killer. And speaking of such, why didn't you tell me you were killing a cop?"

"You wanna help the whole place know what you think I did?" I expected the cops to jump out from all over the restaurant at that point.

Nome was visibly flustered. "My bad," he said, lowering his voice. "That was foul, Angel. You should've told me that you were gonna smoke a pig."

"Didn't you get paid just to just drive the getaway car?"

"Yeah, but damn—"

"Damn, what? What the fuck? I told you exactly what you needed to know. I did what I needed to do, and you got paid for your services. So, what the fuck are you mad about?"

"You should've given me the option—"

"*Option!* Slim, are you on a pill or some shit? The less you know the better. All you know is that you picked up a friend at the courthouse and that's it. I did you a favor by not using you with the whole lick. I protected you. Had you not seen the news and put two and two together, what difference would it make? And what the fuck is up with you anyway? Calling a bitch all shook and shit? You scared, nigga?"

"I ain't never scared, boo. Just cautions, I'm older now. I like to be informed about what I'm getting into, that's all. If I'ma be your codefendant on some shit, I want the choice of whether I'm trying to be on the case. What's shook about that?"

"I feel that, but shook is you calling my muthafuckin' phone ranting and raving about some shit that just happened and is being investigated. Phones are being monitored and conversations inter-cepted and all that shit. That's bad behavior."

"Call it whatever you want. I didn't appreciate you keeping me in the blind."

"*In the blind?* Did you hear anything I just said? You know what? Fuck it, what's done is done. It's water under the bridge. We are sitting here arguing about milk that's already spilled."

"What if some cameras caught you on the act and they traced you to my car?"

"Not going to happen. I cased that garage days before. I knew the layout. I knew exactly where the cameras were. I did what I had to do, and nothing can be traced to you, I promise you that. And it if was somehow connected to you, all you did was give a friend a ride. I'd swear under oath to that. You can rest well, Nome. That was a smoky mission and mine alone. If I go down on either one of the bodies, I go down alone."

Nome just nodded his head.

"Have you eaten yet? Ordered anything?" I asked.

"Naw, not yet. I was too fucked up in the head for all that. But I'm good now. You tryna eat something?"

"Naw, I'm good on the food, but this spot had the best Sangrias in Virginia. I ordered a few, I need a stiff one."

"I can dig it," Nome replied with a hint of a smile. "I'ma order food and a few of them Sangrias myself. Your drinks are on me."

"Listen, I'm sorry about not telling you about the cop. Straight up, I should've given you the right to choose whether or not you wanted to be with that shit. I thought that I was just looking out for you by not telling you what the lick was. Won't happen again. Now with that out the way, do you accept my apology?"

Nome stared at me for a second and I couldn't read his eyes. "Of course, I forgive you. Just give me a heads-up next time you wanna off a cop."

"Will do. But listen, I got one more person I need to see before I can fall back. You've been with me this far, you down for another 187?"

"Your ass sounds like O-Dog from Menace to Society," Nome said and laughed. Then he imitated Larenz Tate saying the words I'd said to Tyrin Turner's character, "Of course, I'm with you. I have been riding this long, I might as well ride until the wheels fall off. Who is it? And do I get another ten gees?"

"The target is a dude named Lonnell that hangs on MLK Avenue. I'm tryna get at him tomorrow. And you always get ten when you rock with me. I got you. I see you down? You sure you ain't shook?"

"Tell me when, where, and what time. You can miss me with all that other shit. You hip to me."

"For sure."

Chapter 4

Angel

"This nigga Lonnell is a vicious nigga. He had something to do with some shit that happened back in the day. I didn't find out about it until I went over the jail back in the day. I always told myself that I was gonna kill him, but I never saw the perfect opportunity until now. I wanna get up on him and let him see me kill him. See that parking lot over there next to the red brick store?"

"Yeah, I see it."

"See the dude with the blue and black ski coat on in that crowd? He's wearing a blue and black baseball cap. See him?"

"Yup."

"Well, that's my man. But I can't hit them out in the open because all the stores on both sides of the street have cameras mounted on them. So, I gotta get him when he comes to his car."

"What car?" Nome asked.

"The black Range Rover over there at the top of the parking lot that leads to the alley. The alley lets out onto Talbert Street. We can post up in the woods up there," I pointed to the woods adjacent to the alley and caught him when he headed for his cat."

"And what exactly do you need me to do?"

"To just be my eyes in the woods and keep me company. That's it. And of course, you gotta drive the getaway vehicle. You with me?"

"For ten more bands, why wouldn't I be. When do you wanna get him?"

"Is tonight too soon for you?"

"Naw, I'm ready when you are."

"Good, well, tonight it is."

"Cool. Let me go home, change my clothes, and get everything that I need. I'ma meet you back here tonight. Meet me over there by the school right there."

"I'll be there. What time are you talking?"

"He'll be out here all afternoon because he sells weed by the store. I'll say about eight. Yes, eight o'clock. Meet me by the school."

"You got that. Peace."

It was dark out now and under the cover of the night, I pulled onto Shannon Place by the school. I saw Nome waiting beside a car that I didn't recognize. He nodded when he saw me, and I exited the car I was driving. Without a word exchanged between us, we walked to Howard Road and headed to MLK Avenue. There we crossed the street and walked inconspicuously up to the woods. I looked all around, satisfied that I wasn't being watched and stepped into the woods. Nome followed me in.

"I'm tryna smash this nigga and get back home. My show comes on at eight."

"What show is that?" Nome asked me.

"Empire, that's my shit. Cookie is my bitch. Sorta reminds me of me."

"No doubt, I can see the comparison."

"All the sons are some wild niggas though the gay one be throwing me off like shit. It seems to me like TV is always tryna force feed us that homo shit. That's why I don't watch a rack of those other shows."

"Yeah, me either. I watch them reality shows—"

That was all Nome was able to say before I blew his brains all over the tree beside him. Stupid ass nigga. Tricked by a bitch. Another one bites the dust.

I never intended to kill Nome. I never wanted to, he was a long-time friend. But that one phone call that he made sounding shook, sealed his fate. I knew I had to kill him after that. He had become a witness to a crime and I never leave witnesses. In my mind, all I could see was Nome sitting in a room telling the detective that I killed Sean Jones and others. I had a Fatima flashback and decided to smoke his ass. Good for me, bad for him. I laid in my bed after taking a shower and plotted my next move. The next person on my list was Tina Brown, Honesty's mother. I referred to my notes and studied the papers that I had printed. Then I visualize the area that

Tina lived in. It was time for me to come up with another clever ruse to get up on Tina.

Tina Brown's house was a beige brick two-story one that sat sprawled on about an acre of land. The lawn was manicured and well kept. I parked my car across the street from her house and watched it for days. The first time I saw Tina exit her front door and walk down the walkway to her Brenz truck, I had the high urge to leap out and kill her in broad day. After watching Tina for a few days, I saw her pattern. Out of the house by 7:30 am and home by 6:00 pm. Every day, the same thing, but what trolled me the most was that I never saw Honesty.

Does She even live here? Is she still on Howard's campus? I'd have to find out from her mother.

Checking my watch, I saw that it was now 6-o'clock on the nose. I sat across from Tina Brown's house in a van that I borrowed from my girl Cheeks. Cheek 2 Cheek balloons were a good side hustle for my girl. *And for me, because I need her van. It's time for me to come back from the dead and surprise an old friend.*

I was halfway through the book I was reading by Lauren Horner when I spotted the Benz truck coming down the street. Putting the book down, I watched Tina pull into her driveway and exit the Benz truck. A dark-colored briefcase in one hand and in the other her keys. A large purse was strewn across her shoulder and her walk was purposeful. She sashayed with confidence and sex appeal. From my position in the van, I could see that Tina had aged gracefully and was more beautiful than I remembered. Once she was inside the house, I saw a light on in all the rooms. It was now or never, so I chose now. I hopped out of the van with the array of balloons in my hand. When I reached Tina Brown's front porch, I rang the doorbell. The balloons partially covered my face.

"Who is it?" Tina Brown asked through the door.

"Cheek 2 Cheek Balloons, ma'am. I have a delivery for Ms. Tina Brown."

"From who?" Tina asked as she opened the door. Her eyes were all over the beautiful array of multicolored balloons. The part of my face she could see, she didn't recognize.

"I believe they're from Ms. Honesty Phillips," I responded.

Tina blushed. "That's my daughter. She shouldn't have. Please come in and sit them down somewhere. I think that—"

I dropped the balloons showing the silenced gun in my hand, recognition set, and Tina Brown's color drained from her.

I smiled. "Long time, no see, huh?"

"You! It can't be."

"Oh, yes it can be. Because it is me. Thought you'd never see me again, right?"

"What do you want? Tony didn't leave any money here. And there's no money. So, you might as well just leave. We have nothing for you to rob us for. You've got all you're gonna get—"

"*Rob you?* Bitch are you retarded? I'm rich. You don't like Facebook much, huh?"

"What do you want if you're not here to rob me?" Her eyes were now locked in on my gun.

"Let me ask you this. Did you send your daughter to kill me or was that her bright idea?"

"You're crazy. Nobody sent anybody to kill you. What in the hell are you talking about? Tina Brown's confused look was genuine.

She hadn't sent her daughter after me. Shooting me was Honesty's idea. "You really don't know, do you? You have no clue about what happened eight years later? Your daughter came to my salon after it closed for the night and tried to kill me. She shot me four times. I was pregnant with my daughter then. Honesty almost killed us both. But Allah had other plans and he's the best of planners. I would have retaliated and killed your daughter years ago, but I thought she was already dead. My uncle couldn't kill her, so he lied and told me Honesty was dead. The other day I saw Honesty again. She was graduating from Howard. I knew right then that she had to die."

"Please! Please, Lord, please! Please don't kill my baby! She was just a kid. She was grief-stricken about her dad. She didn't mean to hurt you. Please leave my daughter alone. Leave us both alone. We won't bother you. I won't say a word to anybody about you coming here. No one will ever know. My daughter and I will leave the city, the state. Please! Listen to me. Leave us alone!"

"I'm sorry, Tina, I can't do that." I lifted the Ruger and shot Tina repeatedly until her body fell straight back and broke the small table behind her. I quickly searched through Tina's things until I found her cell phone. It was a Galaxy S6. The lock screen on was the fingerprint kind. I walked over to Tina and pressed her index finger of her right hand onto the screen. The screen unlocked and gave me access to Tina's contacts. Scrolling down the contacts, I saw a number for Honesty. I left her a simple text message. *//: Hurry home.*

Chapter 5

Honesty

The mirror on the closet door was a full-length one and I couldn't help but look into it. There was something inside me that made me a freak. I loved watching myself getting fucked. That's why I always ended up at his house. In school, around my friends, family, and my mother I was the sweetest person around. But there was one person that knew I was living the Clark Kent side of Superman. There was one person in my life that knew exactly what to do to make me come out of my shell and turn into a super Freaky Woman. His name is Trigga.

Trigga was on his knees behind me slowly pushing his dick into me. I was on all fours on his aunt's bed, in her bedroom, coming repeatedly. I put down on my bottom lip to stifle the screams that wanted to burst forth from my mouth.

"That's right, baby, take this dick like a big girl! Take this dick, True!"

Since my name was Honesty and there was no way to really shorten that, Trigga nicknamed me True. It all meant the same thing he said and the name just sort of stuck. But it really didn't matter to me what he called me as long as he called me. Tyrone Turner was the most popular dude in my high school and all the girls were on him. But for some reason, he was on me. He relentlessly hounded me every day until I agreed to go out with him.

I was afraid at first, but then I said, "Fuck it." What could he possibly do to me?

About a month later, I got the answer to my question. I played hooky from school one day out of every week and spent all my weekends with Trigga. The boy was smooth, fine, and thugged out. That was what turned me on so much about him. Tyrone Turner was the epitome of street and I loved him for it. He's everything I had missed growing up in suburban Maryland. His whole swagger was Mick Jagger like Kanye West said in a song.

"Why do they call you, Trigga?" I asked him one day.

"If I tell you that, I'll have to show you. Then I'd have to kill you," he replied.

The crazy part about it all was that I remember laughing at his response, but he never did. I never asked him about this nickname again. After a month of heavy dating and kissing, Trigga was begging for my sex.

Being a virgin who originally planned to stay that way until I got married, I folded under pressure. I weighed the pros and cons and the cons were outweighed. Plus, I was plain old insecure. I didn't want no other girl to have him. We went to see the movie, *The Family that Preys* and then to a restaurant. At sixteen-years-old, I had my first drink. Since Trigga was eighteen but looked older, the alcohol was no problem. I ended up full, tipsy, naked and broke in. Having sex for the first time wasn't as bad as people said it would be. I enjoyed it. Even begged for it some more once we finished. I had discovered something that I loved more than dancing and dancing was my passion. But after Trigga put that dick on me, my passion became him.

I think back to that day when I asked myself, *"What could he do to me?"* He turned my young ass out that's what he did to me. I dreamed about him fucking me, touching me, and eating me. He was like a drug I was addicted to. I looked at myself again in the mirror and moaned loudly. Trigga's hands were both on my waist, pulling me into him so that he could penetrate me deeper and deeper. His dick felt like the long, fat length sausage that I saw in the meat section of the Farmer's market the last time me and my mother went there. He was so deep in me and it hurt like hell, but it fell heavenly at the same time.

"Ohhhh! Fuck me, Trigga! Fuck me!"

I watched the sweat run down my baby's forehead onto his chest and got even wetter just looking at him. Trigga was 6' feet even and muscular. He was built like Lebron James but looked like Ray J. He kept his hair cut neat in a temper taped and fade with enough waves to make you dizzy. His goatee was always trimmed to perfection. The clothes that he wore were all designer and his shoe game was better than mine.

Having been born and raised in D.C. everything about Trigga screamed, *"Hood."*

D.C Public Schools kicked him out of their system, and he had to go to school in Maryland. If I was a praying person, I would've thanked God for D.C. Public Schools, but I'm not. The platinum link chain with the iced-out S.E. pendant, bounced off Trigga's chest every time he bounced off my ass. It was mesmerizing and hypnotizing all at the same time.

"I'm about to cum! I'm about to cum, again! Damn!"

I felt the tremors start in my toes and work their way up. When they reached the center of me, I shuddered. Trigga sensed that I was knocking on an orgasm's door so he increased his speed and intensity. He pounded into me with the ferocity of a crazed rapist and I loved it. We had become one entity. Our limbs were in sync and our aims were the same. My whole body shook and then I was icing. As if on cue, Trigga told me that he was coming with me. I felt his dick throb and explode inside the condom. I laid in a wet spot on the bed in an orgasmic glow that made me feel like I could fly. Then reality hit and I jumped off the bed. I grabbed my watch off the floor and looked at it. 7:40 p.m.

"Oh shit!" I exclaimed as I jumped off the bed and shot to the bathroom.

When I came out fully dressed, Trigga asked, "What's up? Why are you rushing to leave like that?"

"I promised my mother I'd come straight home so that she and I could go out and get a celebratory buffet of seafood. She's gonna kill me."

"Call me later," Trigga said.

"I will," I replied and bounced up outta there.

I was still fixing my hair as I pulled onto my street. My heart was racing, and I was trying to think of a good lie to tell my mother. I checked my cell phone and read her text again. //: *Hurry home.* Usually, she'd Facetime me, but she hadn't. Maybe she knew exactly what I was up to. Graduating from college was a helluva accomplishment. Maybe she knew that I needed some dick after that. My skin would tell the story anyway if my mouth didn't. My mother knew how I felt about Trigga and she knew that we'd been together for six years and that we'd been fucking each other the entire time. It's always hard to fool your mother. I guess it's because they were your age once. That's what my grandmother always said. I smiled to myself as I thought about my father sexing my mother when she was my age. *He probably used to tear her ass up.*

I pulled my truck into the driveway, right behind my mother's Lexus. Being so preoccupied with fixing my appearance, I never noticed that all the lights in my house were out. I got out of the truck and looked around to the side of the house.

What the fuck is going on? Something's wrong.

The one thing that I hated most sometimes about my mother was that she was a creature of habit. She never deviated from her ways. So, I found it hard to understand why all the lights would be out in the house. My mother never turned all the lights out when she was home or when she was gone. I walked up to my mother's car and peered inside. Her work bag and everything else was gone. She had to have taken it inside the house with her. She never went to bed before 9 p.m. Never.

So, why would all the lights be out? I pulled my cell phone out and called my house. There was no answer. I called again and again but got no response. *Where could she be? And why hasn't she called me?*

I tried not to panic, but I was failing. I walked back to my truck and got inside. My brain was going into overdrive as I lifted the lid on the console that sat between the driver and passenger seat. I kept all kinds of miscellaneous stuff in the console. But that was really to throw people off. I pried my fingers under the plastic casing of the console. Then I grabbed it and pulled it out of its shell. At the bottom of the hollowed-out console was the gun that I put there several years ago. Since I had never heard anything about a funeral for Angel, I didn't know if she was dead or not. Even years had passed, I never left home without. The very first day my mother gave me the Escalade I had a gun in there. Before that, I walked around with it in my purse. I reached down into the console and picked up the Ruger. The feel of it empowered me instantly and my fears left me.

I put my bookbag and purse in the backseat and headed for my house. I entered the house from the garage. Once inside, I called out for my mother. But again, nobody answered. I kept the Ruger behind my back as I crept softly through the hallway.

As I turned the corner to go into the living room, a lamp was turned on in the living room. I stopped in my tracks. The scene in front of me brought tears to my eyes. My mother was laid out in blood surrounded by broken glass and formed what used to be our coffee table. Her eyes were closed, and her clothes were stained with blood. I knew she was dead. Tears welled up in my eyes as I looked over by the fireplace. Standing there in a uniform of some kind was the woman that had killed my father. Now the same woman had killed my mother. An uncontrollable rage built up inside me. I bought the gun from behind my back and pointed it at her. Her quickness was amazing. At the exact same moment that my gun locked on her, her gun locked onto me. Not even 10 feet from one another, we both stood ready to kill. Everything that I had been through in the last few years flashed through my mind as I stood ready to die. My index finger rested on the Ruger ready to give out one ounce of pressure. That one ounce would be enough to end it all. My mind began to race.

"See we meet again, huh, Honesty?" Angel said.

Through my tears, I replied, "It sure looks that way, huh?"

"The sad part is that we were never really introduced. Hi, I'm Angel."

"What did my mother do to you? Why kill her?" I asked.

"Your mother and I go way back. She sold me a rack of death many years ago. After I survived your attempt on my life, I always wondered if she had groomed you and sent you on that mission. But, either way, she had to go because after I kill you, she would have become a very bitter enemy. Besides, now she can be with your father again."

"We're all about to see him again. Me, you, and her. Are you ready to die because I am."

"Naw, I got a lot more living to do before I die. But you can tell me what it's like once I get there. Be a good girl and put your gun down."

"Not in a million years."

"Well, go ahead and shoot me then. Oh, my bad, you already tried that once, huh?"

"Even a cat has nine lives. You killed my father. Fair exchange ain't no robbery."

"Fair exchange!" Angel shouted and I could see the spit fly from her mouth in rage. "You almost killed my daughter. I was pregnant, she was innocent.

"And so was my mother. But you killed her anyway," I calmly replied ready to pull the trigger.

"I like your style, Honesty. You remind me of myself when I was your age. I killed my own father when I was fifteen- years old. So, we sort of have something in common. My father was a piece of shit that raped me and then peed on my little sister. All while hiding behind a beautiful religion. I killed your father because I needed his connection and I couldn't get it while he was still alive. I killed your mother because of what you did to me and for that same reason, I'm about to kill you."

Something in my head screamed, *"Move!"* I did at the exact same moment that Angel fired her gun.

I heard a soft cough and then the glass from the picture frame on the wall behind me shattered. I dived onto the floor and hid behind the wall. I shot a couple of shots in the direction where she stood from my position behind the wall. The thing I knew was that she had picked a bad position to be in. There was no exit out of the living room. The only way to go past me. I swiped at the tears that fell on my face with my free hand. I got down low and peeked my head out around the corner. Angel had reduced behind the couch. I aimed at the couch and fired repeatedly. Then chipped pieces of the wood where I was, started flying and I knew that she was shooting back. I tried to figure out my next move as I stooped, but she forced me to hell on the run.

Chapter 6

Angel

I had to respect the woman's gangster, but that didn't mean, I wasn't gonna nail her ass. When I fired my gun at her, I noticed that the wall must've been made of something like drywall, because my bullets were gone through the wall. When the dust cleared, I could see the light that shines in through the window. The house security gate came with floodlights and lit up the whole circumference of the house on the outside. Then I saw that my shots were going through the wall, I fired at the spot where I knew Honesty was.

Then I heard footsteps retreating to the back of the house. I followed the sound and ended up in the hallway. She had run somewhere in the back toward the kitchen. I realized then that I was on foreign ground. I didn't know the house as well as she did. It would be foolish of me to chase her through her own house. She had the advantage of knowing it backward and forward. I was about to try my hand at a game of cat and mouse when I heard the faint sound of sirens.

I put my back on the wall and strained my ears to hear clearly. I heard it again, it was sirens. They were getting louder which brought me to the conclusion they were coming to the house. Someone had heard the gunshots from Honesty's gun and called the cops. I glanced over at Tina lying on the floor and decided I didn't want to go back to jail, so I ran. I couldn't run out the back way because I didn't know where the back was. I hadn't done my homework properly.

Plus, Honesty was somewhere back there lying in wait for me like the hunter who corners and traps his prey. I made up my mind and ran from the front door. I picked up the bouquet of flowers and my hat and walked calmly out of the door. I was down the street and almost to my van when three cop cars went right by me. I waited for them to get down the block some before I ran to the van and got inside. I started the engine and sped away.

We will meet again, Honesty. The next time we meet will definitely be our last. The next time you die.

The next morning, I got rid of the van, the clothes I was wearing, and the gun that I used to kill Tina Brown. I kept thinking about Honesty as I drove to Rockville where my mother lived. The fact that she wasn't making it easy to kill her intrigued me. Whether she had told the police about me worried me. I stayed up late last night and caught the news.

They mentioned the murder in Kettering but didn't go into any detail. Honesty knew that I killed her mother, but that was all she knew. Besides the fact that my real name is Kareemah and that I was charged with killing her father years ago, she didn't know anything else about me. That worked in my favor. It bought me some time to get the hell out of dodge for a while. I made up my mind to leave town as soon as I laid in my bed last night. I knew exactly where I was going.

Before leaving town, I had to stop by my mother's house and say goodbye to her and my daughter. I couldn't leave without seeing them first. I pulled my SUV into my mother's driveway and got out. At the front door, I used my key to let myself in, a bell chimed loudly throughout the house. It was one of the safety features that came with the home security system. I walked in the living room and saw Aniyah lying on the couch fast asleep. Inwardly my heart skipped a beat as I walked over to her. I saw my whole world wrapped up in a blanket. Aniyah slept as she always did, with her thumb in her mouth, I wanted to wake her and hold her and tell her that Mommy was there, but I couldn't. She was sleeping much too peaceful. Instead, I stood there and gawked at my only child. My child that almost never was. My child that was conceived out of lust, not love. I stood there mesmerized by the little girl who looked just like her father. Aniyah's long, jet black, wavy hair was pulled back neatly into a ponytail and tied by a blue ribbon. I wondered what kind of dreams a person so young could have. I was so in a daze that I never heard my mother enter the room.

"She's beautiful, huh?" My mother's voice said.

I turned in the direction of the voice and smiled at my mother. I crossed the room and embraced her. "Assalamu Alaikum."

"Wa-laikum Assalam," My mother said and kissed me on the forehead.

"Ma, she's so special. I love her so much. She reminds me so much of her father."

"Speaking of which, are you ever gonna tell him about her?"

"One day, Ma, one day. When I feel that the time is right. What would it benefit either of them to know the other, right now?"

"I understand, Angel it's your decision to make."

"I just don't see the need to get into all that, right now."

"I said I understand. Insha' Allah, when the time comes, you'll make the right decision. Other than that, what's going on with you? Have you changed your mind about killing that girl—I mean woman?"

I wanted to tell my mother the truth about what I had done but I couldn't. "I gotta leave town for a while, Ma, and I can't explain why, right now. You're going to have to trust me on this and not ask a rack of questions."

"Where are you going?" she asked with a concerned look plastered all over her face. "You did it, didn't you? You killed her, didn't you? That's why you gotta leave all of a sudden."

"I can't tell you anything, right now. The less you know the better. Trust me, Ma, it's better this way. I will call you every day, though. You and Aniyah are all that I care about in this world and nothing is going to change that."

"I will respect your wishes and trust you. But please be careful out there in the streets, baby. No one can lead who Allah allows to go astray. I don't wanna bury another one of my children. You have to bury me."

"Ma, chill out, I'ma be a'ight. You just take care of you and Aniyah and don't burn yourself out."

"Burn out I don't have time to burn out. I'll have to fit that in my schedule. Besides, I relax by doing what you were just doing. That child came in the storm. I still miss my baby, but her death was the will of Allah. It took me a long time to get to this point. The point where I don't cry every time I think about her, but I'm here and I'm making it by the will of Allah. I now feel a sort of comfort in knowing that Adirah is in paradise. The Holy Qur'an says that everyone should taste earth—some just sooner than others."

I listened to my mother speak, I respect her opinions, but mine was a little different. I cannot believe that it was the will of God for my sister to die so tragically at the hands of strangers.

How could it be? It was my fault that Dearaye targeted my family and kidnapped my sister. Dearaye ordered Tommy Guns and the murders to rape and beat my sister because he was mad that I fucked his brother. That had nothing to do with the creator. It would not have happened, had I not gotten into the streets. If I had never killed Tony and took his spot. Adirah would be alive today. My sister's death was a punishment inflicted upon me and my family because of me. I believe that Allah is gonna roast my skin in hell and then exchange the old skin for new skin and roast that, too. I can accept that, but what I can't accept is the concept of the creator of the world writing a script that called for innocent children to die tragically for no reason at all. Some people say that the sins of the parents come back to revisit the children. Was Adirah's death payment for all my father's sins? Only Allah knows.

If Naimah El-Amin wanted to believe that Allah caused or willed Adirah's death that was her right. But me, I wasn't going for it. I continued to listen to my mother in silence but voiced my own opinion inwardly. A sudden movement and ruffling caused me to look over at the couch. Aniyah was wide awake and staring at her grandmother and me.

"Hi, Mommy," Aniyah said.

"Hey, Princess," I replied and rushed over to her. I kissed her all over her face as I hugged her tight. "I love you, baby. I love you so much."

***

By the time the sunset in D.C. that evening, I was on Interstate 95 heading to New Jersey. It took me a couple of hours before I ended up cruising the New Jersey Turnpike. I was tired but otherwise, I was good.

"I hope I'm going the right way."

I took the Highway 1 and 9 exit while reading the signs that directed me to Newark. I couldn't place any of the outer signs, so I called my cousin Aminah and got directions. She was better than SIRI when it came to navigation.

"Hello?" It was Aminah.

"Mina, I'm on the one and nine Highway. Where do I go from here?" I asked.

"Where are you on the highway?"

"The sign up their says Newark International Airport is the next exit."

"A'ight, keep straight until you see the Broad Street exit. Take that and you'll be in downtown Newark. Go over the bridge past the Northern State Prison. Stay on Broad Street until you come to an intersection. That's the Clinton Avenue joint. Make a left on Clifton Avenue and—"

"Hold on for a minute, girl got damn. I'm coming up on Clinton Avenue, right now. You said make left, right?"

"Yeah. Then keep straight until you see a curved street that says Elizabeth Avenue. Take that joint until you reach the Weequahic Park. You got that?"

"I got that, I'm on Elizabeth now."

"Good. You're almost here. When you pass Weequahic Park, make a right on Chancellor Avenue. On Chancellor, you come all the way down the block until you see 1508. I'm walking outside, right now. I'm on the porch. The street is well lit, and the porch lights are on, so you should be able to see me. I should be to your left. What are you driving?"

I saw my crazy ass cousin Aminah waving her hands in the air. I disconnected the call and pulled into a parking space in front of the house right next door to my family's house. I was amazed at how much Aminah had grown since I last saw her. Then I remembered she was twenty-six now. The last time we saw each other she was ten and I was fifteen. It was at the Masjid in D.C. the day my father was buried.

I walked up to Aminah and embraced her. "What's up, lil cuz? Assalamu alaikum."

"Wa-laikum Assalam. You look good, boo. I guess that D.C. weather agrees with you. All them fine ass niggas down there probably look as good as you."

"Girl, a rack of them niggas probably wanna be me. Them niggas fruity ass shit. Don't get me wrong, D.C. got its fair share of gangstas, but the city is overrun by them gay niggas. Them homo thug niggas. They gotta a real gang of gay niggas that be beating up the good niggas. They call themselves the Check-It Boys. Can you believe that shit?"

"Cuz that's everywhere. Them kinda niggas deep in the brick, too. What the hell is the world coming to? When all the good looking niggas want some dick, too. That's crazy, ain't it? Come on in, girl, and see my parents. They are waiting to see you. You can have my room and I'll sleep in the room downstairs until you say otherwise."

I followed Aminah into the house. "I'm trying to rent a spot nearby. I'ma be here for a minute and I'm not trying to have you sleeping downstairs."

"You're going to be here for a while, huh? What happened down there in Chocolate City?"

I killed a lot of people in the last thirty days. The last one being only yesterday.

"I had to get away from my ex-boyfriend. That nigga was driving me crazy. He was gonna make me kill his ass."

"Angel, you wild as shit but I'm glad you're here. My father is in the den offering the Isha prayer. My mother is in the kitchen."

My aunt Khadijah was at the sink washing dishes when we entered the kitchen.

"Ma, look who's here," Aminah announced.

Aunt Khadijah turned around and smiled. "Kareemah! Come here, baby. Let me touch you."

I hugged my aunt. "Assalamu Alaikum, auntie."

52

"Wa-laikum Assalam, Allah is the most merciful. How are you doing child? How is your mama doing?"

"I'm good, aunt. My mother's good, too. She is taking care of my daughter—"

"Don't you think I know that, child? I'm getting older, not dumber. Do you have any pictures of the beautiful child with you?"

"Auntie, I'm a mother, right? What mother doesn't have pictures of their only child in their phone? You wanna see her?"

"Later, baby. We just finished eating dinner. Show 'em to me after I finish in here. I wanna sit down and see everything. Would you like something to eat?"

"Naw, I'm good, auntie. I'm just a little tired from the drive."

"Well, go into the den and see your uncle Basil. Then you can get all the rest you need. Aminah says you are gonna be here for a bit. You are more than welcome here, baby. Stay as long as you like. Insha'Allah, you can talk some sense into Aminah. Aminah, take Angel to the den."

"Come on, Ang." When we got in the halfway, Aminah said, "Girl, I don't know why I stay in this house. It ain't sister Khadijah getting on my case, it's brother Basil. You better hope he doesn't give you the famous. "My father be tripping like shit. He's in there."

"You're not going in with me?" I asked.

"You on your own, girlfriend. Good luck."

Let me get this over with. I knocked on the door and then walked in. My Uncle Basil was sitting on his feet on the floor as he made dua. He looked up at me and then continued his dua. I couldn't believe how much my uncle resembled my father. Basil El-Amin was the oldest brother my late father had. He had to be at least sixty-one. His beard was long and peppered with grey. He wore a multicolored kufi and a robe over his pants and shirts. A few minutes later, he stood up and looked at me.

"Kareemah, come and give your uncle a hug."

We hugged.

"Your ride here was safe, masha'allah. It's been too long. Where is your hijab? Why don't you cover yourself as the Sunnah of the Rasool Allah tells you to? Why must you imitate the kafir?"

I smiled. *Here we go again.*

Chapter 7

Honesty

I would be turning twenty-three soon, but I felt much older. A time-less and ageless calm settled over me as I sat in the back of the funeral home with my mother. I didn't let anyone touch her. I picked out her clothes and dressed her, and I did her hair and makeup. I pulled the platinum linked chain from around my neck that she had given me a week ago when I graduated and placed it on hers. The platinum heart pendant was diamond-encrusted but hollow. Once opened, there was a small picture of us together when I was a baby. The chain meant the world to me, but I figured she should have it. Even in death, we'd always be together.

"Ms. Phillips, everyone is waiting on you. We need to proceed with the service. Everything is on a schedule," the funeral director peeped in and said.

"Give me five more minutes with my mother, then you can come in and get her."

I waited until the door shut before I walked over to my mother's casket. *She looks like she's asleep.* I stared at the silver casket with pink lining and stared at my mother who was only thirty-nine years old. I ran my fingers down her face and the thought of what she looked like the night she was killed hit me. Tears fell down my eyes for the one-millionth time as I said another silent goodbye to her. I kissed her lips. They were so cold and hard. I straightened myself up and dried my eyes, careful not to let my tears ruin my mother's makeup. I checked her body one more time before pronouncing her ready for the world. I chose to bury her in a grown two-piece business suit that she loved. The suit made by Donna Karan was pin-striped and tailored to fit her perfectly. I added a pink Hermes silk dress shirt and diamond earrings to bring out the color that my mother once had. There was a diamond-encrusted *#1 Mom* pin in the lapel of her jacket. Her hair was high, and everything was on point we were ready. I almost dreaded going out into a room filled with my relatives. They were all fake as hell and my mother didn't fuck with any of them. But they were there to pay their respects and that was fine with me. I was still standing over my mother when the funeral director returned.

"I'm ready," I said before he could say a word. Then I walked out of the room and went to face the crowd.

At Harmony cemetery, my mother was interred. I sat up front and listened to the preacher give the final benediction and say a prayer. Then my mother's casket was lowered into the ground. I rose from my seat and grabbed a handful of dirt, threw it onto the casket, and walked away. I walked all the way back to the limousine reserved for me and climbed into the backseat. Then I broke down, I couldn't be strong anymore.

"Honesty, what are you going to do, now?" My aunt Wanda asked me at the repast.

"I'm going to live in my mother's house, it's paid for. I have money in the bank and the money that my father left me. I'll be okay."

"That's nonsense, child. You are coming to stay with me."

And let your crackhead boyfriend get y'all hands on my family money? Not in your life would I do that.

"No thank you, I talked it over with grandma already and she said it's okay if that's what I wanna do."

My aunt said, "Have it your way then." She walked away mumbling, "Grown ass heifer."

I walked over to my grandmother and hugged her. We talked for a while until my cell phone vibrated. I had an incoming message.

//: I'm outside. T.

"Grandma, I'm going to go home and lay down for a while. I'll call you when I get up."

"Are you sure you wanna do that, baby? The police just turned the house over to you. Do you really want to go back in there after all this happened there?"

"It's my home, grandma. I wouldn't feel comfortable anywhere else. If there's a ghost in the house, it'll be my mother and I need to be there to see her. I'll call you later."

"Okay, baby? Call me," Portia Phillips said.

Outside the church, I walked around the corner and spotted Trigger's car. I got in the passenger seat, reached over, and hugged my man. Then I kissed him. Without saying a word. He pulled the car out of the church parking lot after we had been riding for a few minutes, Trigger said, "Your house or mine?"

"Yours. I'm not ready to go there yet. I'ma spend the night with you and then go home in the morning." I recline my seat and thought back to the night my mother was killed—

When I got to the pantry, I checked my gun and saw it was almost empty, I cursed myself for not carrying an extra clip. I only had a few shots left and I was gonna make them fatal. That's what I told myself as I crouched down beside the dishwasher. Angel had to be coming behind me somewhere and I was waiting for her. My ears focused on sound as I willed myself to hear everything and anything. But there was nothing. I heard no sound for a minute. As second, struck into minutes, I finally heard a sound that cut through the eerie silence like a knife. Sirens, I heard sirens. Evidently, I wasn't the only one who heard them because on the second slate I heard footsteps. They were going in the directions away from me. Then I heard our front door open and close. I stayed put for what seemed like an eternity, before finally coming out of the pantry. Slowly, I walked through the house until I reached the front door. Just as I opened the door, the police were right there.

"Put the gun down now!" one screamed.

"My mother—" was all that I could say before I fainted.

I awoke later that night surrounded by paramedics and cops, uniformed and plainclothes. I opened my eyes to focus and saw that I was lying on the couch in the living room. It was the same couch Angel had taken cover behind,

"She's awaking," I heard someone say.

"What's your name?" another one said.

I focused on the face in front of me and said, "I live here. My name is Honesty."

"She's the daughter. What happened here Honesty?"

"And what is your father's name? Where is he? We need to contact him." This was the white, detective that had a gold badge hanging from his neck.

"Anthony Phillips. You can't contact him, though," I responded.

"And why is that?" The black detective asked.

"Because he's dead. He was killed eight years ago."

"I'm sorry to hear that. Go ahead and finish what you were saying."

"My father was in the streets real hard and feared for his family. So, he put guns all over the house. He hid them. I think my mother knew where they were, but not me. I stumbled across one of them about three years ago. I moved it to another spot. The kitchen, Why? I don't know, I just did. So frozen with fear that someone was in the house, I went for the gun. It was loaded already. I took the gun off the safety and walked through the house. I—uh—"

"Take your time and be clear," the white detective said.

"I walked in on the intruder standing over my mother. She was down on the floor. Her clothes were— I could see that she had been shot. The intruder—"

"Let me stop you right here, Honesty. You keep saying, intruder. What did this intruder look like? Did you recognize him?

"I couldn't, he was wearing a mask."

"Honesty, I need you to think about this and answer me as honestly as possible," the black Detective said. *"You said your father was in the streets, right? He got killed eight years ago?"*

I nodded my head.

"Okay. Was your mother in the streets, too? Was she part of what your father was into?"

"No! My mother was a square. She worked at Largo High as a counselor. She loves to help people."

"Well, why do you think this intruder came to your house to kill her? What was he after?"

"I don't know. I don't know."

"What happened once you and the intruder saw one another?" the white detective asked.

"We shot at each other."

True? True, did you hear what I just said?"

I snapped out of my reverie and looked over at Trigger. What did you say?"

"I said come on." It was then that I realized the car had stopped and was parked back at Trigger's aunt's house. I got out of the car and followed Trigger through the basement door that led to his room.

"Are you okay, True?"

"Yeah, I'm a'ight. It's just hard to believe that she is gone. I buried my mother today—"

I dropped to my knees and put my head in my hands. A dam inside me broke and my tears became like a tsunami. Trigger rushed to my side and tried to comfort me. "She didn't hurt nobody!" I cried out in pain. The pain I felt inside was unlike anything I had ever felt before.

"Baby, it gonna be a'ight," Trigger said as he attempted to wipe my tears with his shirt.

"No, it's not!" I exploded. "It's not gonna be alright! Not now! Not ever! So, don't fucking say that to me." I collapsed in a fit of sobs and coughs. I couldn't believe my luck. Both my parents had been killed eight years apart by the same person. A woman, right there on that basement floor, I decided that my tears were useless. I decided that crying and feeling sorry for myself was no longer an option. What I needed was closure. I needed to know that the woman responsible for the deaths of my parents was dead, and this time, buried. I would never again leave anything to chance. I wiped my eyes and picked myself up off the floor. A complete change had quickly taken place inside me. The woman who had graduated magna cum laude from a historic HBCU was gone, repealed by the person that I was the night I thought I killed Angel. The old me was gone forever.

I'm gonna kill that bitch, Angel if it's the last thing I do in life. And anybody else that gets in my way.

Chapter 8

Angel

I wasn't in Brick City two weeks before Aminah had me in the projects over her friend Salimah's house. The Brick Towers Projects were two sixteen-story buildings that seem to pierce the clouds. The landscape was just like one in D.C. The hallways smelled like piss and there were niggas and crack heads everywhere. We walked in building 715 and literally had to step over a muthafucka lying in the path that led to the stairs.

"Is he dead?" I asked Salimah who had come downstairs to meet us.

"I wish. That's hobo Willie. He sleeps right here and or anywhere else he feels like it in this building. Someone needs to kill his tiny ass. Come on. The elevator doesn't work, Angel. So, we have to take the steps. Don't worry, though. I live on the second floor."

Thank God I wore tennis shoes. We walked into Salimah's apartment a few minutes later and I was surprised to see that her spot was clean and laid out. She had leather furniture, big screen high definition TVs, wall to wall carpet, black lacquer glass tables, and all the accessories. The one picture on the wall was a framed enlarged photo of the Kaaba in Mecca.

"Angel make yourself at home. Aminah always does," Salimah said and disappeared in the back somewhere.

Aminah must've read my facial expression as I continued to survey the apartment.

"Salimah's boyfriend is the head nigga in charge around here. His name is Muqtar, but everybody calls him "Mu". Lima got that nigga's nose wide open."

Is that, right? Well, why doesn't he move her out of the projects then? "This place is nice."

"I know, right. He buys her whatever she wants. Salimah is spoiled as shit. They really fuck with each other. They'd probably be married if he wasn't married already."

"Is he Muslim?" I asked her.

"Yeah but his wife Hafiza ain't going for the two-wife shit. Girl-friend will fuck a bitch up. She doesn't even know about Salimah."

A key was placed into the locked door and turned. The door opened and in walked a tall, well built, vanilla complexioned dude that I took to be Mu. he was fine with a capital F. The nigga looked like a thugged out version of Allen Payne. His soft-looking, jet black curly hair was cut into a temple taper, D.C. style and he wore it well. He had several tattoos all over his arm and chest. The wife-beater he wore was saturated with sweat and so was the Gucci sweats he had on. I looked down at his feet and saw that his crispy brand new hi-top Gucci sneakers were untied.

"Mina, what's good ma?" The dude said when he saw us. "And who might you be?"

I didn't like the way Salimah's man was pushing up on me. I didn't respond to him. I simply adjusted my Chanel frames and sat back in my seat.

"Damn, ma. It's like that, huh? You too beautiful to be so evil. Mina, tell Chris to get up with me, I got something for him." He turned and walked into the back where Salimah was.

"Angel, why you do him like that? He was only speaking to you," Aminah said when he was out of earshot.

"Girl, I ain't tryna be up here beefing with Salimah about no man. He belongs to her. So, why even bother entertaining his con-versation?"

Aminah laughed out loud. "Ang, that ain't Salimah's man. Her man's name is Mu. That's Salimah's brother Najee. Fine ass Najee. All the bitches are on his dick. Which I also happened to have heard is about eleven inches. If I wasn't fucking with Chris—"

Before Aminah could finish her sentence, Salimah walked into the room. She was now dressed in a baby blue Dolce & Gabbana top, 7 For All Mankind denim jeans and Dolce & Gabbana tennis shoes that matched her top.

"Let's get the fuck outta here and hit the mall. I gotta cop some fly shit to wear in Atlantic City?"

"What's in Atlantic City?" I asked as I got up and followed them out of the apartment.

"The Kendall Holt-Reggie Yelverton fight," Salimah said as a matter of fact and gave Aminah a look like I was the dumbest person on Earth. "Everybody in the brick is going because one four local fighters is fighting on the undercard."

A good boxing match would do my desire for blood some good. "When is the fight?"

"In three weeks. We can make it an all-nighter."

At the Jersey Gardens Mall, we shopped like teenagers until I grew tired of the scenery. I felt like a third wheel with them and I had to admit even though Aminah was my cousin and Salimah was cool as shit, she and my cousin were two Bama ass bitches. I was ready to bounce. I told Aminah so and she said she'd get a ride home from Salimah. I hugged Salimah and Aminah, then broke out.

Two weeks later I moved out of my relative's house and into a condominium nearby.

The ballroom at the Merv Griffin Resorts Hotel and Casino was packed to the hilt. Our seats were pretty good. I called D.C. and hollered at one of my homies to get a hookup on the tickets. He put me down with Jermaine. Jermaine Fields was an ex-fighter and an ambassador of the local DC boxing scene. After we talked for a while, I found out that my old boyfriend Buck was his cousin. By the time I finished talking to him, we had seats behind the ringside, waiting for us at the Casino Ballroom.

"Angel I don't know how you pulled this off, but boo, you did the muthafucka. I feel like a celebrity or some shit. Look at all the stats in this piece. Salimah said as she sipped a drink of some kind.

"Yeah, Ang, these seats are the bomb. We got better seats than Ludacris and his entourage. They're about two rows behind us over to the right. When we were coming down the aisle I saw Mya, Young Jeezy, and that nigga that sign the hook on that Lil' Wayne joint."

"Bobby Valentino, I saw him. That looks like that girl Nivea with him, too.

"Doesn't she fuck with Wayne?" Aminah asked.

"She supposed to, but you know how they get down in the music industry. Love and Hip Hop, that shit is like a real-life soap opera. Everybody fucks with somebody's man or woman. I could never be a part of all that shit."

I heard what Salimah and Aminah were saying but I was too busy looking around the ballroom, myself.

There were a lot of stars in the building and we did have better seats than some of them. I spotted several notable niggas from DC in attendance, too. Behind me, about three rows back were James and Antonio Bendable, Tone and Erick from First Street, Cat Eye Chico, and Nick Hampton from R street.

I sat back in my seat and waited for the first fight to start. I looked at the program and saw that the first fighters were two brothers from DC named Lamont and Anthony Peterson. Then it was a dude that Salimah and Aminah knew named Khairi, boxing after them. Then it was the main event. Champ Yelverton was a street dude turned professional boxer after he got released from Lorton Penitentiary. He was the mandatory challenger for Zab's WBA/WBC welterweight belts. I was still listening to Aminah and Salimah act like groupies when the lights dimmed and the fights began.

After sitting through two boring fights that both ended by decision, I was suddenly very thirsty.

"Where is the concession stand in here?" I asked.

Salimah gave me directions and I got up in search of something to quench my thirst. A few minutes later I found the concession stand. I ordered a Sprite and a pack of spearmint gum. When I turned around, I bumped into someone and almost spilled my soda.

I was staring into the face of the man that I had thought about often, since the first time I laid eyes on him.

"My bad, Ma. Hold on, don't I know you from somewhere?" he asked me.

I smiled and completely forgot about the fact that he had almost ruined my 1200-dollar Donatella Versace top. "It's Najee, right?"

"No doubt, but I don't seem to know your name. I feel like I'm at a discount, help me out a little bit. I could never forget about someone as beautiful as you. Where do we know each other from?"

"A few weeks ago, I was at your sister's house. You—"

"Words bond, Ma I remember you now. You were in there acting all evil and shit. I spoke to you and you didn't even speak back. I never did get your name, though. So, what is it?"

"I'ma tell you my name on one condition."

"What's that, Ma?"

"Please stop calling me, Ma. I can't stand that shit. You are not my son and I ain't your mother. My name is Angel. You can call me Angel."

"I respect that, m- I mean Angel. I'ma try my best to remember that. Where are you from, Angel? You obviously are not from here?"

"I'm from DC."

"I should've known."

"And what's that supposed to mean?"

"I'll tell you that once we get to know each other better. How 'bout that?" Najee said and smiled.

For the first time, I noticed how gorgeous he became when he smiled. The man was already done, but when he smiled, he took his sexiness and good looks to another level. I checked him out from head to toe in seconds.

Najee was wearing chocolate brown suede Gucci loafers, Rock and Republic blue head denim and brown Gucci button-down shirt, Every time he moved his arm, the iced out watch he wore sparkled. *This nigga got some paper.*

"I'd like that," I finally responded.

"Good. Let me put your number in my Galaxy and I'll holla back."

We exchanged numbers, then I was about to walk away when Najee said, "Let me buy you another drink. It's the least I can do since I almost knocked over the one in your hand."

"That's a'ight, I'm good. But thanks for offering." I tried to leave again.

"One more question. Are you in town on business or pleasure? And do you have a man somewhere that I need to know about?"

"No, I don't have a man somewhere that you need to know about. Would I be here giving you my number if I did? I'm in town on vacation. Is that all you want to know?" I asked him sassily.

"Would you care to join me for the rest of the fights? I came here with a few of my men, but I can easily put one of them niggas in the aisle. I got seats about four rows back from the ring on the far side."

"You'd really do that to one of your men, for me?" I asked sarcastically.

"In a heartbeat."

"That's good to know, but I'm cool. I came here with my girls one you even know. So, I can't leave them, and besides, why would I give up my seat a row behind the ring to sit four rows back on the gate side?"

Before Najee could respond, I stepped off. I added extra sway in my hips just because I knew he was watching. When I got back to my seat, Salimah and Aminah was engaged in a different conversation. I sat down and listened.

"—Girl, that nigga Raheem been stealing cars since we were in grade school. Fake New Jersey Drive ass nigga. I can't stand his punk ass. He probably stole the tickets to the tickets to this fight," Salimah said.

"He and Chris are cool. They set to live in the same projects Chris doesn't even know I'm here, but I know he is going to find out. I don't care, though, Lima. That nigga thinks he's going to be ripping and running the streets all day and night and I'm supposed to sit home and twiddle my thumbs. He is crazier than a muthafucka."

"Oh, you can bet your last dollar that Chris gon know you were here. When we were walking in, I saw Buck from 7th Avenue and that nigga Boz that be on Bergen and Chancellor. You know them niggas cool as shit with Chris."

"Boz? Are you talking about Boz from Weequahic? The one that got all that shit on smash around my way?" Aminah asked.

"The one and only."

"That nigga ain't gon say nothing. Believe that, Boz been tryna fuck me for years now and he knows that snitching on a bitch would fuck up his chances. But that nigga Buck, he'll tell on a bitch quick. I can't stand his lil' baby dragon looking ass. He stay aggie because won't nobody fuck his ugly ass."

I tuned them both out as the ring announcer announced the next fight, it was the local dude from Newark and a DC fighter that I had heard of named Chop-Chop. The bell rang and the fight began. *Damn! Why the hell is Chop Chop wearing them tight ass short?*

The main event ended up being worth the price of the whole ticket. Reggie *Champ* Yelverton knocked Kendall Holt down in three of the first four rounds before finishing him off in the 9th round. Holt never came out of his coma to start the 10th. I didn't tell my cousin or Salimah but I felt a real sense of pride as we left the ballroom. All the DC fighters won their fights. They came to New Jersey and gave out good old fashion ass whippings. I love it.

Angel 2

Chapter 9

Najee

The whole time I was talking to Angel by the concession stand, out of my peripheral view I saw the two dudes on the wall staring at me. They both looked familiar, but I couldn't place them. They stuck out like sore thumbs. Stupid ass niggas. One of the principles of the art of war is to disguise your intentions. These two niggas were at a major prizefight dressed in war gear. Both dudes leaned on the wall across from the stand in all black army fatigues and Nike boots.

I walked back to my seat and put my men down with what I suspected.

"Are you sure, Naj'?" Hasan asked me.

"Aye, Has', have I ever been wrong about this is shit?"

"Naw, son. So, what da hook gon be?"

I glanced at my other man Gunz and sighed. "The streets won't let me chill. I know them niggas was ice grilling me. I know 'em from somewhere but I couldn't place their faces. Word to mother, son, them niggas got beef with your boy. And I'm about to cook it."

Gunz never said a word, he was the quietest nigga I know and the most dangerous. Hasan and Gunz were two niggas that didn't give a fuck about nothing or nobody. Hasan was the most flamboyant of the crew. But he had no problem backing up everything he said while putting on a show. I knew that both of my men had my back, so I was ready to bounce.

Outside of the Casino, we walked the boardwalk until we reached the underpass that led to the parking lot for Bally's Hotel. I immediately scanned the crowded streets for any familiar faces. I pulled the Glock .45 and held it down beside my leg. On Park Place, we made a right and kept walking. I looked behind me and spotted a black Ford Bronco approaching us with dark tinted windows.

"Yo, Has'?"

"What's poppin, son?"

"There's a black Bronco tryna creep up on us from the rear. You see it?"

Hasan looked back, then he pulled two guns from his waist and nodded.

"You ready, Gunz?"

Gunz cocked his .40 and said, "All the time, baby boy."

The Bronco was slowly making its way down the dimly lit street. The one advantage we had over the people in the Bronco was that we had guns and whoever was in the truck probably thought we were unarmed. I saw the passenger window come down and that was all I needed to see.

"Get down!"

I dropped down behind a car to my left. Then rose up and fired at the truck. On both sides of me, Gunz and Hasan did the same. A full assault of bullets sprayed the car that we were behind. The automatic gunfire seemed to go on forever.

What the fuck are they shooting?

When the shots stopped momentarily, I rose up and saw that the truck was idle in the middle of the street. Hearing one of the doors open. I saw that the driver had jumped out of the truck and was on foot. Using the truck as covers, the driver sprayed the car again. I crouched as low as I could and prayed none of his bullets found their mark.

I heard a loud gasp and then, "I'm hit."

I saw Hasan hit the ground and lay flat, dark blood stained his shirt in the front. I grabbed the gun in his hand and put it in my waist, then grabbed his other guns.

"Just breathe easy, Has'. Lay flat and don't try it move I got you, young son." To Gunz, I said, "He's going to need to reload in a minute. When he does, we're gonna hit both ends of each truck and trap him. Everyone else in the ruck must be hit. So only one gun is going off besides ours."

I raised the four-fifth over the hood of the car and fired. *Boom! Boom! Boom!*

When the dude behind the truck didn't return fire, I looked at Gunz. "Now, son!"

Gunz ran out into the street toward the back of the truck and stopped. I ran up to the front end and peeked around the corner. The startled man raised his head, then his gun to shoot but Gunz had him from the back and laid him down. I walked over to the dude and stared into the face of one of my enemies. Tyreek *Reek* Jones looked up at me with fear in his eyes. They searched for but found no compassion in mine. I stood directly over him and emptied Hasan's Sig Sauer in his face.

"Gunz grab Hasan and get outta here. Take him to the car. I'll be there in a minute."

"Yo', son, baby boy hit bad. You need to come on now." Gunz picked up Hasan.

"I'm on my way." I walked around the truck to the passenger seat and opened the door.

The body of a man spilled out. It was one of the dudes that I saw on the wall in the Casino. He was dead, half of his head was missing. Just as I was about to turn and leave, I heard a sound. It seemed to come from the backseat of the truck. I opened the back-door and saw the dude that was on the wall hiding behind the backseat.

He looked into my eyes with tears in his. "Please, don't kill me, I wasn't with that. I just came along for the ride. Don't kill me, son."

"You guilty by association then, son. As a matter of fact, I remember you now. Your name Bones," I said and spotted the gun lying beside him. The way it looked it must've jammed on him. "I'ma let you go this time. But word life, son, if you ever get with some shit—"

"I won't, Najee. I swear on my mother. I'm done. I didn't even fuck with that nigga 'Reek like that."

Thanks, Allah, for the gun. I turned around as if I was leaving then spent back around and hit the dude twice in the face with the four-fifth. I stood there for a moment and marveled at the mess that the hydro shock bullets inflicted and knew that all three men were dead. As the sirens could be heard in the distance, I ran off at night.

"We gotta get son to a hospital asap, baby boy," Gunz said. He drove the convertible through the streets of Atlantic City. "Son don't look like he's going to make it."

"He's going to make it, Insha Allah! We left three bodies back there, son, so we gotta drop Has' off in the brick. He can't go to no hospital in A.C. because they are going to be looking for somebody."

"Three bodies?"

"Yeah, one of us hit the nigga in the passenger seat off the break. He fell out of the passenger door with half his shit missing. I wanted to make sure we left no witnesses, so I check the truck and sure enough, I found another nigga in the back of the truck hiding. A nigga named Bones from Prince Street He tried to beg for his life, but I sent him on his way. We gon have to pray that Has' can hold on." I looked into the back at my man Hasan and said a silent prayer to Allah.

The hole from his shirt was soaked with blood. His breathing was shallow, and his eyes were closed. *Please God don't let my man die like this. Not in the back seat of a car.*

Has', hold on, son we are almost there. Don't die on me," I said. We were about 20 minutes from St. Michael's Hospital in Newark. "Hold on, Has', hold on."

Chapter 10

Angel

The phone on the table next to my bed rang nonstop. I rubbed the sleep out of my eyes and picked up the phone. "Hello?"

"Assalamu' Alaikum." It was Aminah.

"Was-laikum Assalam."

"You are too scared to miss that many salats. You braver than me," Aminah said.

"Minah', I know you didn't wake me up to talk about no prayer."

"Of course, not, I woke up to tell you what happened last night."

I instantly became awake and sat up in bed. "What happened?"

"Salimah's brother Najee and his men were at the fight last night."

I already know that. "And?"

"When they left some dudes in a black truck rolled up on them as they walked to their car. Salimah told me Najee told her that they had to kill three muthafuckas."

So, Najee was a killer, too. "Are you saying that they killed three people last night in Atlantic City?"

"Yeah."

"You bullshittin'?"

"Wallahi," Aminah said and I knew she was telling the truth. "Salimah called me from the hospital."

"From the hospital? What was she doing at the hospital?" I asked.

"One of Najee's men got hit. This dude's named Hasan. He died at the hospital. Najee called Salimah and she went up there. Everybody in the towers is fucked up about Hassan getting killed. Salimah told me that Najee and his men knew who the dudes were and what the beef was about. Shit, it's about to get mad wicked in the streets of Newark. That nigga Najee is a cold-blooded nut. He has been killing shit since the early 90s. He's the reason Salimah's boyfriend Mu got shit on lock in the projects. All I know is that I'm about to chill out for a while. I'm not going nowhere near Brick Towers. I ain't catching no stray slugs for no muthafucka."

I laughed at Aminah, but my mind was really on Najee. He was definitely someone that I wanted to get to know better. "Well, thank you for the news brief, I appreciate the info. But let me get back at you after I get up."

"Ang, you going back to sleep?"

"Girl, I'm tired as hell. You and Salimah wore my ass out last night. I'ma go back to sleep for a little while. I'll call you when I get up."

"You better. Holla back, Assalamu 'Alaikum."

"Wa-lailul Assalhaam."

I hung up the phone and laid back down. I thought about everything Aminah had just told me. The crazy part about the whole thing was that I was turned on in a strange kind of way. I kept thinking about Najee and all the power he allegedly wielded in the streets I imagined that fine ass nigga busting his gun and killing people.

The thought of that shit had my pussy wet as shit. The next thing I know, my hand was in my panties looking for my clit. I couldn't even remember the last time I had some dick. I stuck one of my fingers inside me and felt how tight it was. My fingers had gotten pretty familiar with my sex in the last two years or so, so they knew exactly what to do. I thought about Najee and the way that he looked the day I met him at Salimha's house. I imagined what he'd look like between my legs, beating this pussy up. My right index finger circled my clit gently as I envisioned myself kissing him all over. I imagine his lips on mine. Then his lips were all over me. They were so soft. I purred like a cat. I rubbed my clit with one hand and stopped my session to ease out of my panties. After removing them, I went back to work. I used the fingers on my left hand to massage my clit. Then I thought about something that Aminah had said to me.

"The bitches are on his dick. Which I also happened to have heard is about eleven inches—"

Damn! The thought of 11-inches of dick hanging between the legs of a man that fine sent shivers all through my body. I reached down with my right hand and pushed two fingers into me. That, in conjunction with my left index finger rubbing my clit, had me ready to scream. I envision me sucking Najee's dick and what it might taste like. I took my fingers out of me, put them in my mouth, and sucked on them. I was so turned on, I put my fingers back inside me and grabbed my hips as if Najee was right there.

By the time I imagined him cumming with every inch of that dick in me, I was cumming all over myself. My legs were shaking from the strength of the orgasm. I put my fingers back in my mouth to taste myself, then decided to call Najee. I needed some real dick, even if it was a dick about to go to war. They tasted better anyway.

I got out of bed and found my cell phone on the kitchen counter. His number was programmed in already so I just hit auto-dial. The phone rang and kept ringing. Just as I was about to hang up, someone picked up.

"Hello?"

"Can I speak to Najee?"

"Who this?"

"Angel."

"He can't come to the phone, right now, shorty. But I'll be sure to tell him to give you a call. A'ight?"

"Thank you," I said and hung up the phone. *I made the first move, Najee. The next move is on you.*

Anthony Fields

Chapter 11

Najee

My eyes were bloodshot red, I stood over the sink and looked into my eyes as if I could see into my own soul. I turned on the cold water in the sink and put my hands under the faucet. I doused my face and head with water to cool off the beast inside of me. I had cried myself into a headache and now my head, as well as my heart, was hurting. My man Hasan was only thirty-years young and now he was resting eternally. Hasan and I had grown up together in the projects. He lived in building #689 and I lived in #715.

We became instant friends after we fought twice as kids. We attended McKinley Elementary and Arts High School together. We learned everything about life together in the streets. We learned about love together and we fucked all the same bitches. We were a package deal. When I went and bought a nickel-plated .38 revolver as my first gun, Hasan went and did the same. Whatever I did, he followed my lead. We were more than friends we were like brothers. Tears welled up in my eyes again and I threw water on my face to try and disguise my newest tears. I told myself that I wasn't going to cry no more.

Tears fell from my eyes anyway and I let them. I bent down onto the sink and cried like a baby. Then someone knocked on the bathroom door.

"Najee, son, you a'ight in there?"

Naw, I ain't a'ight "Yeah, I'll be out in a minute."

I dried my eyes with my shirt and got myself together. I took a leak, washed my hands, and left the bathroom. In the living room of my man Gunz's apartment, I paced the floor before speaking to all the men that were gathered.

"The niggas that brought us that move in A.C. was Reek from High Street and Spruce. The one with the white Lexus 460. I know that because I'm the last person he saw before he crossed over. Me and son have been beefing back and forth for years, but never on no murder-death-kill shit, feel me? The other nigga that was busting out of the passenger seat of the Bronco was a dude that used to be with Reek, named Jim Jim. I saw him and the dude Bones at the fight, but I couldn't place their faces right then and there. That fuckin' weed must be killing my brain cells.

"Anyways, I knew them niggas was up to something, I told Gunz and Has' what was up and we broke out. At some point them niggas hooked up with Reek and then they brought us the move. At first, I couldn't understand why them niggas chose to try their hand with us in A.C. Then it came to me Reek and his men grew up under Hashim and Big Rock. When Big Rock got killed last year, the first person that they tried to blame was me. Me and Big Rock had a fallout at Loretta's one night over a bitch. The bitch was on my dick, but she was there with Big Rock.

"I wasn't even paying the bitch no mind when my son came over and tried to grandstand on a nigga. We faced off in the club, but that wasn't nothing. I knew them niggas didn't really want it. I let it go. A few minutes later, I bounced and went home. Two days later, somebody murks the nigga and the first name that comes to mind for his men is me. When word got to me that those Spruce Street niggas suspected me of hittin' Big Rock, I went around there and stepped to Reek and Hashim. I told them niggas that if I wanted to hit their man, I would have done it and let them know I did it.

"And that muthafuckas was mentioning me, bogusly. Then Hashim got on his tough man shit and said some faggot ass shit I can't remember, but I let it go. I knew they were gonna think I had my hand in it. And I did, but not because of what he said to me that day on Spruce Street. Big Rock beat one of my niggas from Vaislburg outta some money. He sold my man Drayco two bricks of bullshit. They had the brick made up of about one-hundred grams of coke layered around the dummy middle.

"The shit looked and tasted official, but when you got somewhere and opened the whole joint, you could see that it was bullshit. Drayco came to me and asked about them niggas. I gave son the four-one-one and directed his path. He and his men put the work in while I watch from across the street. Reek and 'nem went on a few

78

missions tryna get back at whoever for hittin' Hashim. They probably wanted to come through here but knew they wasn't strong enough for that. That would've made them suicidal.

"That's why they brought the most on me, out of town. They knew that if they attempted to hit me anywhere in the city and word got back, their whole crew was dead. So the best course action was to get a nigga in A.C. that way if they succeed, the beef could go to any number of niggas who may have been responsible. But Reek made one fatal mistake, he never thought that we'd have guns on us. He probably figured that catching us coming back to our cars was the best way to get us.

"After all, who would be in a Casino, at the fights, around all them cops with hittas on them. Plus, how would we get heat into the casino? Reek never factored into his equation that I know people from everywhere. Not just the Brick, with all the dirt we do in the street, I ain't never going nowhere without my heat. I know some bitches that work in the hotel adjacent to the Casio. Them bitches took our heat into the Casino the day before, then found us at a pre-arranged spot and gave them to us. But, like I said, there was no way Reek could have known that.

"So, they tried their hands. And even though Reek is gone and we murked two of his men, my appetite for destruction hasn't been fed. Them bitch niggas killed Has' and that right there is unforgivable to me. Even in death. They got about ten dudes left that'll ride for them. We about to fuck them niggas around and by the time we finish, brick Tower niggas will be running Spruce Street. My man should be buried in the next seventy-two hours before an ounce of dirt touches his casket, I want all them niggas dead. Y'all feel me?"

All the men in the room nodded their heads. I stood there for an extra minute and let a solitary teardrop from my eyes. That was for cause and effect. My men knew how close me and Hasan were. They knew that his death affected me in the worse way and that I was about to cause a lot of murder and mayhem.

***

"This is Helen Debrew with Channel 7 Eyewitness. News at 11. Today has marked a gruesome and bloody day in the city of Newark. Early this morning, authorities responded to a call about gunshots fired in the area. Newark police went to the Riviera Hotel and found the body of a black male lying between two parked cars. The slain man is believed to have been in his late twenties or early thirties. That slaying is still under investigation.,

Then fifteen minutes after 12, at the intersection of High Street and Spruce, a dark-colored Cadillac SUV pulled alongside a white Chevy Tahoe and opened fire. Two occupants of the Chevy were killed at the scene. One man was rushed to Beth Israel Hospital, where he later died. Newark police are asking for any tips about the broad daylight murders. The assailants were last seen speeding away from the scene in a new model black Cadillac truck. Approximately two hours ago authorities were called to the scene of a gruesome discovery. A black man was found in a building in the Spruce Street Projects completely decapitated. His body was propped up so it would appear to be sitting and the head was in his lap.

The Neighborhood Watch has contacted the Mayor and requested more police to patrol these dangerous neighborhoods. Eyewitness News contacted the mayor's office and requested a comment about the recent onslaught of homicides in the city. An aide to the Mayor said that the Mayor refuses to comment. As more news becomes available, Eyewitness News will cover it and get all information to you. In other news, today the Supreme Court—"

I changed the channel to a cable channel, Showtime. Then I channel surfed for a little while trying to find something that would take my mind off of my recent pain. But nothing I could watch or listen to took my mind off Hasan's death. The sight of my man in the backseat of my Benz fucked me up for life. I had one of my men take the Benz up to Branch Brook Park and torch it. I could never drive it again, I thought about what the news had said and relived every moment when one of them niggas died. I witnessed each execution personally. I didn't have to beg to watch my men murk shit, I wanted to be there.

I got niggas in the streets shaking in their boots. To them, it seems like I'm everywhere at one time. By the time I'm finished with them niggas, the whole Newark is gonna bow down and respect my gangster. I clicked the TV off and downed the last of the drink in my cup. Then I fired up the half of blunt in the ashtray, inhaling the acrid blueberry haze smoke gave me a coughing fit, but I kept pulling it. I filled my lungs with so much smoke that I thought my heart would burst at any moment. Then I exhaled. It was as if I was exorcising my demons, I felt a whole lot better when I laid down to rest. I was finally able to go to sleep.

"Naj', you up, fam?" Yasir screamed in my ear from the other side of the phone. "Yeah, I'm up, nigga. Stop fucking screaming in my ear. What's crackin?"

"Ayo, fam, I'm right behind that nigga Mike, right now. He's in the car wit' his girl and a kid. What you want me to do, son?"

I thought about what Yasir had just said. The nigga Mike one of the gunners from the 7th Avenue projects that rolled with Reek and 'nem was caught in a car slipping with his family in the middle of a war zone. Fucking fool. "Yeah, go ahead and taste his ass."

"What about the bitch and the kid?"

"Fuck 'em, toast their asses, too. That'll let them niggas know that no one is exempt. Whoever, whenever, wherever."

"I got you, fam. Consider it done."

"You got somebody with you?"

"No doubt. I got Gunz with me."

"Put Gunz on the phone." A second later, Gunz picked up. "Yo' Gunz, hold the phone and let Ya' put the work in. I wanna hear it. When it's done, I want y'all to meet me around the way in about two hours."

"Yo, baby boy, you bugged the fuck out, but I got you." To Yasir, he said, "Ya' go ahead and put that work in at the next light. I'm holding the phone. Naj' wanna hear that shit."

I laid back in the bed and waited. About two minutes later, I heard the familiar spit of the full-auto AR-15. I disconnected the call knowing that everybody in that car was dead and I didn't feel a thing. What I did feel was a hangover from all the Hennessy I had drunk the night before. After I ended the call, I took a shower and thought about the night Hasan died. I thought about the shootout that led to him getting shot. I thought about seeing the two niggas across from the concession stand. The concession stands made me think about her—Angel.

The woman that had been popping in and out of my head since I met her.

"My name is Angel. You can call me Angel."

She was by far the baddest bitch I had seen in a while and the way she treated a nigga was a turn on. All the bitches in Newark who knew who I was, were groupie types. Angel was different.

"—I'm from DC—"

She looked like a pretty version of Lauren London. Her hair was long and hung down her back, and her body was tight. My dick got hard just thinking about her. Then I remembered that we had exchanged numbers. I was tempted to get my cell phone out and call her, but the time wasn't right. I told myself that as soon as the work was over, I was gonna get at her. I wanted to see what she was about, but later for all that.

"Stay focused, Naj," I told myself.

I went into the bathroom and turned the shower water on. When it heated up, I jumped in. Like a regular muthafucka with a 9 to 5, I had a job to do. No matter what happened, that job was gonna get done.

Chapter 12

Angel & Najee

"This bloodbath shit is bad for business, Najee. You think that muthafuckas in the street don't know that y'all niggas have declared war on Reek's crew?" Mu asked me as he counted money at my sister's kitchen table.

I sat on the couch and watched the short, barrel-chested man that I called a friend. He had a money counting machine going as he counted small bills. On the other side of him was a duffle bag with about 50 keys of coke in it. "I don't give a fuck about who knows what. And my war on them bitch niggas that killed my man is bad for whose business, Mu? Yours or mine?"

"You know what I mean, Naj. You know how war is. It's kill on sight and leave no witness." Killing the dude Mike's family was overkill. You scaring the old people, ock. And when the old people in the hood get scared to come outside, the cops gonna shut shit down. I'm fucked up about Hasan, too, but ock, shutting the whole city down is not gonna bring Ha back. And when I speak of business, my business is your business. How you think you copped that pretty ass Bentley that's parked outside."

"True dat. By the way, I'm doing it, it definitely lets everybody know that somebody fucked up. And it puts niggas on point that if you kill one of mine, I'ma crush four of yours."

As of on cue, Salimah came out of the bathroom with a towel wrapped around her head and said, "Did y'all hear about the girl Renita and her son getting killed in a car with that nigga Mike from 7th Avenue?"

I saw Mu glance at me and shake his head. *Nigga fuck you.* "Yeah, I heard about that shit. That's fucked up about the kid. Shorty ain't did shit to nobody."

"These muthafuckas out here are on some crazy ass shit. Killing little kids and shit," Salimah said and disappeared back in the back.

"See what I mean, ock? You gotta ease up, Naj. Let that shit go. You've done enough. Them niggas in the street got the picture.

Muthafuckas going in the house before the streetlights come on, now. Everybody's afraid of their own shadow. And ain't no money being made on Spruce Street. At the end of the day, after family comes money and it's a lot of that to be made in the aftermath of Reek's demise. Think on that young boy, think on that."

What Mu said made a lot of sense to me and I had to admit that my hunger for blood was starting to subside. I thought about the dude that I had just killed over an hour ago. I caught Dahmir shooting dice on Martin Luther King Blvd, with a group of niggas from the Betty Shabazz Apartments. He had the dice and was so caught up in the game that he never saw the looks on everybody's face as I approached him. I walked up on him from the side and waited for him to look up.

"Oh, shit!" he said when he saw me.

"Oh, shit is right," I replied, right before I replied, right before I nailed his ass to the concrete. "Did anybody here see anything? I asked the stunned crowd.

Everybody shook their heads no.

"Good. Because if I hear that someone did see something, I'm coming back for everybody here. Is that understood?"

"Yeah," they all uttered in unison. I calmly walked back to Gunz' Navigator and told him, "Pull off."

***

"Najee? Najee?"

I looked up and saw Salimah's friend Capri standing over me. I was so much in a daze, I didn't hear her come in. She was dressed in booty hugger shorts and a see-through top that showed off her ample breasts. From my position on the couch, I could see straight through the gap in her legs. My eyes found the pussy print in his shorts and stopped there. I openly ogled her pussy as she spoke, but I didn't hear a word she said. The hood grapevine had it that Capri had the best head on the East coast, every time she tried to give it to me, I shot her down.

Not today, though. I stood up and grabbed her by the hand. "Shorty, let me holla at you for a minute." I guided her to the spare bedroom that I usually slept in when I stayed over at my sister's house.

We walked right past Salimah, who knew exactly what I was up to. I smiled a wicked grin, gave her that *stay out my business look,* and kept on moving.

"This ain't no motel, nigga. Get a room," I heard Salimah say as I closed the room door.

"What's your name again, shorty?" I asked as I unzipped my jeans and pulled out my dick.

"Capri," she said and sat on the bed. "Like the pants."

"What were you trying to say out there? When you were calling my name?"

"I was tryna tell you—"

That was as far as she got before I stuck my dick in her mouth. She tried to say something else, but I cut her off. "Didn't your mother tell you not to talk with your mouth full? We'll talk when you finish."

I put my hand on the back of the girl's head and guided her mouth further onto my dick. "That's right, ma. Eat that dick for me—eat that dick!"

***

My cell phone vibrating got my attention away from the crunches I was doing. I was sweaty as hell and my stomach muscles were screaming for a break. I got up off the floor and answered my phone.

"Hello?"

"Girl, I was looking at CNN and they reported something about three people getting killed in a truck after a fight in Atlantic City. Then I put two and two together and remembered that you said you were going to a fight the last time we spoke. I called your ass a few times, but you never answered. Did you get my voicemail?"

"How are you, Tamara? I'm glad you were concerned for me. But whatever happened to good old fashioned, hey, Angel. How're you doing?" I asked.

"Angel, we go too far back for all that mushy shit. Why haven't you called me back?"

"I've been busy, that's why."

"Doing what?"

"Damn are you my parole officer?" I replied and laughed. I knew Tamara meant well. "I've been looking for a spot to lease up here. I wanna own a store in the area. Newark needs a little bit of that DC flavor, these some bamma muthafuckas up here, girl."

"Yeah?"

"Yeah. They sell P. Miller shit in the stores up here."

Tamara laughed hysterically. "No, they don't. Stop lying, Angel."

"I ain't bullshittin', I walked in this spot called Against All Odds the other day and they had a display case with S.D.C. in it and Vokal tennis shoes."

"What the fuck is S.D.C.?" Tamara asked, obviously vexed.

"Snoop Dogg Clothing, I almost passed out in tha joint."

Tamara laughed even harder. "Angel, stop it. You got my stomach hurting, laughing at your ass. They should change the name of the store."

"To what?" I asked her.

"To B.A.C.K."

"Back? What does that mean?"

"Bamma Ass Clothes and Kicks."

"Tee, I'm gone, girl. You're joking and shit," I said after I finished laughing. "I gotta finish working out. I'll call you later. Bye."

I decided to cut my workout short and eat a little something. I hadn't eaten all day. The leftover General Tso's chicken in the refrigerator looked to be the most appetizing, so I pulled it out. I put the plate in the microwave and then stared at my cell phone. I'ma call this nigga one more time and if he doesn't answer fuck him.

Angel 2

Picking up my cell, I scrolled through my contacts. I pressed the call when I found Najee's number. He picked up on the third ring.

"Hello?"

"Najee?"

"Yeah. Who is?"

"Who do you want it to be?" I asked hoping he didn't give the wrong answer.

"The only one person I'd like to talk to right now and she's from DC."

"Why your fake ass ain't calling me, then?"

"It's a long story—I mean it's a long story. Anyway, what are you doing, right now?"

"I'm about to eat. Why what's up?"

"Can I eat with you?" Najee asked.

"At my house? Naw, we just met, we can't do that yet. You might be a crazy dude or something."

"Look who's talking. I'm minding my own business, driving on the highway, when I get an anonymous call from a woman asking me questions and won't even identify herself. That's crazy."

I pushed the leftover Chinese food away from me. "You win. How about we meet somewhere and eat?"

"That sounds like a plan to me, shortly. Do you know where the Jersey Gardens Mall is?"

"I've been there before, but I was with my cousin and your sister."

"Oh, so Aminah is your cousin?"

"Yeah, why?"

"No reason, I just didn't know. A'ight, here's the plan. Meet me at the mail. Where are you now?"

"At the Colonnades Condos."

"From there you have to go straight on—"

***

I was sitting in my new smoke Grey Bentley Continental GT waiting for Angel to show up. I looked down at my watch. When I hung up the phone with her last, she should have been five minutes away. That was ten minutes ago. As I reached for my phone, I spotted the candy apple red Porsche truck pull into the crossed parking lot and cruise around.

A Porsche Cayenne, huh? When she almost drove right by me. I hit the horn. Then I stepped out of the car. After she parked her truck, I led Angel into the mall.

"Let's eat first, then we can walk around for a while. Is that a'ight with you, shorty?" I asked.

"Yeah. I'm starving like Marvin, right now."

Who the fuck is Marvin? "They got a nice little spot on the second floor. A Muslim brother named Halim own the joint. They make the best lamb chops I ever tasted in my life."

It took us about ten minutes to reach the restaurant. Halim greeted us at the door.

"Assalamu Alaikum, Najee. It's been too long since you last came here."

"Wa-laikum Assalaam, Halim. I been busy, ock. I'm here now, though, and I brought a friend with me." I turned to Angel and was about to tell Halim something when I heard Angel say,

"Assalaam Alaikum, Halim. My name is Kareemah."

"Ah, you are a muslimah? Very good for you, Najee. Wa-laikum Assalam, Kareemah. Let me get you a table."

When we sat down at the table and ordered, I stole glances at Angel every few seconds. She was gorgeous. "Damn, shorty, you didn't tell me you were Muslim."

"You didn't ask."

"True dat. That's definitely a good look, though. At least I ain't gotta worry about pork being on your breath when I kiss you."

"Who said anything about you kissing me?" she said and smiled.

"Oh, I'm gonna kiss you, shorty. Ain't no doubt about that. I outweigh you by about eighty pounds and I'm taller than you. If push comes to shove, I'll take the kiss," I replied, returning the smile. "We'll see about that, don't underestimate me because of my size. Anyway, playa, if you play your cards right, I might let you kiss me. So, you're Muslim, too, huh?"

"Without a doubt. I was born a Muslim. Me and my sister. Our parents were on their deen heavy and they instilled that in us. Then both of them got killed on a ferry boat in the Hudson when we were kids. I was fucked up mentally for a long time behind that. Me and Salimah moved in with our grandmother. Our mother's mother.

"Baby girl was on her Christian shit super hard. She didn't understand us or our beliefs at all. She kept tryna feed us swine and stop us from offering the salat. We knew we had to get up outta that joint quick fast. That's when I went into the streets to make a way for me and my sister. In no time, I did that and more. We have been on our own since.

"Salimah is all I got as far as blood go because I don't recognize nobody else on either side of our family. Both of us are still Muslim, we just fasiq, right now. Especially me, I need to make a million talks for Salatal-Tawba. I was thirteen-years-old when I went into the streets. For some reason, shorty, I never left. Brick City has a way of doing that to a muthafucka. You feel me?"

"I feel you. *More than you'll ever know.* My story is similar to yours. When we get to know each other a little better. I'll tell you mine."

"Now, that ain't fair, shorty. I just spilled my guts to you, and I don't usually do that. You ain't gonna tell me nothing about you, huh?"

We were interrupted by the waiter bringing our food. Suddenly I realized how hungry I was. I had not eaten much since Hasan died. I silently tore into my smothered lamb chops as I thought about the woman sitting across from me. There was something about her that made me feel good. I couldn't put my finger on it, but it was there. There was an air of mystique surrounding her and I promised myself right there at that table that I would get to know her better. *A lot better.*

"What's so funny?" Najee asked me as we walked through a store in the mall.

"This shit right here," I said and grabbed a pair of pants from the rack. "Master P needs to stop this shit. Do niggas in Newark really wear this P. Miller shit?"

"Come on, shorty. You are on some funny shit, right now. Real niggas in the hood don't wear that fugazi ass shit. Why do you think the shelves and racks are full of that shit? Ain't nobody buying that shit."

"What about one of them, Sean Jean fits over there? Would you wear that?"

"I'd rather be naked," Najee replied with contempt in his tone.

I'd love to see you naked. I pictured Najee naked and shivered. He had an effect on me that nobody had on me in years. Since Tony or Deandre. I was still picturing him nude in my mind when the ringtone on my phone chirped. I looked at the phone and saw that the caller was my mother.

"Hello, Ma. Wa-laikum Assalam. Yeah, Ma. I'm doing good. I'm thinking about opening a couple of stores. So, I'm up here looking at properties. Where's my baby? When she wakes up, tell her I love her. I'll call you later tonight, Ma. Okay, Ma. Wa-laikum Assalam." I ended the call and turned back to Najee. "Where were we?"

"You asked me would I wear some Sean Jean? And I was telling you that I'd rather be naked. I wasn't tryna eavesdrop on your conversation, but I heard you say something about wanting to open a store in this area. Is that why you're here? Because at the fight you said you were here on vacation."

"I lied, I'm thinking about branching my businesses out into other cities. In D.C., I own three businesses. A beauty and barber salon, a communications outlet, and a clothing store called Top Of The Line Fashions. I want to open a spot up here in Newark. I've been on the phone with a few realtors and I'm close to deciding on a storefront property on Brad Street and Branford Place. Not too far from the Masjid. I'll close on that spot in a few days. In the meantime, I have to take a few trips."

"Related to the store?"

"Yeah. I scheduled a meeting with representatives for the top designers in the fashion industry I'ma be gone for a few weeks."

What Najee said next caught me off guard.

"I'm tryna go with you, shorty. I know a little bit about fashion. You might need a man's point of view. The male eye can see what the female eye can't. You flying, right?"

"Of course. I'm flying—"

"Well, I'm tryna ride. I need to get away for a while, anyway. So, what's good, shorty? You down for me tagging along?"

"I—uh—yeah. You can come if you want to."

"That's a bet, when do we leave?"

"Tomorrow morning at ten. I'll reserve your seat tonight when I go online. You can meet me at Newark International at 9:30 a.m."

"You said a few weeks, right?"

"Yeah. We're going to Detroit, Las Vegas, L.A. Atlanta, Miami, and New York."

"What do I need to bring with me?"

"Nothing. Just bring you, I got the rest."

Anthony Fields

Chapter 13

Angel & Najee

Gunz walked around the living room of his apartment trying to keep himself calm. "Ayo, son, it ain't the time to be lax. What if a sleeping giant awakes while you're gone? Then you don't even know this bitch, son. What if somebody sent her? Huh? If shorty is a jump-off, treat her like a jump-off. You just met the bitch and now you talkin' 'bout jet setting the country with her. You on some coo-coo shit, right now, son. No bullshit."

"If some shit pops off while I'm gone, handle that shit then, nigga. What the fuck? In the last thirty days, shit has been all fucked up. Has' gone, fast money done slow down and we were out there crushing shit to the fullest. I need a break, son. Getting the fuck away from here for a while will do me good. I'll be back in a few weeks and we can do whatever. If shit gets hectic and you need me, I'll hop on the next thing smokin' back home. I already hollered at Mu. He gon' hit you off with his work and you gon' put Tye and 'nem down with the lick on Spruce. All you gotta do is make sure that shit runs smooth and before you know it, I'll be back."

"Whatever you say, baby boy. It's your call."

"I'm about to go home, pack, and get some rest. Then I'm leaving in the morning. I want you to pick me up and drop me off at the airport. You can meet shorty then. A'ight?"

"I got you, baby boy. You got that heat on you?"

"I lifted my shirt and showed Gunz the twin nine millimeters that rested in my waistband.

"Be safe then, son. One Love."

"One love." I hugged my man Gunz and left his crib.

Gunz and I walked toward the American Airlines terminal and spotted Angel at the counter. She glanced over her shoulder and saw us and smiled. Turning back around, she said something else to the lady behind the counter. I watched as the lady typed rapidly on a keyboard while periodically glancing at her computer screen. Three minutes later, she handed Angel two envelopes. Angel walked over to us and set a Louis Vuitton overnight bag down.

"Najee, I'm glad you made it. I see you even brought a friend."

"I would've stopped traffic to get here. This is my man Gunz. Gunz, this is Angel."

I saw Gunz give Angel the once over, then smiled. "What's up., shorty? Aye, Naj, you were right about one thing, baby boy."

"Right about what?"

"Shorty's a beast. I'm feeling her, son."

"Should I be flattered?" Angel asked Gunz.

"Hell yeah, shorty. Naj will tell you, I'm not impressed often. But today, I'm impressed. And I remember your voice too. The day after my man got hit, you called Naj's' phone. I asked you who was calling and told you he couldn't come to the phone. Remember that?"

"I remember that."

"Hold on, son. You never told me about no call on my phone." I was a little perturbed.

"Baby boy, there was a lot going on that day. You were in my bathroom for hours and wouldn't come out. By the time you did, I forgot to tell you that shawty had called. But anyway, this nigga right here," Gunz said to Angel while pointing at me. "—is my man, one hundred grand. I will kill man, woman, and child over him. So, I hope and pray that you come in peace? Because if you don't, I'll be your worst enemy. Feel me, shorty?"

Angel didn't respond to what Gunz said at all. She looked at me and said, "The plane leaves in ten minutes. I'll be over there by the boarding gate." She picked up the bag, turned and left.

I looked at Gunz crazy and bellowed, "Nigga, see what you did? You done went and pissed the woman off. If I had any chance of fucking in the next few days, that's probably dead. I'ma handle everything from here on out. You too much on your gangsta shit. Gangsters got holidays too, son. You ain't a killer every day."

"That's your problem now, baby boy. You are getting soft. Listen to what you just said. That's a bunch of bullshit. Killers can never take a day off. I'll see you when you get back. And make sure shawty knows I wasn't bullshittin' about what I said. I'm out."

I stood there for a minute and watched Gunz disappear in the crowd, then I walked over and caught up with Angel. The look on her face spoke a thousand words and I felt bad about it. "Angel, don't be pissed at the man, he's a little overprotective of me. Especially, now since our partner got killed. Come on, shorty, talk to me. I said he didn't mean anything by it."

I watched Angel's expression soften. "I don't like being threatened. I understand everything you just said, but he can't ever do that again. That's your man, remember that. That's your man."

I was confused by what she'd just said, so I decided to drop the whole thing. We stood there in silence the rest of the time until an intercom announced the boarding of American airlines flight 2525.

"That's our plane. Come on," Angel said and led the way through the gate onto the plane.

As the plane taxied down the runway at Newark International, I closed my eyes and tried to block out the anxiety that I felt when flying. When the plane lifted smoothly into the heavens, the contents of my stomach threatened to make their presence known. Since I had the window seat, I stared out of the window as the plane leveled off at about thirty thousand feet. I looked to my left at Angel and saw that she was asleep. I closed my eyes again and tried to think positive and eventually I nodded off myself.

In Detroit, Angel rented a beige Cadillac XTS. Since we hadn't said a word to each other since that morning. I decided to try and break the ice as we rode. "What's your favorite football team?"

Never taking her eyes off the road, Angel said, "Who else? The Redskins."

I smiled. "You gon think I'm tryna butter you up, but I fucks with them Skins, too."

"Stop playing."

"I'm serious. Ask me anything about them."

"How many Super Bowl rings did we get?"

"Three. We won 'em in '83, '87, and '91."

"Who are the quarterbacks on the roster, right now?'

"C'mon shorty. Really? RGIII, Kirk Cousins and Colt McCoy. Believe me now?"

"Naw, the sports page of any major newspaper will give you that information. Who was a part of the Hogs?"

"Joe Jacoby, Russ Grimm—"

"The Smurfs?"

"Daryl green—"

"The Fun Bunch?"

"Art Monk, Gary Clark."

"A'ight, a'ight, I believe you. How did you end up a 'Skins fan growing up in Jersey?"

"My father was a 'Skins fan. He was originally from D.C. He met my mother and moved to Newark to be with her. I guess you're a Wizards fan, too, huh?"

"Yeah, but they on some shit, right now. They paid John Wall all that money and he stays hurt. We don't have any room under the salary cap to shop for any stars on the free-agent market because of that. Nene is on the decline. Bradley Beal is really the only star left on a team of underachieving rookies. That's why they are ten and thirty-something."

I looked at Angel with newfound respect. Any female that sums up her whole team in a few minutes is a down ass broad. "Do you like baseball?"

"Not at all. I can't stand that shit. That soccer, tennis, and golf. I like boxing, football, basketball, and other things."

"Other things like what?"

"Like I told you before, if you play your cards right, one day you'll find out the answer to that question."

I watch a sly smile crossed Angel's face. I caught the subtle hint that she threw at me, but I acted like I hadn't. "What's on the agenda for Detroit?"

"I got a meeting scheduled for the next couple of days. The first one being tomorrow at 11 a.m."

We pull into the Grand Marriott Hotels across the street from the Kobo Hall. A valet came and got Angel's bag and drove the rental car away. Angel checked us into the Hotel. I wondered if she and I would share a room. I didn't have to wonder long because minutes later, she walked up to me and handed me a room key.

"You're on the fifth floor right above me in five-twelve. I charge the room to my credit card so go ahead and do everything. I was up all night getting ready for this trip and now I'm tired as shit I'm going to lie down. When I get up, I'll call you, okay?"

I indeed agreed, grabbed her bag, and followed Angel to the elevator. When the elevator stopped on the fourth floor, she grabbed her bag and left without as much as a goodbye. I might've made a mistake by coming here.

I walked down the hall until I found 512. When I walked into the room and looked around, I sat down. "Not bad."

Angel never did call me that evening. So, I watched TV and made a rack of calls to Newark. Then I fell asleep. I woke up the next morning a little jet lag so I decided to try out the Jacuzzi in my room before finding something to get into. If Angel was gonna play the long-distance games, so would I. I ended up going to the hotel gym first and working my muscles out until they hurt. Then I had a hotel employee drive me around Detroit and show me the sights. When I went back to my room, I undressed and jumped in the shower. From the bathroom, I heard a knock on my door. I wrapped a towel around me and answered the door. Angel was standing there. She walked right past me into the room.

"Have you ever heard of Mauri, Najee?"

"Naw, who is he?"

"It's not a he, it's a line of shoes, boots, and accessories. All reptiles."

"Naw, shorty, I ain't hip to Mauri," I answered and then realized that I was standing there wrapped in a towel.

Angel must've realized it, too because she said, "I'm sorry. Did I catch you at a bad time?"

"Naw, I was in the shower, but I'm finished now. Why do you wanna join me?"

"Ask me again when I'm in a better mood. Right now, I'm blown. I thought it would be a good idea to bring the Detroit flavor to D.C. and Newark. I tried to negotiate a deal with the manufacturer, and them muthafuckas told me no. All my other meetings went smoothly. Marc Jacobs people guaranteed me a shipment in the next sixty days. I met with the people for BCBG and Miu Miu, they all agreed to do business with me. But Mauri was the one I really wanted."

"Dudes in D.C. are just like Brick City niggas. They don't even wear that reptile shit. I don't see why you fucked up about that."

"Let me tell you something, boo. What I know about the streets, whether it's Brick City or D.C., is this, all it takes is the right people to be in the right spots and they'll make something fashionable. Certain people are trendsetters, whether they wanna be or not. For instance, if you showed up at all the clubs in Newark dressed in crocs and lizards, the whole city would follow your lead. They think that if you wear it, it must be the shit."

I tossed what Angel said around in my head and decided that she was right. If the right nigga in Newark started riding horses through the city, pretty soon damn near everybody would be on horseback. "I'm sorry to hear that the people ain't fucking with you. But can we get something to eat—together? I'm hungrier than a hostage."

"I'm hungry, too. Get dressed and let's go."

Chapter 14

Angel

Our next stop was Las Vegas. I met with the people from Hermes, Ferragamo, and Max Azria. We stayed in Vegas for three days, then flew to L.A. It was Najee's first time in L.A. He was enthralled with the scenery. I booked us into the La Cienega Plaza hotel on Melrose.

"I got us adjoining rooms. Come on, we're on the fourth floor." Before I walked into my room, I told Najee, "Don't try to sneak into my room while I'm sleeping. I sleep light."

"I should be telling you the same thing. You got a nigga all the way over here in Cali. Ain't no telling what you up to."

"Boy, whatever. You want me to do something to you, don't you?" I asked salaciously.

"I'ma keep that to myself. I'm glad I'm making some kind of progress, though."

"What progress are you making?"

"At least our rooms are on the same floor this time."

I laughed all the way into my room. As I undressed, I stared at the door that adjoined our rooms. All I had to do was walk through that door. Then I laid across the bed and felt like we became one. In time, I wiggled out of my thongs and willed Najee to come into my room.

The force that pulled me to him was strong. I recognized that at the airport. Because although I was upset about his man threatening me, the whole incident turned me on. When I buckled my seatbelt on the plane leaving Newark, I made my mind up to give Najee the royal treatment somewhere between Detroit and New York. It was time for me to get busy. The last dick that I enjoyed was Carlos' and that was too long ago. I could've given myself to any man, but my heart and mind wouldn't let me. There comes a time in life where you just wanna settle down and I guess that's where I am now. I want to be with one man, love one man, and make love to just one man. Something tells me that Najee might be that man. Gang-stresses need love, too. Having a child and getting old was starting to have some effect on me. I thought about all the murders that I'd committed and all the pain I've caused.

The jinn on my right shoulder whispers, "When will it all end?" The one on my left told me, "It doesn't stop until your casket drops."

Now that almost all my enemies were gone. I can take care of business on all levels. There's only one enemy left and that is Honesty. I wonder whether or not Honesty told the cops about me. At last check, no one had seen anything on the news or heard anything on the radio about me. I would know by now if the cops were looking for me.

I cleared all the negative thoughts from my mind and played with my pussy for a little while. I did my best positive thinking while washing myself. Then abruptly, I stopped. I walked into the bathroom and ran myself a bath.

Later that evening, I took Najee to Roscoe's Chicken and Waffles.

"I heard about this spot. These waffles good as a muthafucka," Najee said in between bites.

"I know right, I love them."

"I'm loving you more than these waffles, though."

"Don't say that. You gotta be careful with that *L*-word." I got quiet for a moment then said, "The last nigga that told me he liked me had my sister kidnapped, raped, and beaten to death."

"I'm sorry to hear that, shorty. I was joking with you. I Didn't mean to bring back bad memories for you."

"It's all good."

We ate the rest of our meal in silence, then returned to the hotel. The next morning, I had several meetings scheduled so I turned in early.

***

Things went well with the people I met. When I got to the hotel. I went straight to Najee's room. He answered the door in a wife beater and We R One sweats that he bought in Detroit. I walked into his room and sat down in the recliner.

"My feet are killing me."

Najee who was sitting on the bed patted the spot next to him and said, "C'mere. Sit right here for a minute."

I walked over to the bed and sat down.

"Take your shoes off."

I complied and kicked off my burgundy Chanel loafers. "Move over and put your feet in my lap."

I hope my feet don't smell sweaty. I did as I was told. Najee grabbed my left foot and massaged it, then he massaged every toe individually. I was in heaven. From my position on the bed, I realized that it was easy for Najee to look up my skirt. But I didn't care, the foot massage made me horny. When Najee started on my right foot. I took my left foot and sat the heel on his dick. Then I gently moved my foot back and forth. Najee looked into my eyes and saw the look that lived there. It was a look of pure lust. He knew that I was making the first move.

The next move was his and he didn't disappoint. Najee lifted my foot and licked all over it. He put each toe in his mouth and sucked on it. After giving both of my feet a virtual tongue bath, he moved up my leg to my ankles. By the time his lips reached my inner thighs, I was breathing hard and moaning. I instinctively scooted back on the bed and caused my skirt to hike up higher. Najee stood up and stood over me. He reached for my panties and tugged. I lifted myself off the bed so that they could slide right off. Najee's head disappeared between my legs and I gave in to the pleasure. I ended up cumming three times in the first ten minutes and almost collapsed in exhaustion from the release. Lifting Najee's head, I brought him to me. I grabbed both of his ears and put my lips on his. We kissed long, deep, and feverishly for what seemed like forever. Then I reached down and found the drawstring that held his pants up.

My hand acted on its own as it went inside his pants and grabbed his dick. *Damn! What Aminah said about him is true.*

I held his dick in my fist and pumped it vigorously while we kissed. I took my thumb and ran it over the head of his dick. When I pulled my hands out of his pants it was saturated with pre-cum. I broke my kiss with Najee and stuck my thumb in my mouth. My eyes never left his as I tasted him. Pushing Najee off me, I stood up erect. Face to face, I reached for his sweats and pulled them down as I dropped to my knees. He wasn't wearing underwear, so his dick sprang free and saluted me. My tongue saluted back as I put him in my mouth.

"Angel! Angel, I'm about to cum! It's coming!"

Najee' dick throbbed in my mouth and I knew he was about to blow. His body jerked and shook as I continued to use the muscles in my throat to get every drop out of him, and I swallowed it all. Real bitches still do real things. I wasn't ready to let him go just yet, so I kept his dick hostage in my mouth. It didn't take long for it to get hard again. I sucked his dick long and deep until it was as hard as it could get. Then I pushed Najee back onto the bed. Wiggling out of my skirt, I left my shirt on and climbed up on the bed. I bent down and gave his dick a few deep pulls and a kiss, and then I squatted over Najee. I rubbed his dick head in between my pussy lips a few times before sitting on it gradually.

I had to take my time and sit on it because I was so tight. "Ooohhh—ooohhh!"

Najee's dick was thick and curved. I tried to relax the muscles inside me to allow me to wake the whole thing, but they weren't trying to work with me. I felt so in control as I rode Najee. The look on his face and the sound he made kept me determined to sit on the entire length of his dick. It took me a while, but I eventually released enough to get most of him inside me. My pussy was stretched to capacity and the muscles in my legs cried out as I opened up and down. My feet were flat on the bed and my hands both rested on Najee's chest.

"*A-a-an-g-g-e-l!* Your pussy is so tight!"

I wiggled my hips and sat down further on Najee. He was going crazy and I loved every minute of it. Our eyes never left each other's and I finally rested my clit at the base of his dick. The whole 11-inches was in me and I wanted to cry. I wanted to scream and shout and or speak Spanish. His dick was literally inside my stomach. I bit down on my lip in an effort to not scream. I couldn't scream. Not the first time at least. I had to maintain control. I felt Najee's dick twitch, saw the screwed up look on his face, and knew he was ready to bust. So, I jumped off the dick and kneeled in front of him. I sucked Najee's dick like a professional porn star until he came for the second time. For the second time that day, I swallowed his cum.

After all that, I thought we were finished but obviously, Najee had different plans. He stood me up and bent me over the bed. His dick entered me semi-erect and picked up its own rhythm.

"Najee! Na-a-j-ee-ee! Yes! F-u-c-k m-e!" I put one foot up on the bed and pushed back on his dick.

Najee grabbed my waist and pounded into me and I loved it. Pushing too hard one time, I fell on the bed. Not to be deterred, Najee told me to get on all fours. So, I did. He started fucking me doggy style and all I could do was gather the comforter on the bed and bite down on it. Every time he thrust deep into me, I balled the comforter up in my fists and bit down harder. I was determined not to cry out or scream. Najee was fucking me roughly and I wanted to beg him to stop, but I couldn't. When he pulled my hair and smacked my ass, it was over. I came in tidal waves. I came from the bottom of my toes to the top of my head. My feet tingling and vibrations shot through my body like I was having a heart attack. Nobody has ever made me cum that hard and that long. Najee came again not too long after me. He pulled out and came all over my back. As his warm cum ran down the crack of my butt, I knew I was keeping him.

Chapter 15

Najee

I woke up in bed with Angel. My body ached like I had gone twelve rounds in the ring with Mike Tyson. I rolled over, grabbed the phone, and ordered breakfast from the kitchen. When the food arrived, I took the syrup off the cart and got back in the bed. I moved the covers off Angel and poured the syrup on her stomach and made a trail down to her pussy.

"Najee—what is that?" Angel asked waking out of her sleep.

I didn't respond, instead, I licked the syrup that had rundown her clit, then ate the syrup out of the middle. Angel's hand gripped my curls and pushed me further into her.

"B-a-a-ab-y-y, stop! Oh, Najee stop it!" Angel moaned.

I stepped up my head game and put it on Angel. She started moaning so loud that I thought she was having a fit. She grabbed my hair in her hands and pulled hard. Pressing my head down further and then grinding her pelvis in my face. Angels came all over me.

It took her a minute to get herself together. When she did, she said, "Damn it, boy! What did I do to deserve all that?"

"Breakfast in bed turned into breakfast and head. That's what that Lil Wayne joint stated," I said and smiled. "I felt like a different kind of waffle with my syrup this morning."

"Don't spoil me like that. I'll get addicted. Speaking of breakfast, I got a taste for some beef sausage." Angel rose up and grabbed my dick.

"I ordered breakfast for us to eat—"

"I'm eating this, you can have this food."

All I could do was lay back and enjoy the view. Watching somebody eat never felt so good.

In Atlanta, we booked a single suite at the Radisson Hotel on Peachtree Avenue. We shopped, went to a few clubs, and made love all day. I was really feeling shorty and I wanted to let her know it.

But I knew that she was an independent woman. They weren't looking for niggas to fall in love with or so I heard. If the opportunity presented itself, I decided to put my cards on the table and let her know what I was feeling.

Our second day there, Angel went and met all the people she needed to see. By the time the American West jumbo jet airplane landed at our next destination, I was positive of one thing and one thing. I was in love.

The ride in the rented Ferrari was the smoothest I'd ever felt in a car. *I'ma have to cop me one of these.* I maneuvered the sleek sports car around the streets of Miami with Angel by my side. For some reason, she had been quiet all evening and I decided to leave her alone in her thoughts. A song came on the radio that I liked, so I turned it up—

"When I'm with you/ I hear a sound/ that makes me laugh and smile and sing to you/ When I'm with you/ I feel so free/ I love that love is going to take control of me—when I'm with you it—it's for real/ It's for real/What I feel/ What I feel/ When I'm with you/ When I'm with you/I wonder why/people do stop and stare and smile at us/When I'm with you/ the sun shines my way/Baby, our loves reflect its rays of light on everyone in the world/when I'm with you—"

"Najee pulled over by the beach. I want to walk on the shore and feel the sand in my toes."

I parked the Ferrari and followed Angel to the beach. We walked along the shore in silence until her words broke the stillness of the night.

"I told you back when we first met, that if you played your cards right I'd let you kiss me. Well, you've kissed me, so that means you played your cards right. I also told you that when we got to know each other better, I'd tell you more about me. Remember?"

"I remember that."

"That time is now. I was born and raised in DC. My family is Muslim. My father named me Kareemah, but he nicknamed me Angel. He always said that I was *Daddy's little angel.* But what nobody knew, and I never told was that daddy liked to creep in my room at night when nobody was around and molest me. When I got older, he raped me. As time went on, I guess he decided that I wasn't good enough anymore. Because he went after my younger sister.

"Something inside me snapped one day and I knew that I couldn't let my father do to my sister what he had done to me for years. I put a plan together in my head and carried it out. I lured my father to a park one night and I stabbed him to death. I never told anyone what I had done except my best friend Fatima. I was fifteen-years-old, then. When I took my father's life, a dark cloud fell over me and changed me. I was a totally different person after that.

"Then some years later, I went away to college, I met a dude name Andre Ford my first year there. He was the type of dude that preyed on young girls, freshmen. I thought he really liked me—so I gave him my body. He didn't give a shit about me, I found out later. He's no longer amongst the living. You can figure the rest out.

"After school, my life became normal. I got a job and lived a little. Then I got hooked up with a big-time drug dealer named Tony Bills. Somebody killed him during a robbery-home invasion. I learned a lot about the drug business from him. After he died, I hooked up with the connect and flooded the city with work. The newspapers would later call me a Queen pin. You know that with money come problems, right? Well, I wasn't exempt. Some niggas came for my head, but couldn't get me so they snatched my little sister—"

I was so enraptured by Angel's story that I almost didn't notice she had stopped walking. I turned around and looked at her.

There were tears in her eyes. "Let's talk about something else," I offered.

But she refused. "No, let me finish. I need to get this out. I have never told anyone my life story before. Never. A dude named Dearaye had my sister kidnapped. She was only fourteen-years-old. They raped and beat her, then they strangled her. They found her alone and cold in the woods. She was already gone by then. Dead before she could even begin. We identified her body that same day. My family was devastated. I was angry beyond thought. I wanted blood, I paid two dudes to find anybody that kidnapped people for a living and skin 'em. I wanted answers and they got them for me. I killed everybody involved with my sister's death, personally. Dearaye had a twin brother named Deandre. He heard that I killed his brother and wanted revenge. What he got was a shallow grave.

"I heard a saying somewhere that said, *Please God protect me from my friends, I can handle my enemies.* That saying proves to be true in my case. I told you that when I killed my father, the only person that knew was Fatima. Well, I confided all my business to Fatima. She was even present the day I killed a few people, she ended up getting caught up with this dude she was messing with. The police tricked her out of information about me. I was arrested and charged with four counts of first-degree murder.

"I did a year in jail before being released because the witness was no longer available. Fatima got killed two months before I was to start trial. When I came home, out of desperation and stupidity, I allowed myself to be seduced by the connect I was copping form. The next thing I knew, I was six months pregnant with my daughter.

"One night I was inside my beauty salon, getting ready to close up for the night. A young girl that had been in the salon earlier knocked on the front door. I didn't think anything of it at the time and I didn't recognize who she was. I let my guard down and almost lost my life—"

"Hold on you lost me. The girl knocked on the door and—" I asked.

"I let her into the salon—I thought she needed help or—she shot me."

"The young girl?"

"Yeah, but she wasn't just any young girl. She was the daughter of one of the dudes I killed. To make a long story short, she shot me four times, but my baby survived and so did I. I spent almost two years getting myself and my life back together, my daughter is my everything and I worry about her safety. I've done a rack of ill shit in the streets and for that reason, she's with my mother. The two of them are my lifeline. If something ever happened to them—"

"That's why I needed to get away for a while. So much has happened in DC, but for some strange reason, I can't stay away. I got big plans for the streets, the streets just don't know it, yet. I'm thirty-two-years old and my favorite color is red. There you have it. Now you know as much about me as I do."

Listening to Angel's story had me feeling like I had stepped into the pages of an urban novel. Her story is similar to mine minus the rapes. I couldn't believe that the drop-dead gorgeous woman walking beside me was as deadly as she proclaimed. *Hadn't I just done the same thing that she did? When the dudes shot at us in A.C. and hit Hasan. Hadn't I reacted the same way Angel did when she avenged her sister's murder? I killed a dude before to protect Salimah, so I knew how it felt to kill for a purpose. I had killed for so many reasons, they were too numerous to count. I couldn't even remember all the people I killed. So, how could I pass judgment on her? We were birds of one feather. If there was such a thing as a soul mate, was I walking with mine?*

"Are you gonna say anything?"

"What can I say? I'm feeling everything you said. It's hard for me to believe that you've been through so much and still look this good. I'm a street nigga all the way live and I love women. I have been with a lot in my life but never one like you. We have so much in common, that it's crazy. I never thought that I would meet a woman that I can see me in. It's like looking in a mirror. There's a lot that I can't explain or even understand, but what I do know is that I dig you, shorty. I say that with all honesty and not because your head is a torch."

Angel playfully punched me in my arm

"On the real though, I need you with me on some real Bonnie and Clyde shit. I been waiting my whole life for you."

Instead of saying anything, Angel led me up an embankment to a small patch of woods. Then she leaned up against a tree and slid out of her panties. She lifted her skirt and motioned for me to come to her. I did, we made love against that tree in the woods with only the stars and moon as the audience.

"Give me a call when you get this message."

I checked the rest of my messages and discovered that Salimah and Gunz had called me. I called my sister back first.

"Hello?"

"Lima, what's the deal, ma? How you?"

"Najee, why you ain't tell me that you were going out of town with Aminah's cousin, Angel?" Salimah said with much attitude.

"Hold on, baby sis. Are you drunk or high or something?" I asked her.

"Don't play with me, Najee. You don't even know her. What's the deal with you?"

"Ayo, Lima, the last time I checked my mother was in the ground. Stop, fall back with all that Louis Jefferson shit, ma. You my little sister and we both grown. I don't owe you no explanations about nothing I do. I don't question you about you and Mu."

"Ain't nothing to tell about me and Mu."

"Ain't nothing to tell about me and Angel. We are out of town, enjoying ourselves. I know her well enough to know that we are going to be together."

"*Be together?* She must've put something in your food. I'm a deal with—"

"Damn, Lima, what's really good with you? This ain't like you, ma. All this stressful ass shit. I thought you and Angel were friends?"

"*Friends?* I just met her. You just met her."

"What's your point, ma? And yo, who the fuck told you me and Angel was together anyway?" I exploded.

"Gunz told me. What? Was it a secret of some shit? Gunz also told me that y'all was at the fight that night and you saw Angel there. My question is why didn't she tell me and Aminah that she had seen you and y'all had exchanged numbers?"

"There you go with that conspiracy ass shit. You and Gunz need to fall back and let me do me. I got me. Y'all get y'all. Don't call me anymore stressing me about my business. Do you understand that?"

The phone disconnected on the other end and I knew my sister had hung up the phone. My next call was to my right hand.

"Speak on it."

"That's what the problem is now, son, you spoke it."

"Who did, Naj?"

"Who else?"

"You got my message, huh, son?"

"What the fuck is eating Lima, son?"

"I don't know, baby boy. She has been tryna reach you and she couldn't. So, I told her you went on a trip. So, what?"

"Fuck it, son. What's the deal? Is everything gravy?"

"So far, Mu gave me the work and I hit everybody off. I put Tye and them niggas out there on Spruce like you said. It's all hood for the moment, but I hear that you still got muthafuckas that ain't feeling the way we gorilla the projects over there. I might have to holla at a few niggas and put some hot shit on their minds. I got his, though. Where are you at, baby boy?"

"In Miami, son, and shit is mad lovely down here. I rented a Ferrari, nigga, and guess what?"

"What?"

"That joint is blue, and my president is black," I said and laughed. Gunz laughed, too.

"What's up with the bitch?"

"What bitch?"

"Fuck you mean, what bitch? The bitch you with."

"Ayo, son, ease up with that shit. Shawty ain't no bitch. Watch your mouth big boy."

"Man get the fuck outta here. Don't let me find out you have caught feelings for that bitch."

"Son—I just told you, son, to watch your mouth."

Gunz laughed me out. "Sucker for love ass nigga! Yeah a'ight, baby boy. I'ma watch my mouth. That's wifey now, huh?"

"Could be, I think so. Shorty ain't no regular chick, son. She owns shit and she caked up."

"Like I always say, baby boy, it's your call. But proceed with caution because you don't really know the bit—chick and she could be the police. Either way, if a hair on your head gets harmed, I'ma slap her and you know that."

"Ease up, killa. Brush your shoulders off and kick your feet up for a while. Let them other niggas put the footwork in. I'll be home in a week or so. One love."

"One love, baby boy. I'm out."

Anthony Fields

Chapter 16

Honesty

The overcast skies looked like a sad-faced child that wanted to cry. I looked into the vast grayness of the sky and knew that it was gonna rain soon. I wanted to leave the gravesite before the rain came. Staring at the tombstone for my mother made me angry and sad every time I came to Harmony Cemetery.

The glass-encased photo of my mother was the one that we ran in the Washington Post newspaper when she died. The picture depicted my mother in a good light. She looked happy and so full of life. The tears in my eyes came without provocation and I let them fall. I need to stop crying, I dried my eyes and fixed the flowers that were arranged neatly all over the market and the ground. Pink roses were my mother's favorite, so there were tons of them on her grave. When the first drop of rain hit me, I rode from my kneeling position and said my goodbyes. Goodbye, mom, I'll see you later.

I walked briskly back to my truck and jumped into the passenger seat. "Where are you going now?" Trigger asked.

"The detectives that are investigating my mother's case want to meet with me, again. I have to go to the police station on Livingston Road. You can drop me off and come back when I call you."

I laid back in the leather seats of the Escalade and thought about what I had told the cops the last time we spoke. I had to make sure there was no deviation in my story. There was no way they could ever find out who the real assailant was. That would throw a monkey wrench in my plans. I would literally die if somehow Angel was to go to jail before I could kill her, couldn't let that happen. I wanted to kill her, I needed to kill her. I had to kill her, it's my destiny.

"Have a seat right there, Ms. Phillips," the black detective named Mitchell Bell said pointing to a chair across from his desk. "I'ma get my boss from down the hall and let him sit in on our meeting. You do know that this meeting will be recorded, right?"

I nodded my head and looked away.

"I'll be right back."

About five minutes later, the black detective walked back into the room with the fat, white detective that questioned me the night of the murder.

"Hello, Honesty, my name is Sgt. Able Voss. I am the lead detective on your mother's case. There are a few things that I need you to go over with me again. Just so that we're clear, okay?"

"Okay."

"Good. From the very beginning tell me what happened tonight. You came home and found your mother dead?"

"I was supposed to come straight home so that me and my mother could take care of some post-graduation stuff," I told the story the exact same way that I did that night. Then I rested my case.

"When did you get the gun from the bathroom."

"The kitchen. The gun was hidden in the kitchen, not the bathroom," I corrected him.

"—uh, yeah, right. When you went and got the gun, where did you get it from in the kitchen?"

"In the kitchen, there are several drawers that hold different things. When you take those drawers out, the space in the back is just enough to hide something small."

"And you were able to get to the kitchen and retrieve this hidden gun and the intruder never heard you?"

"I don't know what's in the intruder's head. All I know is that I went and got the gun—"

The white detective put his hand up as if to stop me. "I'm sorry. Go ahead and continue."

"I got the gun and went down the hall. I walked in on the intruder standing over my mother."

"Okay. Let's focus on this intruder for a minute, Honesty. When you reached the living room where your mother was—there was a person there, right?"

"Yes."

"According to you, the person had a mask on, right?"

"Yes."

"And what else was he wearing?"

"I don't recall. I just know that the clothes were dark."

"Did you see any shoes?"

"No."

"Who fired the first shot? You or the intruder?"

"He did. Then I return fire."

"Do you think your mother may have known the intruder?"

"I don't think so."

"The reason that I ask is that we check out every door that leads into your house and all the windows. And we found no signs of forced entry. That tells us that either your mother knew the person and let him in or the intruder had a key. Either way, it led us to believe that this was not a random murder.

"So, again, I ask you. Is there anything we don't know?"

"No."

"Did you go over the whole house when we released it to you?"

"Yes, I did."

"Was there anything missing, that you know of?"

"No."

"So, it wasn't a robbery gone wrong. Your mother's death was an execution and we need to find out who did that and why. Are you absolutely sure there's nothing else that you can tell us?"

"I told you everything I know. So, can you please stop harassing me and find the person that killed my mother and tried to kill me!"

"We're trying our best. We'll be in touch, Honesty. Thank you for coming."

"I know that Mitch, I know."

Fuck y'all. I walked outside and called Trigger on the phone. "Come and get me, I'm ready. I'm out front. Bye."

The cops knew I wasn't being straight up with them but fuck it. What could they do? The Escalade pulled up ten minutes later and I hopped in. I glanced over at Trigger as he pulled the tuck into traffic and realized how sexy he was. He was the strong, silent type and that really turned me on. His Solbiato sweatshirt was off and now tied around his neck. I looked at his muscular arms and knew exactly what was missing, a tattoo with my name on it. I vowed to myself it would come later.

"Baby, ride down by Blue Plains. I wanna show you something."

"*Blue Plains?* What the fuck you wanna show me down that stinkin' ass joint?" Trigger asked.

"Well, not exactly Blue Plains, but down there by the old Potomac Job Corp."

I sat and waited for us to arrive at our destination. "Pull down there by where they used to do the car auctions."

When we got to the bottom of the road that was a dead-end, I looked around and noted how deserted it was.

Just the way I like it.

"What the hell do you wanna show me down here?"

"I wanted to show you how deserted it is down here in the daytime."

"So?"

"So, I can do this," I said and kicked my Gucci tennis shoes off. Then I lifted and tugged on my jeans. "I always wanted to fuck you." I wiggled out of my panties and then pulled my shirt over my head. "Right now the front seat will do."

I reached over and undid the button on Trigger's jeans and unzipped them. "Lift up some." I pulled on his jeans until they rested down by his ankles.

I put my lips on his dick and locked it. By the time I put him in my mouth, Trigger was moaning like he wanted to cum. I slowly sucked his dick and enjoyed it so much that I came on myself. I was shocked to discover that I could cum from sucking Trigger's dick. When his dick was ready to explode, I kept right on sucking.

"I want you to cum in my mouth, baby. I wanna swallow it."

My word must've really turned Trigger on because the next thing I knew cum was gushing out of him in spurts. I had never swallowed his cum before and I thought I was gonna gag but I didn't. I ended up enjoying the taste of his juices. I kept him inside my mouth until he got hard again. Then I climbed up on his lap and put him inside me. I bounced up and down on that dick until I came twice, and Trigger came for the second time.

116

"A-a-a-r-r-g-h-h! Shit, shit, shit! Ride that dick, True! Ride it. I can't take this shit! You gon make me cum too quick."

"I don't want you to do that?" I said and climbed off Trigger's dick. I walked through the space between the two front seats and sat down on the backseat. "I want you to put my feet on your shoulders the way I like and long dick me before you cum. C'mon."

A few seconds later, I was under Trigger with my legs pressed all the way back. My feet were on his shoulders, but my toes were against the leather panel that trained along the inside of the truck. I was in pain and ecstasy all at the same time.

"Trigger! You're too deep in me!" I screamed and bit down on my lip until I tasted blood.

"Be-careful-what-you-wish-for," Trigger mumbled in between thrust. "You-just-might-get-it!"

I had to accept what he did. I had asked for it. So, like a grown woman, I dug my fingernails in this back and loudly took the dick.

The next day I went to see a family friend.

"Sunnie, tell me something good," I said when I walked through the door of her spacious three-bedroom Condo in Capitol Heights.

"Honesty, I checked everything I could and didn't get much. I know that she has one truck in her name and that's a 2006 Hummer H2, candy apple red. She has several bank accounts in her name and the businesses she owns. There's the Beauty and Barber Palace on Queens Chapel Road. There's Angel's Communication outlet on Good Hope Road and a couple of other salons that she wants. She has a valid D.C., driver's license that doesn't expire until 2018.

"The Hummer and the businesses are all under the same name and address and that's Kareemah El-Amin and the Queens Chapel Road address. Whoever she has that does her accounting and her finances are good. They've hidden everything about her other than what's public knowledge. That's all I can find on Karemah El-Amin."

"And there's no way you can find out exactly where she is now, huh?"

"If I was the CIA, yeah, but I'm not. I'm just a little old Sunnie Simms, Department of Agriculture employee by day and private investigator by night. What you need is a GPS device if you really need to track her movement. Who is she anyway, Honesty?"

"Just somebody that's been all over my man," I lied.

"In that case, I'll look harder. I went through the same thing with a bitch that was after Cadoze. The bitch kept running her ass up to Cumberland to see him and I couldn't catch her. So, I put in a little footwork and came up with her."

"Then what?"

"Then I let her know that I could find her whenever I wanted to and if she didn't leave my man alone, I'd fuck with her taxes."

I laughed in spite of myself. "Did she go for it?"

"I never had a problem out of her again."

"Thanks again, Sunnie. Give my regards to your hubby. Call me if you find anything." I left Sunnie's condo. *Angel, where are you? Show yourself so that I can kill you.*

Chapter 17

Angel

When I decided to tell Najee my story as we walked along the beach, there were parts of the story that I purposely left out. It wasn't that I didn't trust him, because I did, it was just that I didn't want to scare him away. My story had too many twists and turns to give away just because the dick was the bomb and my hormones went crazy every time he came around. I couldn't bring myself to tell him that I had pushed Andre Ford off a roof. That might've made me sound a little barbaric. I also lied about who killed Tony Bills.

I didn't want Najee to feel like he had to sleep light around me or that he couldn't trust me. How could I admit that I killed a dude that I fucked for two straight years and loved? I withheld the fact that I fucked both Deandre and Dearaye, and that was the reason why my little sister was snatched and killed. Why did he need to know that? It would've only made me look like a slut. I didn't want that.

Why I didn't tell Najee that it was me who had Fatima killed was beyond me. I just failed to mention that. But I purposely left out the parts about all the recent murders. Najee was my boo, but confessing was something that I never do. I'll leave that to the Catholics. I couldn't afford to have Najee get cracked in Newark on something serious and then give me up on several bodies in DC. That made me think about Nome, I shouldn't have killed Nome.

I turned my head and stared at Najee as he slept in the bed beside me. I watched his chest rise and fall in rhythm and knew he was tired. I was tired too but for some reason, I couldn't sleep. I had too much on my mind to sleep. The meetings that I had in the last couple of days had all gone well. Najee has accompanied me on everyone since we touched down in New York. Then we rode a horse-drawn carriage through lower Manhattan. We talked, we laughed, we planned, and we promised each other the world.

The promises that I made to Najee, I planned to keep. I hoped and prayed that he kept his. After partying like rock stars at Jay-Z

40/40 club, we called it a night. When we got back here to the suite at the Parker-Meridian, I put this pussy on him and put him to sleep. I couldn't remember ever feeling the way that I felt about Najee, with anybody else. I tried with all my might to fight the feelings that I felt for him. But like the song says, *When love calls you gotta answer.*

"If you look right 'bout your threads, you will notice that the *Fasten Your Seatbelt* signs are lit up. That means that we are about to land. So, please buckle up. We are now at fifteen thousand feet and descending. Our ETA is 1:15 p.m. The weather in Newark is cloudy. It's 77 degrees. We hope you enjoyed your flight and thank you again for flying American Airlines."

At Newark International, me and Najee kissed as if we'd never see each other again and then parted. I called Aminah and had her pick me up.

"Tell me everything, Ang. Gimme all the juicy details," Aminah said before I could even get in the car good.

"Tell you what? What details do you want?" I asked playing coy.

"Is Najee's dick really eleven inches? And how was he in bed?"

"Mina, baby, I never kiss and tell. Did you stop by my condo and make sure everything was okay?"

"I did."

"Did you check on my truck at the airport?"

"Yes sir, boss. I's been a good slave since you've been gone, boss. On the real, though, Ang. You ain't gonna tell me shit, huh?"

"Not a thing."

"That's foul, Angel, that's foul. Well, I will tell you that Salimah didn't like it that you and her brother went away together. She didn't say it, but she thinks you're on some gold-digger shit."

"Do you think I really give a shit about what Salimah thinks about me? And what does her brother have that I want? Beside that luscious dick of his. Fuck Salimah and her assumptions. She's your girlfriend, not mine."

"She's just a little overprotective with Najee, that's all. Half the bitches in Newark want him. They have been chasing him for years and here you come out of nowhere and snag him. She called you sneaky, though."

"Like I said before, fuck Salimah. I bagged her brother and we're a couple and that's that. End of story."

"Y'all are a couple?"

"Yeah, I think I love that nigga, Mina."

"Damn! There's gonna be a whole lotta broken hearts in Brick City. I can't believe it. My cousin from DC came to town and stole the crown jewel. That's some fly shit. I might write one of those street novels about that shit."

"Go ahead and write it. I know somebody that will publish it."

"Just answer one question for me, Angel and I'ma leave you alone," Aminah begged.

"One question, Mina, just one," I replied.

"Is his dick really eleven-inches?"

"Yeah, but it feels much bigger when it's inside you. Now leave me alone until we get to my spot."

"Damn! Big dick ass nigga. Bigger than eleven inches? I know your insides gotta hurt?"

"Leave me alone, Mina."

The first thing I did when I got him was run water into the bathtub. I needed to sit back and relax. I did my best thinking while bathing. I needed to sit back and relax. I added a few scented beads to the hot water and stepped in. The water was a little too hot at first, but as I wiggled around a few times, I got acclimated. Where does me and Najee form here? How could we maintain a relationship from two different cities? Could we make it work? Was it even worth trying? I settled all the way down in the tub until my head was almost immersed in the water. Just as I was about to fall asleep, my cell phone rang. I reached out, grabbed it, and checked the caller ID. It was Najee.

"What's up, baby?" I cooed into the phone.

"What's good, shorty? You miss me?"

"Like you wouldn't believe."

"What are you doing?"

"Taking a bath and missing you all at the same time. I'm multitasking," I said with a big smile on my face.

"I feel you, shorty. Plus, I miss you, too. No bullshit. Nevertheless, I'ma see you soon. I gotta tie up a few loose ends out here in the streets and then I'ma get up with you. As a matter of fact, let's make plans. By tomorrow evening all my business should be handled and I will be free. Why don't you meet me at Justin's in New York? It's right over the George Washington Bridge. That's the joint that separates New Jersey from N.Y. I'ma call you in the morning and let you know exactly when to meet me, a'ight?"

"A'ight, shorty. One Love, I'm out."

I hit the end button on my phone and dropped it on the floor. Now that Najee and I were together, I silently prayed that all the stuff he did before we left, did not come back to haunt him. *Be careful, Najee, be careful.*

Angel 2

Chapter 18

Najee And Angel

"All the time, shorty, all the time. One love. I'm out." I disconnected the call and put my phone back in my pocket. "Now what were you saying again, son?"

"I was saying that you need to holla at your men. They feel a little abandoned, fam. We were here putting this work in while you were getting your Hugh Hefner on, naw mean? Gunz is cool, but his son is different. He doesn't have the people skills that you have. The breed of young niggas that's on the team today don't understand scare tactics, son. The young cats bustin' their guns, too, and Gunz just don't understand that. You can't be wildin' on 'em young cats like he is doing. Feel me, son?"

"I feel you." I hit the blunt and passed it back to my man Supreme. Supreme was a good dude that I trusted to handle my hands-off business. He was from 18th Avenue. Before I left, I told 'Preme to watch out for Gunz and my men while I was gone. He was a man of respect and I accepted what he said, straight teeth no chaser. "I told Gunz about that gorilla shit a million times. I'ma handle it, though. Other than that, what's poppin?"

"Ain't nothing poppin' with me, son. I'm just putting you down with what's been going on the streets. This is your world, I'm just in it."

"We in it together, son. Remember that, with Has' gone, we all we got. You, me, Gunz and the crew, we all we got. Let's hit Spruce Street and see what's cracking."

"Sure thing, son, and welcome home."

"—*Ayo, fuck y'all niggas/crush y'all/ rush y'all/with the four drawn and I touch y'all/ plus y'all little muthafuckas ain't ready for war/I seen your team in a Chrysler before/but I forgot/ the same rules apply. Don't try to switch up your style/ Y'all niggas is pumpkin pie. And that's as plain as I/much better than you cats/shocked when I got the news that/this nigga ready for war/Well/where that fool at? I bruise niggas/ severely punish them/Especially those that get fucked for their publishing."*

"Ayo, 'Preme, I gotta piss, son. Pullover and let me out." I said as I turned the music down in the car. "Go 'head and pull around the corner, son, and stop at the corner store. I need to get me some blunts and something to eat. This blueberry got me greedy."

I jumped out of the Bentley and walked over to the wall. The two cups of Grey Goose I drank earlier was ready to come back up out of me. As I let myself go. I saw 'Preme put both windows up and pull the Bentley away from the curb. Not even two minutes later, I heard the rapid-fire spit of automatic rifles. That caused me to jump. I leaked piss all over my jeans in an attempt to zip up and get to the corner. My heart raced along with my legs and I covered the distance in seconds.

When I got to the corner, all I could do was watch helplessly as two gunmen fired, round after round into my car. One gunman was on foot, standing at the hood of a grey Chrysler 300M and the other was inside the car with the rifle aimed out of the window. I couldn't do anything to help Supreme. Before getting out of the car to take a leak, I put my gun under the passenger seat. When the gunshots finally ceased, I saw that my brand new Bentley was Swiss cheese. I knew that whoever had come and shot up the car thought that I was behind the wheel. Since the windows were mirror tinted, there was no way they would have known that the person behind the wheel of the Bentley was Supreme. As tears came to my eyes and fire burned in my heat, I knew those two cups of Grey Goose had saved my life.

***

"What happened?" Salimah asked.

I ignored her as I pulled the Armalite/Colt AR-15 from under the bed. The .223 caliber assault rifle fired seventy 5.56mm rounds in less than six seconds.

"Najee talk to me! What happened to you? Where's your car?"

I went to the closet and reached up to the top shelf. I felt around until I felt the bag I wanted. That bag contained a Heckler and Koch

33K with a collapsible stock, and a .40 mm grenade launcher attachment. I pulled the bag from the closet and loaded the AR-15 into it along with several extra clips for both weapons.

Salimah was openly crying by now, but I didn't have time to talk to her. I needed to hit the brick and find whoever had tried to end my life. I zipped up the bag and put an arm into each of the straps. By the time I reached the door, Gunz and Mu were coming in.

"Yo, what the fuck is going on, ock?" Mu asked.

"Fall back, ock, I got this," I said and made a beeline for the door. Gunz got blocked my path. "Get out my way, son. Word life, son, y'all need to fall back and let me do me."

"What's the deal, baby boy? Something happened?"

"Them niggas tried to murk me, son. They missed but I won't. Get out my way, son."

"Who, son? Who tried to murk you?" Gunz asked. "Who's they?"

I searched my mind for an answer, but strangely I couldn't find one. Then reality hit me. I had no idea who had tried to kill me. I didn't recognize the Chrysler the dude was standing at its hood. The dude that was firing into the Bentley was wearing a baseball cap pulled low over his head. Who was I gonna kill?

Defeated, I walked over to the couch and sat down. I dropped my head into my hands and wept. My tears flooded my hands as I released all my pent-up frustrations. I wanted blood but didn't know whose to take. I thought about Supreme behind the wheel of the Bentley listening to the Jay-Z CD. He didn't stand a chance and he probably never knew what hit him.

Rest in Peace, son.

I got myself together, dried my eyes, and told Gunz and Salimah everything that happened.

***

"What can I get for you two, tonight?" the waiter asked as Angel and I sat at a table inside of Justin's restaurant in Manhattan.

"I'll have the Chicken Cordon Bleu and a strawberry ice tea," Angel said. Then she looked at me.

"Gimme the Chicken and broccoli Alfredo. A side order of buffalo wings and a Sprite."

When the waiter was out of earshot, I said, "I just wanted to tell you upfront what's going on. I'm not gonna let you get hurt under any circumstance, ya feel me? There's a lot of shit going on in Newark and it's about to get outta control. Last night, somebody tried to kill me."

"Let's leave here, Najee. Let's—"

"I can run but I can't hide shorty. I have to stay here and finish what I started. I have never run from a nigga in my life and I'm not about to start now. The streets won't let me chill, that's all I can say."

"What happened last night?"

"My man Supreme was driving me around town. We were talking and checking out a few traps. The liquor that I had earlier started trying to come out of me and I had to piss. I told 'Preme to let me piss and go head around the corner to the store. I wanted to get some more blunts and some other shit. As I stood there pissing, I heard the shots and ran to the corner. Two muthafuckas were unloading rounds into my car. They thought it was me—but it wasn't. They killed 'Preme. He was a good dude."

"Najee, I'm sorry, baby. That's why we need to leave and go somewhere else. What if you hadn't stopped to piss? What if you had been driving the car? Answer me, Najee. What if?"

I didn't know what to say to Angel and I was glad when the waiter finally showed up with our food. We both ate in silence. After I had eaten enough, I broke the silence, "Angel, I need you in my life now more than ever, but I have to deal with them. I didn't want to tell you this over the phone. So, I kept our date to tell you all of this in person. I'm not saying that we ain't gonna be together. I just have a few loose ends to tie up first. Trust me on this. I'm not gonna let anyone do anything to me."

"If that's the case, why don't you spend the night with me? If I'm not gonna be able to see you until this shit in the streets is over.

At least give me the chance to really show you how much you mean to me."

"You got that, shorty," I said and pulled out a wad of money. I put a couple of hundred dollars on the check pad and got up." Let's bounce, now."

Angel smiled a lascivious smile and stood. "What about my food?"

"Leave it, I got something better for you to eat. Let's go."

We walked out of the restaurant and something caught my eye. Across the street, a dude was leaning against a wall with his hands behind his back. He was wearing a black hoodie and dark pants. Then, on the same side of the street, appeared another dude similarly dressed. At first, I thought I may have been paranoid, but when the dude on the wall started coming across the street. I was sure about one thing. It was a hit.

"Angel when I say run, I want you to run away from me. Get back to the restaurant and stay there. Do you hear me?"

"Najee—"

"Run, Angel! Run now!"

I pulled my twin Glocks from my waist and started blasting. The dude across the street produced what appears to be a Mac 11 and fired in my direction. I ran over to a parked car and tried to keep my eyes on both men, who were now coming in my direction. I fired at the one closest to me, then heard shots being fired behind me.

"What the—"

I looked over my shoulder and gasped. Angel washed my right side with a gun in her hand. She was gunning for the dude in the street. I rose from my position and walked the dude on the sidewalk down. My heart was bigger than his and eventually, he turned to flee. But I was on his heels. I looked into the street and saw the other dude fall. I wanted to catch the dude I was chasing, but I decided to stop. I turned and met Angel in the street as she stood over the fallen killer.

Just as she raised her gun to finish the dude off, I fueled, "No!"

Angel turned and looked at me and then lowered her gun. I ran up on the fallen dude. He was still breathing. I kicked at the Mac that he had been firing and bent down to remove the baseball cap from his head. The dude was young and his face looked familiar. *Where do I know him from?*

"Who sent you?" I asked him. I looked down and saw that the youngster was bleeding profusely. His hands were holding his stomach, but they were filled with blood."

"Najee, we gotta get outta here, baby. The police will be here, soon."

"If you tell me who sent you, I promise that I will call an ambulance for you. I know you don't wanna die out here in the street like this. You didn't do this on your own, tell me who sent you."

"Don't—"

I looked into the eyes of the frightened young dude and said, "Last chance. Tell me who sent you and I'll let you live."

The young dude coughed once and spit up some blood. Then he said something that chilled me to the bone, "Mu sent us—it was Mu."

I couldn't believe my ears. I had been betrayed by the very person that I believed was protecting me. I shot the dying youngster twice in the forehead and then I turned to run. I heard the unmistakable sounds of footsteps and knew that Angel was right behind me.

I drove around in a daze until my mind focused and led me to where I needed to be. Where I had to be.

Angel had dropped her car off and was now riding with me in the passenger seat of a black Yukon Denali XL. I pulled up to Mu's house and saw that all the lights were out. I wondered who was inside the house. I knew that he wasn't there because he was at Salimah's house. He was there when I left, and he always stayed with her on Thursday nights. I didn't want to confront Mu at Salimah's house or anywhere near Brick Towers. Although I gave Mu the power to get money in the towers and in the area, he was still a connected dude with ties to an alleged powerful Muslim cartel of heavy hitters. I wanted his death to be untraceable to me, so I chose the place where he truly resented. The good part about it all was that Mu didn't think I knew where he lived. *Stupid muthafucka.* When he first started messing with Salimah and giving me coke, I followed him home. That was my way of having an insurance policy just in case a night like this ever came, and it did.

"Climb over in the driver's seat and don't get out of the car for nothing. Lean your seat all the way back, so that nobody looking out of a window can see you. I should be back soon. I gotta make Hafiza get Mu home. Then I'ma kill him and we can be out. When I come out of the house, start the truck up and be ready to roll out. Earlier, I said something about leaving here and going away. When all this is over, where do you wanna go?"

"I wanna go home."

"To D.C.?"

Angel nodded her head.

"That's where we're going then." I reached over and hugged Angel. Then I kissed her long and hard. "You think the Nation's Capital is ready for me?

"We'll have to see. Go handle your business so that we can go."

I got out of the car and walked to the back of the house. I found the breaker box circuits for the alarm on the house. As expensive as the house had to be, I was positive there was an alarm. I opened the breaker box with my house key. I pulled the wires that I knew would enable the alarm. Then I found a small back window and lightly shattered the glass in the pane. I was inside the house in seconds. I pulled my gun and crept through the house. I found a staircase and ascended the stairs. The upstairs had two bedrooms and two bathrooms. I quietly looked in each room until I found the one I was looking for. The bedroom door was ajar. I looked in and saw a lone sleeping figure in the bed. I tiptoed to the end and pointed a gun at the head of the woman I knew to be Mu's wife, Hafiza.

"Wake up, Hafiza!" I said and tapped her on the side of the head.

The startled woman opened her mouth to scream when she saw me, but I shushed her with a finger to my lips. "If you scream or make a sound, I'ma kill you. I want you to get on the phone and call Mu. Tell him to come home. Make up an emergency. Keep your words short and concise. Don't try and secret code shit or you die instantly. Do you understand me?"

"Good. Now make the call."

Chapter 19

Mu

"Hafiza, what are you talking about? Why didn't you call an ambulance? A'ight. I'll be there in about twenty minutes. Bye."

I hung up the phone and went to Salimah's bed. When the call came through on my cell phone, I thought it was somebody else. Hadn't I told Rahmel to call me as soon as it was done?

"What's wrong, baby?" Salimah asked.

"Hafiza is sick. I gotta go home."

"That bitch ain't sic—"

"Didn't I tell your ass to never speak her name?" I exploded.

"I didn't speak her name," Salimah said defiantly. "I said that bitch."

I didn't feel up to Salimah's shit, right now, so I ignored her and got dressed. Why hasn't Rahmel called?

"I know you hear me talking to you, Mu."

I grabbed my car keys off the dresser and my phone and walked out of the room.

"Fuck you, Mu! Don't come back! Do you hear that? Don't bring your ass back here!"

I tried Rahmel's cellphone one more time before I got out of the car. Just like all the other times, I received no answer. Where the hell are you, 'Rah? So, far no news has gotten back about whether or not Najee had been killed in the attack. He hasn't called and told Salimah anything either, so that was a good sign. Najee being out that meant I could put the rest of my plan in play. There were always plans and bigger plans being made and Najee was too small-minded to see that. The plan was to take over every project in Newark starting with the strongest one—Brick towers. Having already done that it was time to get rid of the old vanguard and replace it with a new one. Najee had to be eliminated for this to happen. He loved Brick Towers too much to stand by and let me bring in my own people to run it. The original plan was to use Najee and his men to wipe out all the competition in all the projects around Newark. Then I would simply walk in after the smoke cleared and put people in place to govern.

It was like playing a game of Monopoly. But only the stakes were higher, and the players were real. But as time went on the plan changed. Najee was too loose a canon to keep on a leash until the ultimate goal was reached. I made the decision to get rid of him a long time ago. I was the one who had Big Rock killed and supplied Hashim with the fake keys of coke. I sat back and predicted each outcome as if I was a master strategist. I was the puppeteer and everybody involved were my puppets.

I dropped the hint to 'Reek that Najee was behind all the recent deaths of his men. Then I told Najee that 'Reek and his men suspected him of killing Big Rock and Hashim. Najee getting away in Atlantic City wasn't expected but it served another purpose altogether. He, like I knew he would went on a killing spree and got rid of all my opposition at the Spruce Street Projects.

His partner Gunz was also on my payroll, so the people he put in place on Spruce Street works for me as well. Mission accomplished. The hit on Najee yesterday was well planned but poorly executed. The stupid ass niggas that I recruited for the job never checked to make sure Najee was in the car. So, I had to try again. I had to get rid of Najee. My plans could not come to total fruition with him alive. I walked up the steps in my front yard and stopped at the front door. I tried Rahmel's phone one more time and then went to my house.

When I walked into my bedroom the scene in front of me stopped me in my tracks. My wife Hafiza was tied to a chair, with her mouth duct-taped. She was wearing the thin nightgown that she always wore to bed and her large breasts and nipples could be seen through the material, beside her chair sat a five-pound bag of potatoes. On the other side of her stood Najee, dusty, and slightly bruised. He had a gun in each hand. The look on his face spoke a thousand words.

The look on my face must've spoken volumes as well. I felt like the wind had been knocked out of me. As I stood there and traded looks with Najee I knew in my heart that all campaigns had failed.

Angel 2

I also knew that my life as well as my wife's life was about to come to an end.

Anthony Fields

Chapter 20

Najee

"Mu, what's really good, son?"

"Najee, what are you doing, ock? Whatever it is, you making a mistake."

"First off, don't call me, ock, no more. In Arabic, that means brother and you are definitely not my brother. You might be fuckin' my sister, but we ain't brothers. And I'm not making no mistake, son. You made the mistake. All I wanna know is why?"

"Why what, ock? Najee what the hell mistake did I make? Talk to me."

"Oh, I'm talking to you alright. All three of us are going to talk to you. Me and these two Glocks, right here."

I put one of my guns in my waist. "I know you're probably wondering what the bag of potatoes is sitting here for. Let me show you."

I grabbed a potato out of the bag and shoved it onto the barrel of the gun in my hand. "They serve as a good makeshift silencer. This is how this is gonna work. I'ma ask you a question and then you answer it. As simple as that. If I don't like the answer, I shoot your wife. Since I asked you a question already and you didn't answer—" I pointed the gun at his wife's leg and fired. She tried to scream, but her muffled cries died in her throat because of the duct tape,

"Please, Najee, don't kill her. She's innocent in all of this. She doesn't have anything to do with this."

"Why did you do it, Mu? Why did you cross me?"

"Najee, it wasn't me!" Mu cried.

I put another potato on the end of the gun and shot his wife in her other leg. "Don't lie to me, Mu. That's only gonna get your wife hurt more. I'm tryna spare her life, but you're making it hard for me. Why'd you try to have me killed?"

"Najee—I—I"

"Think about your wife, Mu."

"Okay, okay, I got greedy. I figured that I could control things more with you out of the way."

"Was that your work yesterday, too?"

"No—"

I pulled another potato from the bag and removed the old one from off the barrel.

"That wasn't me, Najee—no! Don't!"

I shot Hafiza in the foot. "It was you, Mu. I recognize some of the shooters. The one standing outside the car. He was one of the dudes who tried me outside of Justin's. And you were the only person besides Salimah that knew I was going there."

I put another potato on the gun and shot his wife in her other foot. "Where is the coke and the money, Mu?"

"What coke? And what money?"

I turned to Hafiza and said, "Your husband cares nothing for you. Go ahead and say a dua before I kill you. You got one minute." I replaced the potato on the gun.

"Okay! Just don't kill her! Kill me, not her! The money is in the closet over there. There's a safe in there, all the way in the back. It's built into the wall. You have to remove all the clothes hanging on the pole.

"Then you have to pull the pole from off the hinge. The false wall will open to reveal the safe. The combination is 21-23-21-07."

"Where is the coke, Mu. I know you got it here somewhere. Give me the coke and I promise you I won't kill your wife."

"Do I have your word as a Muslim and a man?"

"Yes."

"Wallahi?"

"Wallahi."

"In the garage is a Town and Country caravan. The coke is there. Let me make dua before you kill me."

"Go ahead."

"Bismillah-hir-Rahman-nir-Raheem...Inna lillahi wa inna ilaihi raajiun. Remember your promise."

"I will," I said and then shot Mu in the face. I grabbed another potato and walked over to his body. I replaced the potato with a

136

fresh one and then shot him in the forehead. I turned around and walked back over to Hafiza. Her eyes were as big as saucers and filled with tears. "I gave my word that I wasn't going to kill you and I'm not. But do understand this, your husband had my friends Hasan and Supreme killed. He was responsible for the deaths of a lot of people. He wasn't innocent in this. I'm sorry that I had to shoot you, but I had to show Mu I meant business. I could be about to make the biggest mistake of my life, but then again, I might not be. It's on you. If you mention my name to the police, I promise you I will not rest until I've found you and kill you and everybody that you love. Do you understand me?"

Hafiza nodded her head in terror.

I left her tied up and went to get the money out of the safe. There was so much money in it that I had to make two trips and fill up pillowcases. I went out the back way and ran the pillowcases to the truck. Without saying a word to Angel I raced back around to the back of the house. I entered the garage from the back and found the caravan. The windows had dark tints and I knew why. When I pulled open the side door, I saw rows and rows of cocaine. As the sweat beads formed on my forehead, I stared at the most coke that I had ever seen in my life.

All I could say was, "Ching-ching!"

Chapter 21

Angel and Najee

"The name of the community out here is Beacon Hill. These are the Beacon Hill Apartments the street that we live on is Southgate Drive. The city is Alexandria and the state is Virginia. You got that?" I asked Najee as we laid in my bed basking in the afterglow of great sex.

"I got you, shorty. Beacon Hill Apartments in Alexandria, Virginia. Southgate Drive. The address on the building is 3100 and the apartment numbers G4. Just like the jet."

"Yeah, just like the jet. You are gonna pick up on all the shit quick but for the time being, you need to know this. Southgate Drive, once you leave the parking lot and make a right, will run you all the way into Route One. Route One will take you all the way to DC. Depending on where you tryna go is where you exit. But all that'll come later, right now, I wanna make sure you know where you put that work.

"When you leave the parking lot outside, make sure you turn left. Take Southgate all the way down to the intersection. When you go straight through the light to your right will be a small shopping center. In the back of the shopping center is the storage place we just left. You saw the place and you got your key to the spot, so you're good. Just be careful when you go in and out of your area because somebody might get nosy and try to go in it. Always take something or bring something out that they can see.

Like a small piece of furniture or a box of some kind. Our next order of business is getting you a valid DC driver's license. I know some people in the DMV, that won't be a problem. The new cop gives you something low key to push. You don't wanna attract any unwanted attention to yourself. So ain't no more Benzes and Bentleys for a while. You in DC, now, these cops are a little more vicious than they are in Newark. So, you gotta be careful. We got about five different police agencies that patrol the streets. You got Park Police, Metropolitan, Housing authority, Metro Transit, and Capitol Police.

Since DC is surrounded by Maryland and Virginia, we gotta duck their cops, too."

"Got damn, shorty! You ain't tell me all that on the way here. You tricked me," Najee joked.

"Boy, ain't nobody tricking you. Besides, it ain't as bad as it sounds. Trust me, you got fifteen thousand, five hundred and fifty bricks that you need to unload. In one-hundred and eighty days they'll be gone, mark my words."

Najee reached over and grabbed me. "Right now, I'd rather mark my territory."

"And what territory is that?" I asked and kissed his face.

Najee never responded. He positioned himself between my legs, grabbed a hold of each of my ankles, kissed both of my feet, one at a time, and then entered me.

"Whose pussy is this?" Najee whispered to me as he dipped and dug deep into me repeatedly.

I felt my toes tingle as I replied, "It's your pussy! This your pussy! Mark your territory, nigga, mark it."

I traded my Porsche truck in for a BMW760i. We copped Najee a midnight blue Lincoln Navigator. Then Najee followed me all around town to try and familiarize him with the city. We ended up on Martin Luther King Avenue. Since we were in the neighborhood, I decided to drop in on an old friend.

K and P Barbershop was still a fixture on MLK, and Fat Doodie was still the man on that side of Southeast. I silently prayed that he was in the area because I needed to see him, so I pulled into the Amoco gas station across the street and motioned for Najee to do the same.

"I know a dude that we need to see. He owns that barbershop, right there. I wanna introduce y'all. C'mon."

The sidewalk in front of the barbershop was still packed with dudes that were out there hustling. Just as it had been over four years ago when I first came and hollered at Doodie. We walked into the barbershop. I didn't recognize any of the faces that stared back at us.

"Is Doodie in the back?" I asked the dude cutting hair closest to me.

"Who are you, sweetheart?" The man asked.

"Angel, he knows me."

I watched as the dude went to the back and disappeared. He came back a few minutes later with Doodie. Doodie was notably thinner, but still well dressed and handsome. His head was bald now but overall, he still looked the same. He smiled when she saw me.

"Angel! What's up, boo? It's been a long time."

"I'm hip, Fat Boy. Damn, I can't call you that no more, huh?"

"Not at all. One of these diets finally worked."

"Which one?"

"That one called high blood pressure. The doctor told me to both change my diet and lose some weight or I suffer a stroke or heart attack. I took him seriously and the rest is history."

I heard Najee clear his throat as if to tell me to hurry up. "Doodie, let me holla at you in private." Doodie looked from me to Najee and then said, "Come in the back."

When we got into his office and the door was shut, I introduced Najee. "Doodie, this is a friend of mine named Najee."

"What's up, dawg?" Doodie said and extended his hand.

"Hi you, son?" Najee replied.

"I'm good, dawg. I'm Doodie."

"Doodie, I need you, baby," I said.

"What you need, boo? You know how we do. Even though you got ghost on a nigga, I still fucks with you. What's up?"

"Are you still in the business?"

"Somewhat. Why? What's up?"

"You know I've been gone for a minute, but I'm back now and I'm ready to rock and roll. Me and my people got them things dirt cheap and I wanted to holla at you before anybody else."

"Dirt cheap?" Doodie repeated.

"Dirt cheap. I made a few calls and caught up with the most dudes who are paying for a brick, right now. If what I heard is true, the recession got the prices of coke sky high. According to some friends, everybody pays between twenty-two and twenty-five grand a bird. Is that correct?"

"Somewhat."

"You come back on board with me and I can guarantee you whatever you get now at a better price. Depending on how many you buy. Throw me a number."

"Sixteen a joint. You step it up to fifteen a week and the price comes down to fifteen apiece. You can't beat that. Holla at your girl. Fast money is slowed up but if you run fast enough, you can catch it. What's up?"

"You never seem to amaze me. Did these doctors put some bionic parts on your ass when you were in the hospital? Because every time you fall you bounce right back. They can never keep a good woman down, huh, boo?"

"Never."

"Angel, I never went wrong fucking with you and you my buddy from the sandbox. So, you know I can't refuse that kinda offer. I'm in. When can I get that work?"

"Tomorrow. You remember how I used to do it? I pick up the money and then tell you where to get the work from?"

"Yeah, I remember."

"Well, the same rules apply. But only this time you'll be meeting with Najee. Is that alright with you?" I asked.

"If you say he is your people, then by all means it's cool. Gimme some numbers to call."

I turned to Najee. "Write both of our numbers down for him." I turned back to Doodie. "I need to know something, Doodie."

"What?"

"Is Scrub still doing his thing down Park Chester?"

"Nah, Slim went broke fuckin with them young bitches. There's another nigga down there doing the muthafucka. His name is Jamal, but everybody calls him J.T."

"You fuck with him?"

"Shorty alright."

"Is that a yes or no?"

"That's a yes."

142

"A'ight. What about J-Rock down the Farms? He's still the man down there?"

"Yeah, Jay is still down there. His men Sterling and set Trippin' got killed while he was still standing. Wack came back and helped him keep it together."

"*Wack?* I thought he went straight?"

"Well, he's back crooked."

"That's good to know. Do me a favor and I'll look out on the next one?"

"What?"

"Holla at J-Rock and Jamal for me. Give them the same prices I gave you and tell them to holler at me."

"You got that. I'll do that today."

"It's good seeing you again, Fat Boy."

"You too, boo. Tomorrow."

"Tomorrow."

I walked out of that barbershop feeling better than I had in a long time. The stress was calling my name and I was listening. I looked around at all the poverty and filth and remembered my up-bringing before all the money and notoriety. I remembered how me and Fatima used to strut through the streets as if we owned them. I thought about all the money and power that I used to have. Then I thought about the 15,500 kilos in the storage area out in Virginia and smiled, I'm back.

The next day I walked out of the smash All Hot Niggas apparel store with three sweatsuits for Najee. I also got a commitment from Antwan and Poo to cop five bricks a week for us. Then I picked up Doodie's money and sent Najee to drop off his bricks. While Najee was doing that I rode through Condon Terrace and found out that Black was dead. He went to some dudes from 3rd World about Nome after his body was found out Maryland.

Black allegedly went to two brothers named Lloyd and Keith because they had a beef with Nome. Somehow shit backfired and the brothers ended up killing Black. From Condon Terrace, I drove to Valley Avenue. I caught up with a young dude named Whistle who everybody said was the man out there. He promised to call me later that day. I decided not to fuck with the Congress Park niggas because they were fresh off beating a conspiracy. The government was probably videotaping their every move and I didn't need to be on candid camera.

By the time I hooked back up with Najee it was getting dark outside and I was hungry. "Najee, I'ma take you where they sell the best turkey burgers in the city."

Inside of Ben's Chili Bowl, we ate and talked about everything that we'd accomplished for the day.

"I talked to my man Gunz a couple of hours ago. He told me that the streets are still tryna figure out who killed Mu. As far as Gunz knows, the wife never snitched on me. He said Salimah is fucking with a nigga from Prince Street named Que."

"That was fast wasn't it?"

"That's exactly what I said. Other than that, he said that shit is all love."

"That's good. Look, when we leave here, I wanna try and catch one more nigga. I heard that he went to jail but got out after the case was dismissed due to an illegal search warrant. You ready to go?"

"No doubt, let's bounce."

Chapter 22

Najee

I sat back in the plush seats of Angel's BMW and looked out the window. Riding through the streets of DC was no different than riding through Newark. That showed me that ghettos were the same all over the world. As we rode up Georgia Avenue, Angel pointed out a few sports that I wanted to see.

"That's Howard University over there. We just passed the Hospital. The dudes I told you about, Robbie and Duck. That's their store right there, The Gangsta Gear Shop. They have been hitting the whole city off with coke ever since the late eighties. I used to— hold on, boo—that's my song, right there."

I laughed as Angel reached over, turned the radio up, and started singing, *"Silken dream take flight/ As the darkness gives way to the dawn/You've survived/Now your moment has arrived/ Now your dream has finally been born! Black butterfly sailed across the waters/Tell your sons and daughters/what the struggle brings/Black Butterfly set the skies on fire/rise up even higher/ so the ageless winds of time can catch your wings—"*

"You don't know anything about that," Angel said and then hummed the rest of the song.

"While you slept/ the promise was unkept/ But your faith was as sure as the stars/ now your free and the world has come to see/ Just how proud and beautiful you are/ Black butterfly sailed across the waters/Tell your sons and daughters/what the struggle—"

There he goes right here."

"Who?"

"The dude I need to see."

"Which one?" I asked curiously.

"Faceman. The Don of Uptown," Angel replied and pulled down to a small street that looked to be a dead-end street. I read the sign at the corner. It read 600 blocks of Morton street. There were two dark-colored Range Rovers double-parked beside a Mercedes

Benz S63 AMG. That's a mean joint there. I watched from the passenger seat of the BMW as Angel got out and walked up to a crowd. Then she and one of the dudes walked toward the Benz and leaned on it. That must be Faceman.

A few minutes later, Angel motioned for me to get out of the car and come over. I felt the butt of my newest purchase since being in DC a .51 caliber Desert Eagle automatic. Then I got out of the car and walked to them.

"Face, this is Najee. Najee, this is Face."

"What's the deal, son?"

"What's up, Moe? Angel, tells me that you got them thangs for the low-low, huh?" Face said.

"No doubt, son. What do you need?"

"That shit some butter?"

I looked at Angel for some help. *What the fuck does butter mean?*

"Fish Scales, son. I got the fish scale shit."

"I'm tryna cop like fifty of them, right now. What's up?"

"*Fifty?* Shit, it's all good, son. You cop fifty of them bricks, right now and I'll give 'em to you for fifteen a pop. You got three quarters of a mill ticket, son?"

The dude Face laughed in my face. Then he called out of one of his men.

"Aye 'Lil Man, go around the corner and get three of them duffel bags out of the spot.

A short, brown-skinned dude walked over to one of the Range Rovers and hopped inside. Then he pulled off.

"Angel, I trust you with my life, boo. You one of the realest bitches I ever met—no disrespect. You know how I get down and I know how you get down. When my man gets back with that money, take it with you. That's a sign of good faith. You got my numbers. Call me when you are ready to drop off them."

Me and Angel stood by the Benz and watched Face walk back to the crowd and camouflage himself. We got back in the BMW and waited for the dude to return. He did about ten minutes later. He exchanged a few words with Face and then drove over to us.

"Here you go, cuz," The dude said as he got out the truck with two big bags in his hand.

Angel hit the trunk button as I climbed out of the car. I put both bags in the trunk and waited for the third. Then I put that in the trunk, too. I hopped back into the car with Angel and said. "Ayo shorty, I respect my son gangsta. Son a real-life nigga. Ain't no way I'ma part with that much paper on a nigga work."

"Boo, that nigga been getting money for so long, he probably spends what he just gave us on clothes, cars and bitches."

"When do you want me to give him that work?"

"Get up early tomorrow morning and see him. Take him one-hundred bricks. That'll let him know what he did ain't shit and that you can cover whatever. Tell him that you decided to give him fifty extra since he paid for fifty of 'em upfront. That'll reciprocate the trust that he showed and then he'll have to respect your gangsta."

My respect for Angel was growing daily. "Shorty, you were the man out here for real, huh? I thought you were bullshittin.'

"Najee, baby, I laugh and I joke, but I never bullshit. I wasn't the man out here I was the woman out here and these streets weren't mine. I borrowed em for a while, then gave 'em back."

"Well, fuck the streets; I'm tired of them right now. I need to borrow you for a while. How about that?" I asked and reached over and rubbed up Angel's leg.

"If you borrow me that means that at some point you gotta give me back. I don't want that. I want you to keep me." Angel unbuttoned her pants and unzipped them. Then she grabbed my hand from her leg and put it inside her panties. "See how wet you make me?"

"No doubt," I responded and rubbed around her pussy for a minute before finding the clit and circling it. "Um-m-m- hm-m-m! Kee-p-p me, Najee! Ke-e-e-p-p m-e-e, ba-b-b-y!"

When I saw Angel close her eyes, I pulled my hand out of her pants. "Shorty, you gon fuck around and crash this car. You keep closing your eyes while you drive."

"You sure right, I wasn't even thinking about no cars or nothing, you were about to make me cum. Let me hurry up and get home so you can finish what you just started."

***

I successfully hooked up with the dude face and dropped off the one-hundred keys. Then Angel called and sent me to a greasy spoon joint called White Corners to see a dude named George Forman. At first, I thought she was talking about the boxer, but she wasn't. The dude George was a good friend of Angel's. He drove me to his hood in Eastgate and showed me much love. By the time I left, we agreed on him copping twelve keys and me giving him eight more on consignment. He gave me two-hundred and sixteen thousand upfront with the promise to have the other one-hundred and forty-four thousand within the next week.

My cell phone vibrated it was Angel. "What's crackin', shorty?"

"I'm just checking in with you. How did everything go with George?"

"Son a live nigga. I noticed that a lot of them cats in the hood treat son like a made nigga."

"They better, the whole city knows about George. He went to jail on more murders and beat 'em than anybody in the history of the city. Don't let the light-skinned pretty boy look fool you, he's a dangerous muthafucka. But he's an honorable nigga and he can be trusted. Where are you now?"

"I'm—on—Benning Road."

"That's my hood. Where is Benning?"

"Shorty, I don't know—hold on—I'm at the light now. There's a—gas station on both sides of the street. I see a Denny's—"

"I know exactly where you are. Go through the light and make that left into Denny's parking lot. You hungry?"

"No doubt."

"Well, go ahead and order some food and I'll be there in twenty minutes."

"Aight, shorty. One."

Chapter 23

Angel

Disconnecting my call with Najee, I turned back to my homie Marvin. "I miss shorty, Ang," Marvin said.

"Who? Lil' Chucky?"

"Yeah."

"Me too? I miss Big Squirt, Lump, Tye, Spider, and Chyno—everybody that ain't here. Anyway, God bless the dead and all that, but we gotta keep on living, boo. The bills gotta get paid. I got some folks that just got in town with the best coke in the city. What type of numbers you doing now fucking with whoever you fucking with?"

"I been fucking with that boy, Pretty B."

"Michael Wonson?" Marvin nodded his head. "When will he get home?"

"About a month ago and Slim on like a muthafucka. The streets say that he fucking with Carlos Trinidad and nem."

"How did he do that?" I asked, vexed.

"The way I hear it is that Pretty B put some work in the Feds for somebody close to Carlos Trinidad. To return the favor, Trinidad put some people on Ronnie T's family, and they forced him to take back all his statements against Pretty B in court. On appeal, he got out and the case was dismissed."

"So, Ronnie T home, too?"

"Naw, his hot ass got shot down on appeal. He left Arizona somewhere on PC."

I was coping five bricks quality keys at fifteen a joint. But it's just for you. What's up?"

"Angel, say no more. I'm ready when you are ready," Marvin said.

"Call me later on and I'll tell you where to meet me, a'ight?"

"That's a bet."

I left Simple City and went straight to the Denny's. I found Najee seated at a table near the window in the back. A sense of deja

vu overcame me. Najee was sitting at the exact same table that Carlos had sat when we first met four years ago. I looked at Najee and
stopped cold. My throat got caught in my chest. It was the first time
that I noticed the uncanny resemblance. Najee and Carlos would
definitely go for brothers. The same curly hair and exotic good
looks. The height and build. I took a moment to gather myself before getting to the table.

"Hey, baby. What's good?" I asked as I sat down.

In between bites of what appears to be an omelet of some kind,"
Najee said. "It's all good, shorty. You are looking as beautiful as
ever."

"And you fine as shit, now what? I guess that makes us special,
huh?"

"More than that. We like Jay-Z and Beyonce out of this piece.
Divided we are just two natural born killers."

"Together—can't nobody out here stop us."

"I know that's right."

Chapter 24

Angel

By the time the ball dropped on New Year's Eve in Times Square, we were firmly holding the reins that controlled most of the horses that ran in DC's underworld fast track. On the Eve of 2015, shit was lovely for real. In the five or so months that it took to get there, a lot changed.

Najee had so much money that living in Beacon Hill Apartments no longer suited him. My old friend James found him a house in Potomac, Maryland that he loved. So, I moved in with him. The house cost 1.2 million dollars and was situated on over 4 acres of land. It was made strictly for MTV cribs. There was a four-car garage that held his Navigator, my BMW, a purple Ferrari Medina, and a black on black Mercedes Benz S700. We kept the money and other stuff in the Beacon Hill spot, we just didn't like it there. I had successfully turned Najee on to all my old customs in DC, Maryland, and Virginia. The prices we were offering couldn't be matched and money poured in from all over.

I always preached the idea of investing your money and one day Najee listened to me. His dream was to build a nightclub in Suburbia Maryland that could rival the fame and fortune of Club Love in DC. Then he hooked up with a local dude we both knew named Eric *Big E* Miller and started an independent record label. They called it RNR or Real Nigga Records. The influx of drug money and Najee's pride afforded RNR the type of focus and promotion that rivaled the big companies.

Me, I traveled back and forth to Newark and oversaw the construction and grand opening of my clothing store. Since I worked so hard to get everything I wanted for the store in Newark I named it Modus Vivendi II. I talked my uncle into quitting his dead-end job at the factory and running the store. The first person that he hired to work there was Aminah.

In DC, I kept in touch with Tamara who was running the B and B Palace for me. I dropped in on Kia every now and again to make sure that she was making Modus Vivendi as successful as it could be. Kia Ransom was a godsend. She was nicknamed Kia the Diva and she always knew what style was hot and what was not.

Thanks to her my store was turning a helluva profit. So, most of my days were free and I spent them showing Najee how spontaneous I could be. When he was working on something, I fucked him. When he wasn't, I fucked him. All I did was play my part as Bonnie to my Clyde and fuck my man. I felt like such a slut every day but I loved it. Every day I went past my mother's house to check on her and Aniyah. My daughter was getting so big that it was scary. I never thought that I could love one person so much. My daughter was what I lived for.

I raced my BMW around the Capital Beltway and thought about the situation that I had created. In my hast, I never to stopped to think about the toes Najee would be stepping on when he flooded the city with coke. I guess I never realized just how big he would become. The streets are always watching and talking but I never realized how much until now. The conversation that I had overheard while at my clothing store came back to my mind—

"—baller nigga. I'm so tired of these broke ass wanna be gangsta niggas that look like Rastafarians. They need to put a nationwide ban on niggas with dreads. And they always end up in a bitch face. All day, every day. I always attract the wrong kind of dudes. All the wild niggas love me to death. But I need one of them out of town niggas like the dude, Najee," the pretty young girl said to her company who she called Star.

"Najee? Who the fuck is Najee?" the girl called Star responded.

"Girl, I swear. You green as shit. Who doesn't know who Najee is? That nigga got shit on smash for real. He and his people own Real Nigga Records. Them niggas caked the fuck up and I'm tryna get me on of 'em. You hip to the nigga Madd Flow, Lil Stew, Southeast Soldiers, Lil' Swipey, and the Chocolate City Cartel?"

"Bitch, I might be a little behind but I ain't retarded. I watch TV just like your groupie, 106 and Park ass, yeah, I'm hip to them."

"All of them are on the record label that Najee owns. Everybody in the city fuck with them niggas. That's what I mean all these niggas out here with real paper and I get stuck with Marco bamma ass."

"You got B.F. too, don't you? He got money."

"Now you got jokes. B.F. is what I call a 'keep up' kinda nigga. He is so busy tryna keep up that he can't catch up to save his life. It's 2014 and that nigga still pushing the '06 Caddy truck and think he the shit. Somebody needs to introduce him to Najee and nem."

Since everybody was talking about Najee, it made me wonder how many people were listening and who? I knew then that we were back in the big league and that every negative element in the game would now be waiting to pounce at any sign of weakness.

I think it's time for Najee to slow down. I need to tell him about the conversation that I overheard and exactly what it means. He went from hustler and killer to Kingpin

How long will it be before the cops and robbers come knocking? Was I wrong for bringing Najee here?

Does he think that he's impervious to the pitfalls of the fast life? How lucky can one man be? I'm going to have to talk to Najee. He was a street dude before he was anything else. He knows how niggas in the streets think. In the blink of an eye, Najee had become the person that he had killed to eat here. Only he probably didn't realize it. If Najee will listen to anybody, it'll be me and I have to let him know that it's time to give up the street side of the game and focus on the legit side. *The 48 Laws of Power* said it best—*Do not go past the mark you aimed for. In victory, learn how to stop!*

I couldn't get Robert Green's words out of my head. Najee and I had set a goal in the beginning. The goal was to get rid of the coke, put the money up, and live high off the hog forever and ever. The coke was almost gone, so we were a stone's throw away from reaching our goal. Then I had another thought. I thought about all the people that couldn't eat while Najee was housing shit in the streets. He had been taking a lot of food off a lot of tables for a while now. That meant that he was stepping on a lot of toes. Even though I never said a word to Najee I knew some of those toes belonged to a dude that wore way bigger shoes than Najee.

No matter how much I tried to forget him, whenever I looked at my daughter, I saw him. His name was still mentioned in several circles in the city. He was rarely seen and myth-like, but I knew he was there. I'm willing to bet that he's not taking too kindly to the new kid on the block. What does he know? How much does he know? Does he know about my part in it?

If I was sure of anything in the world, I was sure Carlos had to notice that somebody besides himself was pocketing millions of dollars off of coke in DC. The sad reality of it all was that almost overnight, Najee had become Carlos' only competition in the city. That brought the 19th Law of power to mind—*Always know who you're dealing with. Do not offend the wrong person. Choose your opponent carefully then never offend or deceive the wrong one.*

Najee had no idea what he was up against and it was all my fault. He had probably heard Carlos's name mentioned in hushed tones in the streets everywhere, but to know him was to know his real power. To know his power was to fear him. The police had questioned me about him, and the media were in love with the idea of him. He helped me get out of jail and for that I'm loyal. But I am also loyal to Najee and my heart lies with him. Is it possible to divide your loyalties? At some point, I knew that the two men in my life would clash and that it was a war Najee couldn't win.

Chapter 25

Carlos & Benito

Three more miles to go. I looked at my sports watch, thirty-six minutes. Seven miles in thirty-six minutes means that I'm on pace to beat my personal record of ten miles in fifty-two minutes. I was smoothly running a 5-minute mile. Not bad for an old man. Out of the corner of my eye, I spotted Benito at the entrance to the Washington Racquet and Fitness club. On my way back around the track, I saw Enrique riding a stationary bike trying to look inconspicuous. But I knew the young hot-headed Latino was watching me and everybody in the area. But I thought that was all unnecessary because nobody in the club knew who I was.

To the personal trainers and regular clientele, I was Mr. Venegas a wealthy businessman. I kept to myself and worked out hard, 2 miles left. Running is like therapy to me. It's the only way I can completely ease my mind. I was always able to rationalize myself better while running. I constantly pushed myself, on the track, and in everything that I do. It's my release plus, it was my way of trying to keep the doctors away. Running thirty miles a week had to keep the doctor from trying to stick a finger in my ass.

"I'm checking you for prostate cancer," they always say.

Once a man turned fifty it was all downhill from there and I am determined to beat those odds. One more mile to go. I looked at my watch again, forty-six minutes, ten seconds. I stepped up my pace and pushed myself to a little over a 4-minute mile. My muscles ache and my body threatened to quit but I made it. I walked a couple of laps to let my body cool down then I hit the showers.

After a shower, I stood in front of the mirror and dressed. The only part of my body that betrayed me and showed my forty-seven years of age were my eyes. My eyes were old, if I allowed anyone to stare into my eyes, they'd be able to see the pain that still lived in my eyes and the cold blackness that covered my heart. It was all there in my eyes on display for the world to see. The pain, the heartache, the losses, betrayal, and death. I was an open book if you could get close enough to me to read them. That was the key. You had to get close enough and I never allowed that.

I put my Dolce & Gabbana shades on and gathered my sweat-soaked clothing. I handed my bag to Enrique as soon as I left the shower room and checked the messages on my iPhone. Personally, I hated modern communication devices because they were so open to taps but the information age insisted that I stay connected to the world. The silver and black Maybach appeared as soon as I stepped out of the club. Enrique sat upfront with Manny the driver and Benito climbed into the back seat beside me. He opened the small refrigerator and handed me an energy drink.

"We're taking a beating in the street, my amigo. DC no longer belongs to you. The money that we take in now is laughable. More peanuts in comparison to what we used to do. While we were away getting fat someone else filled our shoes," Benito said and grabbed another drink. After popping the top and taking a generous swallow, he said, "This shit tastes awful."

"But it's good for you, old friend."

"Someone has their finger on the pulse that controls the city's heartbeat, comrade, and that someone is not you."

I calmly sipped down my drink as I thought about what Benito had just said. "How much of a beating are you talking about?"

"How much? Let me see." Benito went into his pocket and retrieved his cellphone. He read from it, "In Anacostia, we did a little under a million, Petworth a million-five, Shaw a million even and everybody else gave us a million. That's under nine million this month alone. The last couple of months the numbers have been steadily declining."

"Maybe people have stopped using drugs, Benito. Have you thought about that?" I joked to keep my mood light but inside I was furious. If the money was mysteriously falling shorter and shorter every month that could mean only one thing somebody in the city was moving seriously. But who? "What do you suppose is going on, Benito?"

Benito reclined in the luxurious leather seat, put his hands behind his back, and became silent for a moment. "Carlos, you know the answer to your own question. It is as simple as one-two-three. There is a new supply of cocaine in town. Someone is moving major coke in the backyard of your humble abode."

"How could this have happened, Benito? It is understood amongst our associates that the Nation's Capital belongs to me. Who would violate such an agreement? Who would challenge me in such a way?"

"I do not know, mi amigo."

His answer was unacceptable to me. "Benito, you are my eyes and ears in the streets. There is a reason why you don't know such things. Tell me."

"I will find out for you. Give me a little time and I will have all the answers you seek."

"Don't let me down, Benito."

The lock on Face's door was one of the easiest to pick. I had become quite skillful at picking locks over the years. Picking locks and killing. It is what I was made to do. I walked into the backdoor of the large two-story home in Fairfax, Virginia without making a sound. Being able to move about undetected is another skill I honed to perfection over the years. I crept through the house and counted three people inside three different bedrooms.

The person that I had come to see was not home. I looked at my watch and knew that it was still early for a person in life. So, I decided to sit and wait for the man that I needed to see. He had to come home. Like a good husband and father, he always did. Carlos wanted answers and answers he would have. I pulled out one of my Cuban cigars and lit it. I inhaled the acrid smoke and held it in for a while then exhaled. *Face come on home to Poppa.*

I heard keys turning in the lock about thirty minutes later and knew that it was Face. He walked right past the living room at first but then doubled back, I heard him sniffing the air and then he turned the light on. He looked me in my face and jumped.

"Benito, what the fuck are you doing here? You scared the shit outta me. How did you—"

"I needed to talk to you."

"Shit man, you could've called a muthafucka."

"I could have but I didn't. Sit down, Face."

Face took the sofa seat opposite me and sat down. "What's up?"

"When you were frustrated with your situation a few years ago. Who did you come to for help?"

"What do you mean?"

"I mean when those fucks in the Gangsta Gear Shop were selling you twenty bricks at twenty-five apiece. Who did you come to?"

"I came to you."

"Right, I didn't want to fuck with you but I did anyway because of your reputation as a money getter. Who fronted you fifty keys at a time consistently at twenty a key?"

"You did."

"When Cujo and those crazy cowboy putas wanted to bring you love, who declared you off-limits?"

"You."

"So, haven't we been good to you, Face?"

"Definitely."

"When the last shipment got fucked up. Didn't I still give you more coke to straighten it out? And with no hassles?"

"You did that."

"Well, tell me then, mi amigo. Why have you betrayed us?"

"*Betrayed you?* What the fuck are you talking about, Benito? I never betrayed you. How?"

"I talked to my people and they told me that in the last five months or so, you've brought no coke from us. None. Nada. And I said to myself, There's something wrong with this picture. I am too wise to believe that suddenly you have turned over a new leaf. So, either you quit the game, or you now buy cocaine from someone else. Which is it, Face?"

"I couldn't resist the prices. But I never thought I was betraying you. I was just tryna do me. I get a hundred bricks every forty-five days at fifteen a key. I buy fifty and I get fifty. That's the deal. No offense to you, Benito, but I had to go with the better price. I had no idea that I'd come home one day, and you'd be sitting in my living room. How the fuck did you get in here, anyway?"

158

"I have my ways. Tell me, Face, who is the new supplier of cocaine that offered you this good deal?"

I sat and listened to Face break everything down for me. "You are a smart man, Face. I don't blame you for going with a better price. I would have done the same thing myself—had I not been involved with people who don't like to be betrayed."

"I didn't—"

"You don't have to explain anything to me. I understand. I understand." I rose from my chair with the silenced 10 millimeter in my hand. "But Carlos Trinidad does not understand betrayal." I shot him twice in the face. Then I walked over and shot him once in the forehead. I left his house through the same door that I came in through.

I drove to Chevy Chase and told Carlos everything that I had learned from Face. Carlos never said a word as he listened. Even when I spoke her name, I knew it was a name he would be interested in.

"Benito, I want you to find out who they are getting their coke from. I will make a few phone calls myself, but I need to know. Once we have an assessment of the whole situation, I'll decide then how to act."

Over the next seven days, I paid visits to at least five other major dealers in the city. I was given the same answer by them all. The others were not obligated to the Trinidad Organization, so I spared their lives for the time being. But I promised myself to come back later and kill everyone who opposes us. In the meantime, I had to find out who was backing the man with the Arab song name. He had to be backed by someone powerful to supply the demand that he was, and *without permission.*

Anthony Fields

Chapter 26

Angel

"Blow out the candles, baby," I told Aniyah.

Individually she blew out all nine candles on her birthday cake while everybody laughed and snapped photos. Then we sang happy birthday to her. Even at nine years old, you could tell that she loved the attention. I looked at my child as she tore through her cake like a child possessed and smiled. The older Aniyah became, the more she looked like Carlos. It was surreal. Her long hair was pulled back into a ponytail, held in place with a red hair tie. She was chubby with the cutest cheeks imaginable and she was an extension of me. That face never ceased to amaze me. For her birthday, I gave my baby a platinum charm bracelet with tiny teddy bears on it and purple carat diamond earrings.

I thought about everything I had gone through over the years to get to this point and it made me emotional. I never even knew I was crying until I heard a voice say, "Mommy why are you crying?"

I looked down into my daughter's eyes and knew that they were her father's eyes. I wiped at the tears in my eyes and hugged Aniyah.

"Mommy is happy, baby. You make me so happy and I love you, baby, with all my heart. Do you hear me?" As I held my baby close to my chest, I felt her nod her head.

"City Under Siege Fox News, I am Maria Wilson reporting to you live from the corner of Martin Luther King Avenue and Malcolm X Blvd. Behind me here about one block down, a local business owner was ambushed and shot to death as he left the shop that he owned. Sources close to the scene say that De'lonta Bethea was seen closing up the K and P barbershop, a shop that he has owned for over fifteen years. Witnesses say that a dark-colored car pulled up and two men approached De'lonta Bethea. A tussle ensued and both men pulled weapons and shot Mr. Bethea to death."

When I walked through the door, I heard the TV going in the day room and went to see what Najee was doing. He turned around and faced me with a look of concern on his face.

"Did you catch that?" Najee asked.

I nodded my head, I couldn't believe what I had just heard. Doodie was dead. Two dudes had killed him in front of his barbershop. *Doodie what did you do?* "Najee, I'm starting to get a little concerned. Be careful with your offense."

"Concerned about what? Be careful about offending who?"

"Listen, when I brought you here, I thought I had it all figured out. But I was wrong. Miscalculated something and now it might be about to come back and haunt me."

There was a look of concern on Najee's face. "What are you talking about, shorty?"

"At first I thought you could just come in and set up shop for a while. In my mind, I didn't think that over fifteen thousand keys were a lot of coke. Until I saw what type of money you were pulling in. The 48 Laws of Power says, Be careful who you offend. Lately, I've been thinking about the toes you're stepping on to get that money—"

"I hope you ain't saying—"

"Let me finish. You got niggas in this city that ain't gon' take it too well when the new guy comes in and sets up the whole strip. I forgot about them. Well, he."

"*He?* He who?"

"His name is Carlos."

"Trinidad."

"Yeah, that's him. Najee, muthafuckas can say whatever they want but Carlos runs all this shit. He controls everything that comes in and out of DC."

"Not everything, he doesn't control me. Why are we even here having a conversation about that nigga? Fuck Carlos Trinidad! Son don't put no fear in me. And all the 48 Laws of power shit, I ain't tryna hear that shit. You ain't gonna do nothin' but make me revel. I'ma do what I want, when I want, with who I want and ain't nobody gonna tell me different."

"Baby listen to me. What I'm tryna tell you is that all this shit is connected. Face getting killed in his house out Virginia a week ago.

And now Doodie gets killed coming out of his shop. I'm telling you, it's Carlos and he ain't gon' stop. We have—"

Najee stood up and exploded. "We ain't gotta do shit. If that nigga is killing muthafuckas because he mad about a little paper, that's his problem. Son don't know me and he doesn't wanna get to know me. Fuck son and I'm through with the conversation."

I stood riveted to my spot by the wall and watched the man that I love walk away from me. What just happened was exactly what I wanted to avoid. A pissing contest, men always wanted to prove whose dick was bigger and who could piss the furthest. I was defeated. I didn't know what to do or say to get Najee to see things from my perspective. I'ma have to let the pieces fall where they may.

***

Pope's funeral Home on Pennsylvania Avenue was packed with people by the time me and Najee walked through that door. Everybody in the city who was anybody was in attendance. The scene was reminiscent of Tony Bill's funeral. I asked around after Doodie's death and the word that I got was that Doodie had fallen out with an old acquaintance. The part that caught my attention the most was the fact that Doodie's prior connect was some dude named Enrique. According to the streets, Enrique was a part of the Trinidad Cartel. All kinds of warning bells went off in my head. I wanted to make Najee understand the severity of the situation, but he was too stubborn to listen.

Am I responsible for Doodie's death? That thought was too much for me to bear. Was Carlos now killing the people that he once employed? Or was Doodie and Face's death purely coincidental? Slowly, we made our way up to the casket. Doodie was dressed immaculately in a cream-colored button-down Cesare Paciotti shirt and jeans.

His cuffs were bound together by two exquisite yellow diamond cufflinks, they matched the canary yellow diamonds in his watch and chain. I kissed his face. The body is so hard and cold in death.

I stared at Doodie and saw no visible signs of what caused his death. Then I thought about all the people that I had sent to their deaths. When a person is born, he or she is promised nothing in life but a chance to die. I started to cry then, Doodie was one of the only people to come over DC Jail consistently and see me when I was locked up. He came to the hospital all the time while I convalesce. I loved him for that.

"Until we meet again, Fat Boy. Rest in peace," I whispered, then walked down the aisle and exited the funeral home.

Chapter 27

Carlos

"The District Attorney's Office is vigorously pursuing all avenues that will directly lead to the arrest of all persons connected to the Trinidad Crime Organization. We hope to file charges against these people in hopes that the infestation of the individuals will lead us to indict and eventually convicting the leader of the organization— Carlos Trinidad," Deputy District attorney Susan Rosenthal said. She then turned around from the mirror and faced me. "How does that sound?"

It turned me on immensely for Susan to recite her D.A. office sound bites for me. "That was marvelous, baby. Come here and let me show you how much I like it."

Susan stepped out of her Caroline Herrera two-piece business suit. After shedding the skirt, shirt, and blazer, she salaciously danced while stripping for me. Susan seductively simulated dancing on a pole in a strip club and she had my dick as hard as granite stone.

I walked across the room and picked up her pantyhose, ripping them in two. I grabbed Susan and kissed her. I led her to the bed and laid her down. I tied both of her wrists to the brass bars on the bed's headboard. Then I moved down between her legs and started the foreplay. I knew how much Susan loved to be dominated and bound. If that was her predilection, I was there or service that. It was a small price to pay to keep her loyal.

Her wild sexual fantasies bordered on the extreme at times, but every time she came in abundance, that was like money in the bank. She did whatever I asked her to do. The woman who is second in command at the District Attorney's Office fought for the weak and prosecuted the bad guys all day long, but at night she loved to be fucked royally by the most notorious criminal that she claimed to hate. I will never understand that one, and as long as she stays on my side, it ain't meant for me to understand. Every day, Susan publicly castigated me to the media. She initiated fake investigations into my dealings and championed the cause of bringing me down.

But then she would come to me, speak nothing of her job and give me the best blow job known to man.

Every time, I watched her head bob up and down on my dick, it turned me on. When she swallowed my semen, it made me truly feel like the powerful person that she portrayed me to be. As I laid between her legs with her pussy in my mouth, I thought back to the day we met.

It was at a fundraiser for a local politician. Morgan Whitley was his name. Everybody at that table knew who I was and allegedly what my business was. Susan newly appointed to the D.D.A. position talked of crime in the district and criminals all benign as if to unnerve me. But what she didn't know was that I am unflappable.

She asked me incriminating questions and it was plain for all to see that she loafed me. My sitting at that table was like a slap in the face to her, she said, but what everyone at that table couldn't see was Susan's hand under the table inside my pants gently rubbing my dick. I was intrigued by it all and the next day, I called her office. We arranged a rendezvous for later that day and that's when our relationship began, over six years ago.

"Ooohhh, yes baby! Don't stop!" Susan moaned.

I continued to lick and suck on her pussy. Susan Rosenthal, the quintessential politician, the hero of the weak, loved to get her pussy eaten. Over the years she helped lead her office on wild goose chases that led further away from me and my associates. She secretly destroyed evidence being used against my soldiers and business partners. She supplied me with the names of anybody who dared to turn against me and become a rat. The strange thing about it was that she never even told me why she does it and I never asked because I know that powerful people need powerful friends. If it were not for her, my downfall would have been hard, long, and steep. Having Susan on my side was a definite plus. It was she who had introduced me to my femme fatale, Dorothy Benigan my U.S, Marshal, and another lover of mine.

The next thing I knew, Susan got loose from her binds and pulled me up to mount her. She grabbed my zipper and unzipped my pants. Freeing my dick, she guided me into her. She was tight and wet, and I felt young and strong as I fucked her. In minutes, I was on the verge of cumming.

"A-a-a-r-g-g-h, I'm about to cum!" I informed her. "Get up, baby, and let me suck you dry."

I rolled off Susan and watched as she dived head-first for my dick. Using no hands, she deep throated me and swallowed every drop of cum that left my body.

"Mmmm, that was so good," Susan announced as she sat up on the bed.

"Susan, do you remember a woman that I did business with years ago that was arrested on several high-profile murders? Her name was Angel?"

A pensive look crossed Susan's face. "Kareemah El-Amin. She was charged with the *Tourist Home* murders in '05. I got rid of the DNA evidence on her for you. I haven't heard her name since the night she was shot in her beauty salon. I thought she left the street life?"

"Well, apparently she's back and playing ball for another team. I never released her from her contract or gave her permission to sign with another team. What I need you to find out for me is this—"

"Benito, have you been able to find out exactly where our friend is getting his coke from?" I asked my comrade as we sat in my living room later that night.

"I am on the verge of knowing everything there is to know about Najee. Give me a little while and I will have the answer for you. Have I let you down yet?"

"No, you haven't old friends, no you haven't."

Chapter 28

Najee

I stared at the watch as I turned it over in my hand. "What kind of watch is that? And why are you always buying me watches all of a sudden?"

"That watch is an Audemars Piguet. I saw it in a shop up Georgetown and thought it would look good on you."

The watch was a platinum calendar skeleton design. "How much did one of these run you, shorty? If you don't mind me asking?"

"I don't mind. That one cost ninety-seven thousand. It's from their *Royal Oak Grande Collection*. And I bought it for you to keep you time conscious. Have you thought about what I said to you a few weeks ago?"

"About what?"

"About knowing when it's time to get out. Knowing when to stop and all that."

"Yeah, I thought about it. How could I not? And although I understand everything you said and respect the fact that you're just looking out for me, I still say *fuck him*. Be careful who you offend—ain't that what you said? I still can't see how I'm offending that man. I don't even know son and he don't know me. Are you tryna tell me that I'm not supposed to eat because that nigga mad? Fuck that, shorty. I ain't feeling that shit."

"Boo, I'm with you one hundred percent. I feel you on everything you just said. Believe me, I do. But all I'm saying is—a beef between you and Carlos is inevitable, I know it. I blame myself for not factoring all that into the equation when we started this shit. You know what's inside of me. I feel the same way you feel. Fuck Carlos Trinidad, but this is not 'bout him—to a degree.

"It's about you. You've almost accomplished your goal of getting rid of the coke. In the process, you got rich, made a lot of friends, started a business, and bought some prime real estate. You're worth over a million dollars—you're set for life. How much more do you want, Najee? Greed, ignorance, and overconfidence is pushing you past the goal you aimed or. You have everything that you've wanted and more. And most importantly you've got me. I wanted to get back into the game, too.

"Before I met you, I told myself that I wanted my spot back. I wanted to feel the love of the streets again. But now it's different. Meeting and falling in love with you has changed my whole outlook. I no longer want the streets. Looking at the potential of a beef between you and Carlos has really made me realize that the streets love no one. They don't love me, you, or Carlos. If he wants the streets, boo, let him have em. We are both enterprising young multi-millionaires. We've made it already. Look around you."

I sat down on my desk and pondered with what Angel had just said. My eyes roamed around the room of my office in the headquarters of Real Nigga Records.

"You know what? You're right, I'm on some coo-coo shit for real. The Feds are probably investigating me as we speak. There's a lot about the street that we don't know, but what we do know is that thirty percent of the niggas in the streets are tryna get rich. And the other seventy percent of niggas in the streets are tryna tell on the thirty percent. I made the situation personal when I entertained the idea of a beef with Carlos Trinidad. But fuck that shit. You're right. Son can have that shit. When I sell the last five-hundred or so bricks, I'm out of the game. That's it, that's all. I'ma let everybody know that. That's my word."

"That's your word?"

"I swear by Allah. I'm finished as soon as the last brick is gone." I thought about something Angel said earlier. "So, you're in love with me, huh, shorty?"

Angel smiled and came toward me. "You ain't know?"

"I had an idea, but I wasn't sure," I replied as I unbuttoned the buttons on the shirt. "I mean, I kinda felt that you might—" I unsnapped her bra. "Love me. Judging from the way you are."

"Go lock your office door."

"—making *love* to me. Are you scared to get caught?" I asked as I put one of her nipples in my mouth and sucked on it.

"Boo, I ain't never scared."

"Show me, then, I dare you—"

Angel pulled her nipples out of my mouth, took my hand, and led me to my chair. Then she unzipped my pants as she kissed me. When my dick sprang free. Angel bent over and put my dick in her mouth. When my dick was wet with her saliva, she straddled me.

"Don't ever dare me."

All I could do was sit back and enjoy the ride.

A week went by and I was still unloading coke without incident. Angel called me one day and asked me to come to her clothing store. She needed to move some stuff that was too heavy for her to lift. When I walked through the door, I was met by a beautiful young woman that had to be every bit of 4'11 or 5 feet tall. She had a body for days and she was impeccably dressed in Dior from head to toe.

"May I help you, sir?"

"I'm looking for the owner," I replied.

"Oh, you must be Najee." her features softened. "I've heard a lot about you."

"Don't believe anything you hear and only half of what you see."

"I'll remember that. Angel is in the basement. Go through that door right here and go down the stairs. He won't be hard to find from there." She went to assist someone else that had just come through the door, just before I descended the stairs. I looked through the plate glass window and saw a black Cadillac Escalade pull up.

"Come out, come out, wherever you are," I shouted once I reached the bottom step.

Out of nowhere, Angel appeared. "Baby, come on around the wall," she said disappearing back around the wall that divided the basement into sections.

I followed Angel to a wall of boxes that were labeled with different designers.

"I have to move all these boxes from this end of the basement to that end. I have some plumber people coming in that need to break the concrete right here to get to the water main underground. It was a short notice and I didn't know who to call, so I called you."

"Gee, thanks, I guess."

"What were you up to before I called?"

I unbuttoned my shirt and took it off. "I was celebrating with Big E."

"Celebrating what?" Angel asked. "Najee, start with them boxes right there, first."

"We just signed two local artists that have a helluva buzz all over the East Coast."

"Who?"

"Elliott Johnson and Ronald Randolph also known as District and O.G. Them niggas are next to blow watch what I tell you."

"I ain't never heard of them."

"You will, shorty. Trust and believe me, you'll hear about 'em."

I manage to move all the boxes in a little under two hours. I was tired, sweaty, and geeking for a shower.

We walked up the stairs and prepared to leave the store.

"It was nice meeting you, Najee," the diminutive woman said.

Angel looked from me to the woman who ran her store. "Baby, I see you've met the Diva?'

"We met," I said, glancing out the window and shocked to see that the black Caddy truck was still outside.

Only now it was parked across the street. "I didn't know her name was Diva, though."

"It's not. My name is Kia. But everybody calls me Kia the Diva."

"I'll remember that. Take care, ma."

"Kia, I'm outta here. I'll call you tonight sometime, okay?"

"Do that. Bye, Angel. Bye, Najee."

We walked out the door and started to separate when I stopped to tell Angel something that I forgot to tell her. But before I could open my mouth, gunshots rang out. I pushed Angel down and laid on top of her until the shots ceased. I got up just in time to see the black Escalade speed off up the street.

"That was a close—"

I turned around and noticed that the Angel hadn't gotten up. She was still on the ground on the side.

172

"Angel?" I cried and got down on my knees.

I rolled her over and saw that her blouse was stained with blood. His eyes were closed, and my mind flashed back to the night Hasan got shot.

"Please don't die, Angel." Putting my ear to her chest, I heard her heart pumping. I heard a scream and looked out to see Kia with tears in her eye.

"Call an ambulance, now!" I shouted to her while holding Angel's hand. "Stay with me, baby, stay with me."

Anthony Fields

Chapter 29

Angel

Believe it or not, I looked worse than I actually felt. All I'd been hearing for the last hour was how scared I had everyone. It wasn't my fault Najee doesn't realize how strong he is. When he pushed me down and laid on me in an attempt to protect me from the gunfire. I hit my head and blacked out. What Najee didn't know and neither did I was that I was already hit. A single bullet found its mark and entered my shoulder. The bullet went clean through me and exited out of my right arm. I looked at my arm that was now in a sling and sighed. The questions of how and why wouldn't leave my head. I thought about the beef that was percolating between Najee and Carlos.

We're those bullets for me or him? I tried to understand a person in Carlos's position and asked myself what would I do? Then I wondered if Carlos knew about me and my role in Najee's ascent to the throne as DC's new kingpin. Getting' shot wasn't new to me, but it always managed to convince me of just how vulnerable I was. I silently thanked Allah again for sparing my life a second time.

"Stop at the CVS drugstore, so that I can get this prescription filled," I said to Najee.

Najee did not respond, instead he stared straight ahead and kept driving. When the sign for the CVS came into view, he pulled the car into its parking lot. Once the prescription was filled and I had popped two Tylenol with codeine. I was on my own. Before I knew what hit me, I was asleep.

I didn't even remember being carried into the house by Najee. I didn't remember being undressed or put to bed. I woke up and overhead Najee talking to someone on the telephone—

"That's it, son. Work-life, I'm ready to go off down here, son. Some clown ass nigga named Carlos. Yeah, son. Snatch Tye up and y'all niggas get down here in the next thing with an engine. No, doubt—no doubt. Get that bag from over Salimah and bring that, too. I'm about to show these DC niggas how we get down in the

Brick. Yeah, she's a'ight though, son. If something would've happened to shorty. Ayo son, I don't even wanna think about that. You, son, I found my queen and I ain't tryna let no pussy ass nigga fuck that up for me, feel me? Let me go, but call me when y'all ready to bounce and I'ma direct y'all path. A'ight yo', word is bond, son. I'm out, son. One!"

I laid in the bed and replayed Najee's conversation in my head. He had told somebody to come to DC, and bring somebody named Tye. I had no doubt in my mind that the person Najee had just spoken to was his man Gunz. The bag that Najee requested had to be filled with weapons and the reality of the situation hit me. Najee had decided to take the war to Carlos and that was something I couldn't let him do.

"Najee?" I called out to him.

He came to my side of the bed and sat down. What's up, shorty? How are you?"

"Najee, I heard you on the phone just now. What are you doing? Are you tryna start a war between you and Carlos Trinidad?"

"I ain't tryna start nothing, shorty. He did. That nigga started it yesterday. That bullet you caught was meant for me. I know it was. I saw the black Escalade pull up to the store behind me. They let me go inside and tried to get me to come out. That'll never happen again. From now on, you only get one shot. If you mess that up, that's your ass. We ain't gotta keep playing these games—you feel me.

I sat straight up in the bed. "Najee, I'm begging you, please don't do this."

"You begging me what? Please don't do what? Preserve my life? You begging me not to take care of me? I gotta protect me. The first law of nature is self-preservation and you outta all people you know that."

"You can leave here and walk away from it all, baby. I should've never brought you here. We can and go somewhere else and live—"

"Listen to yourself, right now." Najee walked away from the bed and leaned up against a dresser. "We had this same conversation in New York, remember? Right before we walked outside and nig-gas tried to end my life. My right-hand man lost his life. And for what? Because one muthafucka got greedy and corrupt.

"One muthafucka wanted to run it all. That's what Mu said to me the night I killed him. With me out of the way, he could run everything. To him, my life, my love, my loyalty, it all became worthless. I lost too much blood, sweat, and tears to turn away from that then and I can't turn away now. This shit is like deja vu. It's New Jersey all over again minus the love and loyalty.

"I could've walked away and let Mu live, knowing that he was the cause of it all, but I couldn't. That would've been uncharacteristic of me. Angel, it's just not in me to walk away, to leave something undone. This nigga almost killed us—not just me, but you, too. And again-for what? Because he is greedy, conceited, and selfish. What the fuck kinda nigga wanna kill another nigga for getting some money? Every dollar in the world ain't his."

That nigga on some mega maniac shit. Who the fuck he thinks he is Napoleon? Hitler? That nigga on some fucked up shit, but he fucking with the right nigga this time. He started it and I'm gonna finish it."

"What about me, Najee? Do I even matter?"

"Of course, you matter. I love you, Angel. Haven't you figured that out by now? This is for us. So, that we can live and not be bul-lied by this nigga. We shouldn't have to leave, run, or whatever you wanna call it. Getting money in the streets is the American way. This isn't about you, it's about him."

Najee was so angry that he didn't even understand the contra-diction in his own words. "This is about me, Najee. If something happens to you—I lose, you lose, we lose. Why would you wanna do that to us?"

"Ain't nothing gonna happen to me. There's a side to me that you've never seen, shorty. Trust me, I can handle me."

"Pick your opponents wisely. Najee, this is a fight that you can't win!" There, I said it. It was out in the open and I didn't regret say-ing it. I had hoped that this day would never come, but it had, and I had to talk some sense into Najee. A war with Carlos on his turf was suicidal. Najee dropped his head for a minute. Then he looked me straight in my eyes and the look he gave me made my blood run cold.

Najee laughed a sinister-sounding laugh and said, "Thanks for the vote of confidence, Ma. That's your opinion and everybody is entitled to one."

I had to lay all my cards on the table for him to see. It was now or never. "Najee, I wasn't totally honest with you—when we first met—well when we first talked about our lives together." The hurt look on Najee's face spoke a thousand words that his mouth didn't. "I never lied to you—I just purposely left certain things out. They never seemed important to me then and I was worried about the way you would view me. But now I feel like you should know every-thing."

I searched Najee's face for any hint of compassion or under-standing but found one. "Remember when I told you about the dude named Tony Bills?"

"Yeah."

"What I didn't tell you was that Tony was hooked up with Car-los Trinidad. I learned a lot about him from Tony and I met him on a couple of occasions, but that was it. I saw how he operated, how he manipulated people, situations, and events. When Tony got killed, I talked to Carlos at the funeral. Remember I told you that I hooked up with some people and started getting bricks? Those peo-ple were Carlos and his organization. I dealt with him directly most of the time.

"We became friends. I told you that I went to jail for some mur-ders and that I beat the case because the witness—my friend Fatima never showed up in court. Well, what I didn't tell you is that she never showed up because Carolos had her killed. He had her killed while she was under armed guards in the witness protection pro-gram. That showed me just how powerful Carlos really was. When I go out of jail, Carlos and I hooked up and one thing led to another. I was caught up in the moment and I was careless. The next thing I knew I was pregnant. Carlos is my daughter's father."

I saw the dejected and confused look that crossed Najee's face. "Don't even think about it, Najee. I've been around you long enough to understand how you think. I never crossed you or intentionally set this up. I don't even talk to Carlos. I swear by Allah, I don't. The last time I saw Carlos was the night I got pregnant by him. And that was over nine years ago. So, please take the betrayed look out of your eyes. I'm not clairvoyant, Najee. I couldn't predict that all of this would happen between us and we'd fall in love. I kept the information about Carlos away from you the same as I did everybody else. Nobody except for my mother knew about Carlos being Aniyah's father. Carlos doesn't even know."

"What do you mean he doesn't know?"

"Carlos doesn't know because I never told him. I never contacted Carlos again after that night that we conceived my daughter. I didn't want to complicate the situation or put him in a situation where he felt I got pregnant on purpose. I would have aborted the pregnancy, but I didn't. I decided to raise the baby on my own. At the time, I was out of the game, anyway. So, there was no need for me to contact Carlos. I'm not taking anything away from your gangsta, Najee. That is what's in question here, isn't it? If we leave all this shit to Carlos, you'll still be gangsta. Gangstas are born, not made. Carlos has the advantage of you, Najee. He has cops, politicians, judges, and all kinds of people in his pocket. He dictates to the city council here, not the other way around. That's why I say you can't win. I know Carlos, Najee, and I know how powerful he is. The deck is stacked against you, baby. Please listen to me."

"I'm listening to you. I heard you out, but now more than ever nothing's gonna stop me from killing your baby father. It's not the money he's mad about, it's you."

"What?"

"I can't believe this shit. Let me ask you something. Do you remember how you felt when you were being molested by your father?"

"Yeah, but—"

"What about the rage you feel when you use your father molesting your sister. Do you remember the rage that propelled you forward even though you knew what you were up against? Remember all the people had died because your sister was taken and killed? If somebody would have told you that the odds were against you, would you have abandoned your position? Would you have swallowed your hunger for revenge? Didn't you know that the twin nigga would eventually have you killed, too?"

I was defeated and I knew it. Everything Najee had just said was a message well received. I remembered the pain and my desire for retribution. Najee was right about Dearaye. Had I not killed him when I did, he would have killed me but I couldn't bring myself to admit that to Najee. "That was different."

"*Different?* How's it different? Dudes that I fuck with, the ones that you introduced me to are being killed in the streets. Then this muthafucka brings me a move and almost kills you. What's so different about that? And what about Doodie? Didn't you cry on my shoulder about how much of a friend he is to you? Where's his justice? If we walk away who's to say that Carlos won't still bring us a move? Especially when he finds out that you're his baby mother."

"Najee, don't even go there. Don't even fucking go there. If you got something to prove to yourself, go ahead. There's nothing I can say to stop you. If you wanna throw that baby mama, baby father shit in my face go right ahead. I can deal with that, but don't try to imply that I'm the reason for this or that I'ma means to end it. I love you, Najee, and I've only loved one other dude in my life."

"And you killed him. The night you told me about the dude Andre, the one from college. You said you loved him. You said that you thought he really liked you, so you forced yourself to him. Then you said he was no longer amongst the living. You told me that I could figure the rest out. I never said anything, but I figured that you killed him. So, did I figure right, Angel?"

"Yeah," I answered meekly. "I killed him. Is that what you wanna hear? I fucking killed that son of a bitch. But that doesn't mean that I didn't love him."

"I know and that's what I'm afraid of. And you knew I'd be afraid of the fact that you can kill the people you love as easily as the ones you don't. That's why you neglected to tell me that part.

How can I beef with your baby father and still lay in the bed with you every night? How do I know that I'd be safe from your wrath if I kill him?"

"Najee what the fuck are you tryna say to me?"

Najee pulled his car keys out of his pocket. "What I'm saying is it's a vote between us. I can't trust you. And my survival depends on me being able to trust the people around me. I have to get away from you. When this is all over, I'm going back to Newark. But not until I kill Carlos Trinidad. Forget about me Angel and I'ma do the same. When this shit heats up, please stay outta my way because I'm not gonna have time to decide if you are friend or foe. One love. I'm outta here."

I sat there stupefied, outraged, and numb at the same time. I watch Najee gather a few things and leave. *Where is he going?* The scream that came out of my mouth started at my heart and went upward I never meant for things to end up like this. Things had gone all wrong. Terribly wrong.

Anthony Fields

Chapter 30

Najee

I didn't know where I was going or what I was gonna do. All I knew was that I had to get out of there. I couldn't stand there any longer and look into Angel's face. Everything she said to me repeated itself in my head. My emotions were going haywire and I didn't know if I was gonna laugh or cry at any given moment. I didn't know whether to feel betrayed or honored. The only thing I knew for sure was that I love Angel, but I can't go back in there until this thing is over with. How can I trust her? How can I love a woman that will kill without impunity at the drop of a hat and then stand over you and say, "I love you?"

I sat in my truck and went through a sea of different emotions before I got myself together and pulled me out of the garage. I put my Bluetooth earpiece in my ear and told my phone to dial a number. I knew Gunz and Tye would arrive sometime later that day. But I needed a dude to direct my path and lead me to Carlos Trinidad. I needed someone who was unafraid to challenge the stronghold the powerful Latino had on DC. I needed a local natural born killer.

"Hello?" a voice said.

"What's the deal, son?"

"Najee, what's up, moe?"

"You, son."

"I was about to take care of some small shit but it can wait. Where are you tryna meet?"

I'm out Maryland, right now, but I'll be in the city in a little while. Tell me where to go and I'll be there."

"A'ight look, do you know where Eastover shopping Center is?"

"Naw."

"Just go to White Corners and wait for me there. You do remember where that is, right?"

"Of course, son. I'm on my way here. One."

I was standing on Southern Avenue in front of the old OBO Shop when I saw George Forman's pearl white Infiniti M35 make a U-turn and park on a side street. I walked toward the White Corners restaurant and met him.

"Let me order me something to eat before we talk. You want something?" George asked me.

"Hell naw, son. The last time I went in that place they had a whole pig on the grill. I ain't fucking with that joint. That's why I miss Jersey. We got mostly greasy spoon spots."

George laughed and went inside the restaurant. A few minutes later he came out and said, "Let's walk and talk."

Once we had gotten to Marlboro Pike, George said, "What's up, moe? Talk to me."

"Do you know a dude named Carlos Trinidad?"

"Not personally naw, but I'm hip to him. Why what's up with him?"

"This nigga fucked up with me because I'm selling weight to niggas, son. Can you believe that shit?"

"Look here, slim, a rack of niggas is probably fucked up about you coming to town and flooding it. That's just how shit is. I've been living in the city all my life and I still can't figure this shit out. We love when out of town muthafuckas come to town and bless us with work but we hate the fact that they are here. I saw niggas do the nigga Alpo the same way. Niggas was loving Alpo for what he brought to the table, but they couldn't stand him and what he represented—a New York nigga. Fuck Carlos Trinidad, slim, he ain't gon get in your business."

"He already did."

George stopped in his tracks. "He what?"

"He already did get in my business. He sent somebody to bring me a move yesterday."

"How do you know it was him?"

"Trust me, son, I know. That's why I called you. I Need some information."

"What kinda information?"

184

I need to know where to look for this nigga, son. I'm not from here, so I need to know certain things about escape routes, good places to hide out, and shit like that. I might need some extra guns, ammo, and etcetera. I got some men coming down and we're about to turn up the heat on this nigga. He tried to kill me, son, and I can't forgive or forget that. Feel me?"

George did not respond right away, instead he started walking again and appeared to be deep in thought.

After what seemed like an eternity, he said, "Fuck it, moe. In the last six months, you showed me more real shit than a rack of niggas. I grew up with that nigga Carlos Trinidad. He thinks he's the original Don Dadda out this muthafucka. I never understood how a Spanish nigga could run shit in an all-black city anyway. That nigga ain't never did shit for me and my men, so fuck him. Give me a few days and I'll get all the info you need on that nigga. And as far as guns and ammo, I'm the man you need to see. My basement is a gun store. You gon need a couple of low-key vehicles—some buckets—disguises—that sorta stuff. I know a broad that can get you an apartment in town where you can lay and strategize. Like I said--give me a few days and I'll have you ready to rock. I might even go with you."

I appreciate the love, son, word is bond," I said genuinely.

"Don't mention it, moe. Let's get back around this corner so that I can get my food. I'm hungrier than a muthafucka."

Chapter 31

Angel

All I could do was lie in the bed and stare at the ceiling. As if the solution to my dilemma was there. The four Tylenol that I had taken was starting to take effect because the pain in my head and shoulder were starting to subside. My body was drenched in sweat and I needed a bath. The temperature outside was in the high 80s. But I never got up to turn the AC on. My mind and body were in purgatory and the hot room fit my mood perfectly.

In the last few days since Najee left, I only moved to use the bathroom and eat a few times. The telephone was disconnected from the wall and my cell phone was turned off. I wanted to be incommunicado. Completely cut off from the outside world. In the outside world was the one person that I love as much as my daughter and mother. As long as Najee was out there and mad at me, I wanted to be inside. I wanted to hide from the world because things were all wrong.

Thoughts of what Najee said to me before he left kept coming back to mind as I lay. *"How can I beef with your baby father and lay in the bed with you every night?"*

Was I wrong for telling him everything? How could I have known that my decision to come clean would turn out so negatively? I kept asking myself those questions over and over again. I should've kept my big mouth closed. But there was something inside me that told me I had done the right thing. When I told Najee about Carlos being my daughter's father, that was a double-edged sword that I thought might have driven Najee to leave the beef alone. I was trying to emphasize my relationship with Carlos to show Najee that I had first-hand knowledge of how powerful the man was.

It would have been wrong to let Najee go into a war half-cocked without the facts. Najee was a student of the streets, but his knowledge of war was a little off. In war, one must always know their enemy. A good general always has to know the strengths and weaknesses of the opposing army. Najee was moving off raw emotion and not wisdom. I tried to tell him just how far Carlos's name stretched in the streets. Najee wanted to go to war with a man that had made DNA evidence disappear in the United States Attorney's Office.

The same man that was bad enough to have Fatima killed while under armed guard by six US Marshals. To pull that off was a demonstration of exactly what he was capable of. I couldn't let Najee jump out there like that, not if I could help it. But I couldn't help it, and that was what had me so depressed. Why couldn't Najee put his pride to the side and accept the fact that he was out of his league?

I wanted so desperately to find him, shake him real hard and say, "Nigga stay in your lane."

The pains in my body were now gone temporarily, but the constant ache in my head was still there. It was almost too much to bear. This must be what it feels like to be truly brokenhearted. I was tired of it all. The pain, the stress, the drama, and the tears. Since Najee left, I cried myself a river and I hated to cry. Crying denoted weakness and I'm far from weak. But it was hard not to cry when you were hurting, so I got off the bed and went into the bathroom. I ran the water into the tube and added a little Epsom Salt. Then I went to the stereo system and found the CD that I wanted to hear. I put the CD in the changer and hit the proper buttons. Then I walked back to the tub of water, undressed, and climbed in. By the time I rested my head on the back of the tub, Usher's voice permeated me to the soul.

"It's gonna burn for me to say this but it's coming from my heart. It's been a long time coming cause we have fallen apart/ I wish that I could work this out/ but I don't think you're gonna change! I do but you don't I think it's best we go our separate ways/ Tell me why should I stay in this relationship! When I'm hurting, baby/ I ain't happy, baby! Plus, there's so many other things I need to do/ I think that you should let it burn—

I listened to the whole *Confessions* CD and cried some more. *What can I do to help Najee?* I turned the question over and over in my mind but couldn't find an answer. Then I remember that Najee didn't want my help.

"I don't trust you." He stabbed me repeatedly in the heart when he went off on me.

What exactly did he mean when he told me to stay out his way? How could he just throw away everything that we built, to prove something to himself and Carlos Trinidad? Especially when it could possibly get him killed?

I contemplated calling Carlos and begging him to kill the whole situation. Too much blood had already been spilled. Some were my own, I was at an impasse. A rock and a hard place. Then another thought hit me. *What if it wasn't Carlos that was behind the attempt on our lives. What if the bullets that Najee was convinced were for him, weren't? What if Doodie and Face's deaths were not caused by Carlos? What if the bullets that I caught were for me and not Najee?* I leaped out of the tub naked and ran to the closet. There were several boxes in there with my things in them. I pulled each box out and went through them until I found what I was looking for.

Inside a small box was the paper that I had put there over eight years ago. It was the paper that Latesha Garrison, Carlos' niece gave me at Bally's moments after our sexual escapade. I opened it and read it.

Dearest Angel,

Thank you for the memorable moment in the sauna. Call me whenever you need anything. My numbers will never change. I hope to hear from you soon.

P.S. The money is from my niece.

Carlos

I read the letter repeatedly. It was as if the letter connected me to him somehow. If the letter was correct, then I still had a way to reach Carlos. I never thought that I'd be contacting him now, especially not about something like this. I always thought it would be about Aniyah. But now that the man I love has declared war on the father of my child, I must talk to Carlos and see if he's behind this. I have to tell him what he doesn't know before everything blows up. My heart raced as I came out of the closet and ran across the room. I grabbed my cell phone and dialed the numbers that I had for Carlos. I prayed that I wasn't too late.

Angel 2

Chapter 32

Najee

"George, this is my man, Gunz. We call him Gunz because this nigga been playing with guns since we were kids. And this right here is, young boy, Tye."

"What's up with y'all?" George said to my men and then turned back to me. "This move you making is big. Nobody has ever gone at this dude and—"

"Gee don't tell me you came here for nothing, son. I could've heard the untouchable stories over the phone."

"Hold on for a minute more. Always let a man finish what he's saying before you speak. I gathered the info you need, I just wanted to let you know what type of challenge you face. I never said that he was untouchable. Nobody's untouchable. History has shown us that. What I was tryna say is that this nigga is rarely ever seen in the streets. He wields power from afar. What you're gonna have to do is draw him out. Hit him where it hurts. You create enough terror in his organization, he'll surface and then you can kill him."

I pondered what George said and respected it. "You right, son. My bad for jumping the gun and doubting you. I'm just ready to kick this shit off."

"I know the feeling, slim. Trust me, I do. You have to learn the streets first. Today we ride around, and I'll show you the places you need to hit. Let's roll this hit off."

We exited the apartment on Howard Road and walked outside to our cars.

George turned to me. "Let's take your truck, slim. We'd be in the Infiniti squeezed together like sardines. As a matter of fact, let me drive. We'll get around quicker that way."

Two days later, we were ready. The hardest part of my mission was identifying Carlos Trinidad. George couldn't come up with any picture of him. I called around and found a dude that had a sister who worked at the Washington Times newspaper company. He said that his sister said they had pictures of Carlos on file. I agreed to

189

hook up with him later and pay his sister for the pictures. But right now, I'm ready to tear some shit up. First things first.

Me and Tye sat in the stolen UPS truck and scoped out the small cafe on 14th Street. I looked at the stuff on paper that George had written for me. His sources hadn't told him who exactly was a part of the Trinidad Organization, it didn't say who to hit. There was just a list of places to target. The place on the list was believed to be places of business that belongs to Trinidad and places where his crew congregated.

The cafe that I now watched was on that list. I watched Hispanic people go in and out of the cafe. I glanced over at Gunz who was dressed as a UPS delivery man. He was inside a laundromat across the street acting like he was making deliveries. We locked eyes and he nodded his head. I nodded back. Then Gunz walked across the street and entered the cafe. Minutes later he walked out of the cafe. He walked over to the tuck and lifted the back door.

"How many are in there?" I asked.

Gunz pretended to be looking at some paperwork in his hand and scratching his head. "From what I could see, baby boy, there's not that many people in there. I only scanned the joint for a minute or so. I counted about ten people, eight men, and two women. Every now and then someone comes outta the back area—I think that's the kitchen. So, we know there's kitchen staff in here. There's one dude at the front counter who makes eleven. I spotted a few doors behind him. They look to be offices of some kind. If so, ain't no telling how many are in them."

"A'ight. Everybody dies except the cooking staff unless they get in the way. If it has on plain clothes, kill it. I'm going to the office."

Gunz pulled the lid off a box and screwed the specially made silencer onto the Mac 90 submachine gun. Then he put it back in the box. "The whole cafe is a one-level joint. I'ma hit everything in the outside area then join you in the rooms in the back. Be careful, baby boy."

"Son, you know how I do. One." I got out the side of the truck and waited for Gunz to walk back over to the cafe. Then I went in behind him. The two Rugers in my waist were loaded, cocked, and ready for some action.

I walked up to the man at the counter and placed an offer while Gunz fumbled with a clipboard. Then Gunz said, "Sir, I hate to keep bothering you, but I just checked my itinerary and delivery confirmation forms. This package is supposed to be delivered here. It is addressed to Mr. C. Trinidad."

The man behind the counter eyes grew wide at the mention of the name and I knew that we were in the right place.

"T-t-h-e-r-ee is no C. Trinidad here."

"Isn't this 1447 14th Street Northeast? Isn't this Mamacita's Cafe?"

"Sir, senor, but nobody here ordered anything from—"

"Frederick's of Hollywood. Are you sure?" Gunz fiddled with the box until it opened. "Nobody ordered the beautiful lingerie?" He reached into the box and pulled out the Mac.

The Latino man behind the counter stood frozen in fear as Gunz swung the gun up and hit him square in the face. Before the dead man's body could hit the floor, I leaped over the counter and headed towards the two doors in the back. I heard screams and shuffling and knew that Gunz was now executing everybody in the eating area.

I turned the knob on the first door. It turned out to be a utility closet. The next door opened revealing two men who were both on telephones speaking in rapid Spanish. I got the drop on them and they never had a chance to react. I shot both men and made sure they were dead. Then I searched all the doors in that room. Finding no one, I sprinted back to the dining area. I stopped when I saw a young Latino kid lying in a pool of blood. I looked over at Gunz. My look shot daggers.

"Baby boy, I told him to get back in the kitchen. He didn't listen, so I murked him."

"Fuck it," I said finally. "Let's roll. They should learn to understand English before they come over here."

Gunz put the Mac back in the box and then we both walked out of the cafe. As we got into the UPS truck, we heard people screaming in Spanish and running out of the cafe.

Two blocks away we both changed clothes while Tye drove the truck. Then we ditched it on Hobart Street and found another vehicle that we stashed there. As the black 2006 Nissan Maxima pulled away from the curb and headed for Georgetown, I said to myself, "Let the games begin."

Chapter 33

Mareya Garcia

I hate this job. The house is shitty, and the wages are low, but they pay the bills and right now the bills have to be paid. The country is in a recession and everybody's feeling it. Some nights I make really good tips and some nights I make nada. I love the nights when all the important men come and go. The handsome men in fine suits and expensive watches. On those nights Mama Caesar would close the store down for them and I'd get to serve them. I knew that they were very important people because Mama Caesar and everybody in the store treated them with the greatest respect. There was one of the men that I especially like to wait on. He was the most engaging man that I'd ever seen. His companions called him Benito and I was in love with him. He lavished me with money and small gifts when he came to the restaurant. I secretly started yearning for the days when they would come.

Besides needing the extra money for school and books, I sent what I could home to my family. My scholarship at George Washington University only covered room and board. No living expenses or books, so Salaazar's it was.

"Mareya, you have a customer!" Mama Caeser yelled out.

"Okay, okay," I said aloud, but under my breath, I said. "Keep your shirt on you, fat cow." I laughed to myself at the hidden joke. But I meant it literally as well.

Everybody in the restaurant knew Mama Caesar had an affinity for the young guys that worked at the restaurant. At fifty years old, time had not been kind to Mama Caeser. The word around the store was that after work when the store closed, Mama Caesar would pay one of the young guys to massage her body from the waist up. She ordered them to lick her saggy breasts and then place their penises between them as she squeezed both breasts together. They would *titty fuck* her while she licked the tip of their penises until they came. Then she would lick their dicks clean until she orgasmed.

I shuddered at the thought of anybody doing anything sexual with tha dirty old hag. I walked over to the table where the black man sat. He was very handsome and dressed like a man from the TV. "Hello, sir. Welcome to Salaazars can I get you anything before you order—water, appetizer, anything? Or do you wanna just go ahead and order?"

"I already know what I want, so I'll just go ahead and order. Gimme the chicken Quesadillas, a plate of soft-shell tacos with chicken, steak, and rice. Bring me some of that salsas stuff, too."

"Anything to drink, sir?"

"Yeah, a raspberry iced tea would be nice."

"Right away, sir." He looks like a big tipper.

I walked into the back and joked with Jore the cook as I placed the order for the black man. My feet started to hurt a little and I desperately needed to sit down for a while but I couldn't. Mama Caesar had strict rules about taking breaks while not on break and I couldn't stand to be fired. I went to the beverage bar and mixed fresh raspberry juice in a pitcher of iced tea. Then I walked back into the room and saw that the table where the black man had been sitting was now empty. My eyes scanned the room for him but couldn't find him. I shrugged my shoulders and set the iced tea down on the table anyway.

Maybe he went to the restroom. It was then that I noticed the small black object on the table. It looked like a cell phone of some kind.

Chapter 34

Carlos & Najee

"There are several brownstones in Brooklyn that have been fore-closed. I talked to DuPont Inc. and I believe that if we act now, we can negotiate acquiring those properties at below premium rate," Jennifer Rizzoti said to her boss.

"Mr. Trinidad," Brett Trousdale harped on. "I must tell you that I believe Venegas Realties is making a big mistake by investing in that Hill Tower project. It's on the lower Eastside for Christ sakes. I know some people down there who say that eventually the project is gonna lose more money than it makes. I talked—"

"Excuse me. I have to take this call." I saw my emergency cell phone was vibrating on the table. I picked it up and answered, "Hello?" I listened for a minute then said, "Jen, Brett, please excuse me for a moment. This is a private call that I must take. I trust you both to make the appropriate decisions on your own."

I held the phone on my shoulder until the room was clear. Then I calmly said, "What happened?" I listened in silence and stunned to the latest report. "I'm leaving, right now! I'll be there in one hour. Meet me at the airport."

Thirty minutes later I was on a chartered plane heading back to DC.

"Benito, what the fuck happened?" I asked as soon as I was inside the Maybach.

"Somebody hit Mamacita's."

"Was it robbed? What? Hit it how?"

Benito pulled out an assorted roll of Tums and popped one into his mouth. Then he chewed it up. "Not robbed, mi amigo, hit. As in fourteen people killed, hit. Roberto and Javier were killed in the of-fice. The room was searched but nothing was taken. Ortega was killed at the counter. Everyone else including the customers were killed Lit—"

"Wait a minute. You said little Manuel. What Manuel?"

"Mrs. Castonas youngest son, Manuel. Emmanuel Vasquez's son."

The words that Benito said pierced my heart. Manuel Vasquez was an only child. His father was killed in the war with Armando Ruelas. I promised his family that I could take care of the boy. Now he was dead. "He was only fifteen-years-old."

"I know, comrade, I know. The detectives say he surprised the killers as he came out of the kitchen with food. Two men were seen leaving the scene. One was dressed like the UPS. We believe that they were the killers."

I was too shocked to respond at first, then I got myself together and said, "Let me make sure I understand you, Benito. Two men walked into my cafe, in broad daylight and killed thirteen people and a boy? And nobody inside the cafe that survived saw or heard a thing?"

"That's exactly what I'm saying, Carlos."

"But who—" I turned to Benito. "Angel? The dude she deals with now?"

"I don't know yet, comrade. We can't rule them out. I talked to some friends about large shipments of cocaine and our friend Najee. Apparently, a large shipment of cocaine was stolen in New Jersey, from a man that worked for Muhammad Farad Shahid. Shahid runs an organization in New York, Connecticut, and New Jersey. His people say that a man named Najee worked under a man named Muqtar Kareem. Kareem was killed in his home as his wife watched. She was spared. The man called Najee took the cocaine and fled. That, my friend, is how he flooded your city with cocaine. At some point, he hooked up with Angel and the shit, as they say, is history."

"Does anyone know anything about this Najee?" I asked.

"Born and raised in the mean streets of Newark. Commands a large organization. A formidable opponent has the city of Newark afraid to sleep at night. He has no idea what he's gotten into and I don't think he cares. I believe Angel has figured it out that we killed Face and Doodie. I'm not one-hundred sure, but I'd wager and say that Angel and Najee are behind these attacks—"

196

Benito stopped mid-sentence and answered his cellphone. I saw the look that crossed his face and knew that whatever he was hearing on the phone wasn't good.

"More bad news, comrade," Benito said and reached for a drink out of the refrigerator. "Salaazar's just blew up. The restaurant is gone. There were no survivors."

I sat back and digested the information that I had just been given. Two of my establishments was attacked on the same day. I couldn't believe it. What angered me, even more, was the possible role that Angel played in it all. What had I done to her, but help her? Why would she turn against me? Doesn't she know that I will crush her whole existence? I silently hoped that I found out that Angel was innocent in all of this. But something inside me told me that she wasn't.

"Go to Mrs. Castonas and give her my condolences. I want you to give her a million dollars for her family. Set up a fund that will pay for all the funerals and burial of all people killed in the cafe and Salaazar's. Go to Marta's father, Javier's wife and children, Roberto's parents and girlfriend, and Ortega's family and extend our condolences and grief. Assure them all that justice for their loved ones will be swift. Then find out if Angel and Najee are at war with us. If they are, find them so that I can kill them all personally."

***

"Ayo, son where the fuck did you learn that shit?" I asked Tye as we rode down M Street.

"What are you talking about, fam?" Tye responded.

"You know what the fuck I'm talking about, nigga. Where did you learn to blow shit up like that?"

"Fam, you'd be surprised what a muthafucka can learn on the Internet. They got all kinds of *How To* websites on that joint. They sell dynamite, C-4, and all that shit. I think I learned that shit because I had too much time on my hands when I was up North. I had a cellphone in my cell that had Internet access. I learned all kinds of shit.

"What y'all wanna do? Call it a night or hit one more spot?" I asked Tye and Gunz.

"Fuck it, baby boy lets hit one more joint. On that list is a street or somethin' where your man said them migo niggas hand over the work for Carlos, right?"

"Yeah," I replied as I checked the list again. "It says here that all them muthafuckas are on 15th Street. 15th and Park Road, Monroe, Newton, and Spring Road. They also hang in a pool hall on 16th Street."

"Let's go through all them shits, baby boy, and fuck shit up."

"That's a bet, son. Tye, let me drive."

AT 2:36 a.m. we hit the pool hall. The pool hall was owned and operated by a Trinidad associate named Vito Marquez. I wanted to send a message to Carlos Trinidad. I can hit all your spots whenever I like it.

"Gunz, let's do this. I'm gonna drive right in front of the joint. You and Tye run up in there and light up everything moving. Then run back to the car and I'll get us outta here."

"You got that, baby boy. C'mon Tye."

I drove the car up to the entrance to the pool hall that was packed with people. I had barely stopped the car before Gunz and Tye leaped out and ran into the pool hall. For the next two minutes, all I heard was gunshots. That Calico fully is a bad muthafucka. A blur in front of me caught my attention. The only thing that registered in my brain was *gun* a Hispanic man was running toward the pool hall with a gun drawn.

"Aye!" I yelled

The man stopped in his tracks, turned, and faced me. I put a bullet in his head and one in his chest. Then I ran over and finished him off just as Tye and Gunz were exiting the pool hall. We all jumped into the car and I pulled off.

"What happened back there, fam?" Tye asked.

"Some muthafucka wanted to be a hero but got sent on his way," I replied.

"Ayo, baby boy?"

"What's the deal, son?"

"How long do you think it'll be before that nigga Carlos figures it out that it's you that's on his ass?" Gunz asked.

"Who knows. But in the meantime, I'ma keep coming at his ass."

Anthony Fields

Chapter 35

Angel

"This is Maria Wilson for City Under Siege Fox News, reporting to you live from the 300 Block of 16th Street N.E. As you can see behind me, the DC Police have cordoned off the entire block here to search for clues as to why a popular Hispanic pool hall was targeted by gunmen. Apparently, forty-five minutes ago, two men walked into Pappito's Pool Hall and opened fire.

Witnesses say that a late model Nissan Maxima pulled up in front of the hall and two men got out. The two men proceeded into the pool hall and opened fire indiscriminately. Moments later, an unidentified man rushed to the scene of the gunfire but was killed by the driver of the Maxima. Fox News is unsure at the time of exactly how many people are dead here. Sources close to the scene put the death toll at close to twenty, with several wounded.

As more about this grizzly crime becomes available, Fox News—wait a minute—Fox News has just learned that authorities are calling this a retaliator crime. We've just been informed that certain Hispanic gangs are said to be at war. The spot here at Pappito's is believed to be in retaliation for an earlier drive-by shooting that took place a few blocks away from here. Fox News has received information on all the recent violence including the killing of fourteen people in a cafe that are all connected. We—"

I clicked the flat-screen TV off and paced the floor. DC Police thought that rival Hispanic street gangs were feuding. DC Police don't know shit. The Latino street gangs in DC were small-time thugs and snatch-a-pocketbook type shit. They killed a member or two every now and then, but not like this. I thought about the cafe on 14th Street that was shot up—Fourteen people dead, the restaurant in Georgetown that Carlos had taken me to one day, blown up—twenty-four people killed, the drive-by shooting on 15th Street that left six people dead and now the pool hall.

None of that was the work of MS-13. Vatos Locos or the 1-5 Amigos. It was Najee. The war had begun, and I was powerless to stop it. After finding Carlos's letter the other day and remembering all the numbers that I had for him I called him, but what he had put in the letter was a lie. My numbers will never change, they had changed and I had no way of getting in contact with him.

Now things were too far gone to stop. Najee and his men had taken the war right to Carlos's doorstep in a way. They targeted all the places where they must've heard that Carlos owned or frequented. There was no way in the world that Carlos would allow what he had done to pass. How had Najee obtained his info about Carlos?

When I first heard about the UPS truck and the fact that one of the gunmen from the cafe shooting was dressed like a UPS worker, I knew it was Najee. That same ruse he pulled here was the same one he pulled in Newark. He told me all about it. As I paced the floor, my heart told me to contact Najee. I needed to make him understand just how much I love him and that we were meant to be together.

I had to make him see that he could trust me and that it wasn't too late to abandon his attack on Carlos. That's when I decided right then and there that I had to hit the streets and find a way to reach Carlos. Somebody in the game must know how to reach him. He has to hear me out, and if he doesn't, I'll kill him myself.

Chapter 36

Carlos & Susan

"Benito, my patience is wearing thin. I want them found today, not tomorrow. Today! I was upset and I had to let that be known. "Would somebody please tell me where I can find this Najee character, his men and Angel? Angel should be the easiest to find. Why can't we find her?"

"Carlos, I am trying my best to locate them. You have to remember that Najee is not from the city—"

"You're right, Benito, he's not from the city. So, please explain to me how he knows that I grew up on 15th Street? How did he find out that I own Mamacita's and Salazar's? How does he know to hit Pappito's pool hall? Please tell me that."

"He has help—"

"Which brings me to my next question. If Angel is assisting him, how does she know my personal business? And why am I not asking her that, right now, instead of you?"

"Angel has done a pretty good job of making herself hard to find, mi amigo. She owns business all over and shows up at none of them. I have people staked out at every place where she's known to go. So far we have nothing."

"You have nothing? *You have nothing!*"

"I miscalculated."

The look I gave Benito shot daggers at him. "You say you miscalculated?" I was unable to believe what I had just heard.

"Let me finish, instead of just killing Najee when we had the chance—"

"And when did you have the chance, Benito?"

"When I knew for sure who it was that was flooding the city with cocaine. Najee owns and operates a small record label based right here in DC. He calls it real Nigga Records. I had knowledge of his whereabouts because I love to party with the groups that he manages. I could have caught him at any number of nightclubs in and around the metro area. But I decided that maybe we should at least try to recoup some of the money we lost. When I was unable to contain the info that I needed, killed whoever I felt had betrayed us or stood against us. I could've killed Najee at any time—but as I said, I miscalculated."

Enraged, I threw my glass in the fireplace. "Benito, we have been friends for over forty years, right?" Benito nodded. "At what point in time did I start an exceptional excuse such as that?"

"Comrade, I am the age iteration you say. I cannot and will not dispute any of it. I have spoken to Muhammad Farad Shahid. His organization wants to come down here and get—"

"No!"

"But Carlos, that would take the whole mess out of our hands and we can focus solely on Angel and her role in—"

"I said no, Benito. I will not have outsiders coming into my city to clean up for me. It makes the Organization look weak and it opens us up for a backdoor play. Before you know it, we'll have all kinds of outsiders here and they will try to stay and drink from our fountain. I cannot accept that. We will deal with Najee ourselves. I want you to call, Mr. Shading and tell him to send us any photos that they have of Najee and anybody else that may be with him here in DC."

"I will do this as soon as we finish here. I know what kind of cars Angel and Najee both drive. I know where they do business. I have a man at each place of business. If either one of them surfaces, they will die. It's as simple as that."

"Is it Benito?" I said sarcastically and left the room.

I walked upstairs to my room and shut the door. I grabbed the phone and placed a call.

She answered on the second ring. "Hello?"

"Susan it's me, Carlos."

"What is it?" she replied groggily.

"I need to see you?"

"When?"

"Now, I need you now."

"Now? I can't—"

"I need you to come here, now. Tonight. Don't disappoint me, Susan. Be here in the next hour. Goodbye."

Rain poured down on the windshield of my car as I maneuvered the Jaguar slowly onto George Washington Parkway. The windshield wipers hummed a rhythm that almost lulled me back to sleep. *What did Carlos want? Why has he summoned me to Chevy Chase at 1:08 a.m.? What could be so important?* I slipped out of bed without waking my husband. If he woke up and found me gone, what would I tell him? How could I explain my absence?

Grant would be frantic. He was an overprotective husband that smothered me sometimes and I didn't like that. But I love him dearly and would never leave him for anything in the world. Being Mrs. Grant Rosenthal afforded me prestige in Washington that opened all sorts of doors for me. My husband is the most powerful lobbyist in the country. He was one of the reasons that I was about to be appointed District Attorney after Samuel Crowder retires in a year. I know that I owe my husband a good deal and I will honor that, but my loyalty to Carlos is just as intense.

I never realized that I had a secret desire for Latinos until I graduated from Law School and came to Washington. I was a fledgling prosecutor working at the US Attorney's Office when I prosecuted a case against a Hispanic man named Ricardo Lopes. His case was a murder for hire case and Ricardo was cooperating with us to get a woman that hired him to kill her husband. Every time I was alone with Ricardo, my hormones got all screwed up. Then one night it just happened. I acted upon my ellipses and fucked Ricardo.

It was the first time I had cheated on Grant who was my fiance then. After Ricardo came other men of Latino descent. But none of those affairs became serious until I met Carlos Trinidad. He changed my life like no other.

"Susan, I need your help," I said as I rose from the couch to greet her. "Take off those wet clothes and let go and sit by the fireplace. It'll warm you as we speak."

Susan shed her coat but left her thin nightgown on. She sat down on the floor and drew her legs up under her. "This must be important. You got me out of bed to hear it. So, what is it?"

"I have a problem. A serious problem. There are people loose in the city and they are killing my friends and associates."

"I'm sorry to hear that, Carlos, but what do you want to from me?" Susan replied.

"The situation is getting out of control. These men are out of control. Are you familiar with the shootings at the crew on—"

"Fourteenth Street?"

"Yes. And the shooting on 15th Street, at the pool hall and a restaurant blowing up in Georgetown—"

"The gangs are feuding—"

"There is no feed amongst the gangs, Susan. The feud is between these individuals and me. Remember when I told you about Angel—"

"Kareemah El-Amin?"

"Yes, her. And remember when I told you that she had joined another team?"

"I remember."

"Well, that team is named Najee and he's making my life miserable. At the moment, my people cannot find him or Angel. They know of places to hide in the city that I don't. I need to find them today so that they can't cause no more harm to my associates or by businesses. That's why I called you here tonight. Time is of the essence.

"What can I do for you, Carlos? How can I help?"

"I am waiting for pictures of Najee and his associates. You have pictures of Angel already. I want you to get the police to put out a citywide watch for all of them. Say that they are wanted for questioning or whatever you have to say to get them to cooperate Once they are in custody, I will send Dorothy to get them and take them to a location of my choice and they will simply disappear. Your office works closely with the DC Police, they'll do whatever you ask. When I give you their pictures you can broadcast them all on TV. I need you to put all of this in effect today, starting with Angel. I have vowed not to rest until they are found."

"I will help you, Carlos. You know I would, I will take care of everything. Now I must go before Grant wakes up and find me gone."

I caught Susan in my arms as she rose from the floor and embraced her. I kissed her soft lips and tasted her tongue. Then my hand went between her legs and the orange sheer material of her panties. My fingers bypassed that and went directly to that warm and wet place between her legs. Her body started to respond to my touch.

"Car-r-l-o-o-s—st-o-p-p—I-t—I h-a-v-e—to—g-g-g-o-o!"

I covered Susan's mouth with my own to muffle her protest. Then I laid her down on the floor by the fireplace and made love to her.

The next day, Benito came to me with the news that the photos from Newark had arrived. He handed me the envelope and I opened it. Finally, I was able to put a face on my headache. I extracted the photos and looked carefully at each one. Each one was attached to a small piece of paper that explained who the person was. The first photo was of the dead man Muqtar that Najee had allegedly killed and stolen the coke from. The second photo was of two men. The man on the left was named Gerald Minnis also known as Gunz.

He was Najee's right-hand man in Newark and was rumored to have several bodies under his belt. The man on the right was Hasan Sharif and he was deceased. The last photo had to be of Najee. I looked at the photo and my heart stopped. I felt as if I was suspended in time. The face that stared back at me was like a blast from the past. But how could it be? I shook my head and tried to clear my eyes as if that would change what I was seeing.

The shape of the face, the complexion, the hair, the nose, and cheekbones. The eyes. It was the eyes that confirmed what I already knew, the face has aged since I had seen it last, but it was the same face. It was the same face that appeared in the photo Maria sent me seventeen years ago. A month before her and her husband's death. Exactly twelve years after she left DC and fled to New Jersey.

Her mother was from Newark and she wanted to raise the baby there, our baby. She later married a man there. He had a funny name. What was it, again? I thought long and hard for a minute and then it came to me. His name was Nadeem. Nadeem Bashir. I stared at the photo and wondered why life had dealt me another set of trick cards? Whose idea was it to place this cruel twist of fate in my lap? I couldn't believe the sudden turn of events. I put the picture of Najee in my pocket before going to my office to fax the remaining photos to Susan. I had to find a way to deal with Najee personally. After all, he was my son.

Chapter 37

Honesty

This bitch has more lives than a lucky cat. What the hell does she have that everybody else doesn't? A guardian angel? I was still fuming about the failed attempt on Angel's life a week ago. Everything had been set up perfectly. The pieces fell the way they needed to, and she was marked. There was no way in the world Angel was supposed to survive that hit. But she did and I was pissed as we drove away from the scene that day I just knew Angel was dead. Trigger and I both fired direct shots at her.

There was a dude with her that eventually pushed her out of the line of fire, but she had already been hit. I saw that with my own eyes. I know for a fact she took a bullet to the chest in the heart area. I told Trigger as we rode away that we should have run over to the sidewalk and made sure she was dead. But he talked me out of that. Now, look at me.

Here I am, hiding out and waiting to get another shot at her. Ain't no telling when that's gonna be. Frustration set in as I sat on the sofa and watched a movie on DVD. *How long must I wait to have my revenge?* Six months have already passed since the day we shot at each other in my house. I was ready to end it all so that I could move on with my life. Rage, vengeance, and lust for justice consumed me every day and it was affecting my relationship with Trigger.

"You sleep, eat, and shit thinking about that bitch," Trigger said to me one day.

I remember getting mad but I knew he was right. What I really wanted to say was, "You wait until somebody kills your parents and then tries to kill you and see how you feel about that."

But I held my tongue. Kept my mouth closed and plotted. There had to be another way to get Angel. The next time I get the opportunity to get anywhere near her, I am not leaving until I know for sure she's dead. I remember how I watched the news all day that day we shot her outside of her clothing store. I was excited and anxious for the news broadcast to announce that a woman had been killed on Pennsylvania Avenue in the Southeast. When nothing was mentioned I knew we had failed. I cried and went off on Trigger.

When I finally calmed down, I was able to refocus and reevaluate. That's where I am today, still refocusing and reevaluating. I had called and texted Kia a million times but got no reply. I needed her to contact me again in case Angel came to the store again. She was the key, I was able to effectively turn a person in each of her businesses against Angel. I used money to conquer them and so far, it has worked. Money was the root of all evil. When big face money spoke, everybody listened.

I picked up my cell and dialed Sunnie. She answered on the third ring. "Hello?"

"Sunnie, it's me, Honesty."

"Hey girl, what can I do for you?

"Sunnie, I wanna redirect my attention."

"Honesty, I am at work, right now—"

'Sunnie, just write this down, okay?"

"Okay, shoot."

"Try and find any people with the El-Amin last name. Angel said that she had a baby. A daughter. Her daughter has to be at least eight or nine years old now and in the system somewhere. She has to have her last name. The name El-Amin is not common. If we can find her daughter, mother, father, brother, whoever, maybe that'll help me find her."

"I don't know, Honesty. They do have privacy laws that have—"

"Please Sunnie! I won't bother you anymore after this, I swear. And I got five-thousand dollars for you.

"Okay, okay. Five grand, huh? Give me a few days and I might have something for you. Bye."

I put my phone back on the jack and relaxed on the sofa. Why hadn't I thought of that before? If I found Angel's mother or one of her relatives, I could be in a better position to find her and kill her. If only Sunnie comes through for me.

Ring! Ring! Ring!

I awoke out of a deep sleep and mugged the telephone as if the phone itself was responsible for breaking my sleep. Beside me, Trigger stirred. I tried not to wake him as I grabbed the cordless received. "Hello?"

"Honesty?

"Sunnie?"

"Hey girl, I got—"

"Sunnie, what time is it?"

"It's four o'clock in the morning. You know I'm an early riser. Anyhow, I did it."

"You did what?"

"I found her."

"Angel?" I sat up in the ed.

"No, not her. Her mother, I think. I ran a check through all the database but came up blank. Then I remembered that you told me Angel had been to jail before. I know that once you catch any kind of charge in the district, you become a part of their system whether you were convicted, acquitted, case dismissed or whatever, you still become a part of their system. That system is called the W.A.I.I.C. system. It's connected to the N.C.I.C computers. Well, I hacked into their system and put Kareemah El-Amin in, and I hit pay dirt. In their system, she has a lot of family members on file. But most are either deceased or have no fixed addresses. Her mother runs a non-profit organization. She's listed as Naimah El-Amin. I took her mother's name and ran it through the DC Tax Bureau and came up with an address and phone number. Although she still pays taxes in the District, Angel's mother resides in Maryland. Get a pen and I'll give you what I have."

My spirits soared as I went to get a pen and paper. Maybe Angel wasn't so lucky after all. "Sunnie, I'm back. Go ahead."

"Like I said, her mother's name is Naimah El-Amin, her address is 6708 Deborah Drive in Clinton Maryland. The phone number is 301-694-2536. Do you want anything else?"

"That's all I need, for now, Sunnie. Let me go before I wake up my boo."

"A'ight girl, call me. Bye."

The good news that I had just receive had me in a celebratory mood. I got back into bed and reached under the covers until I had Trigger's dick in my fist. I stroked his dick until it became hard. Then I put my head under the covers and took him in my mouth. I heard soft moans escape from Trigger's mouth as I put my throat and neck game down. Once I knew that he was fully awake and turned on I pulled him out of my mouth and rose to meet his face. I kissed Trigger long and had.

"Baby I feel a little better now."

"That's good because your attitude has been real shitty lately," Trigger responded as he gently rubbed one of my nipples.

"Do you know that thing you been tryna get me to do for the longest?"

"What?"

"You know. The thing you've been tryna get me to do and I always tell you no."

"Oh, that?"

"Yeah, that. I'm in a freaky good mood and I just realized how special you are to me. It's the least I can do to give you whatever you want sexually. You constantly give me all of you, so I've decided to give you all of me."

"All of you?"

"All of me. When I was a little girl, I did the thing that little girls do. But now that I'm a woman, I must put the childish things away and do the things that women do. So, go and get the baby oil gel and let's make me a complete woman."

"Baby, I love you," Trigger said as he hopped up on a flash and ran to the bathroom to get the gel. He came back into the room with a devilish look in his eyes and passion in his heart. "I'ma go slowly and if it hurts you can just tell me to stop, a'ight?"

"A'ight. How do you want me?" I asked.

"It'll be easier for you if you lay on your stomach."

I complied and completely gave myself to Trigger. We fought for a while and wrestled around until he was inside home. I cried a few tears and then became overwhelmed by the pleasure. It became so intense that it negated all the discomfort and pain. When it was all over, I was in love all over again. Trigger was the sole owner of my heart, my mind, and my body. I was still in pain as I laid there but I didn't tell him that.

Trigger went to the bathroom and came back with warm, wet, soapy washcloths and gently cleaned me up down there. I noticed that there was a little blood on the washcloth. I didn't bleed when he broke me in so I never felt the way I did now. Seeing the blood made me feel like we had crossed a different line. An invisible line that had never been crossed. When a person joined a gang, they had to be jumped in. The blood that leaked was like a rite of passage. That's how I felt. I felt more connected to Trigger now, blood in, blood out, baby. We are forever bonded by my blood.

A few minutes later, my mind focused back on Angel and the info that I now possessed. "Baby?"

"What's up, True?"

"Would you die for me?"

"For sure. And you know that."

"Would you kill for me?"

"You know the answer to that already, too."

He was right. I did know the answer to all my questions, but I wanted to hear him answer them anyway. "Do you know where we can get uniforms, disguises, and costumes from?"

"Yeah. The Sonny Surplus off Minnesota Avenue. Why?"

"I'll tell you when we get there later," I said and grabbed the oil gel off the floor. I squeezed a generous amount onto my fingers and then rubbed the hell all over my ass. "C'mon, let's do it again."

"Do I what again?" Trigger smirked and said.

"You want me to say it, huh?"

"Yeah."

"So, you like it when I talk dirty, huh?"

"Without a doubt. What do you wanna do again? Tell me."

"I want you to fuck me in my ass again. I love that shit."

"Is that right? Well, I'll tell you what. Get up on your knees. I'ma fuck that ass doggy style. You think you can handle that?"

"Do I have a choice?" I asked as I got on all fours and spread my cheeks." Trigger took his position behind me and entered me slowly.

"I guess you don't."

By the time he was all the way in, I was cumming. I gotta get some mirrors put up in here.

Chapter 38

Najee & Gunz

"According to this list, there's a car lot on U Street that's owned by a dude named Felix Cardona. He's an enforcer in the Trinidad Organization. He's next up on my list," Najee announced to his men as they sat around the living room in his apartment. Tye and Gunz were busy playing video games on the Xbox.

"A'ight, baby boy, it's whatever. We can talk about that as soon as I get through beating Tye's ass in Madden."

"Fuck you talking about, fam? I'm beating that ass twenty-one to six. Ain't no coming back from that shit."

"Nigga, I play this shit for bread and meat, if I don't win I don't eat," Gunz said and scored a touchdown. He ran for the 2-point conversion and got that, too. "Twelve-twenty-one, nigga. Like I said, I'm beat that ass."

I laid back on the couch and thought about Angel. If I said that I didn't miss her, I'd be lying. I missed her like hell. I wanted to call her and hear her voice, but I couldn't. That would be showing weakness. I had to stick to my guns and be firm. When Carlos was dead, I promised myself then, and only then would I go to her. Her daughter didn't know Carlos as a father anyway, so I could step right in and fill that position. I wanted to be in her daughter's life because I was in love with Angel.

I accepted her and whoever came with her. I closed my eyes and tried to envision her sitting there with me. I imagined myself holding her. The mind was so powerful that I could smell her perfume as I held her. Then I kissed her and fell asleep.

"Naj! Najee, wake up, baby boy!"

I woke up and see Gunz standing in front of me. I looked around the room and saw that Tye was knocked out sleep on the floor. "I'm up, son, what's the deal?"

"Ayo, baby boy, I'm about to hit the fish spot down the street. I'm starvin' in this bitch. That muthafuckin' tree we copped from up the street was fire. I need to get my grub on, son, no bullshit. You want something from that joint?"

"I'm good, son."

"Baby boy, you ain't good. You ain't shit in about two days. That ain't cool, son. All that lovesick puppy shit, that ain't for gangstas. You going soft on me and that ain't a good look. In the movies when niggas start getting soft, the gang will kill them niggas for that shit. You know that, right?"

"Son, I ain't tryna hear that shit," I replied with a smile. "Fuck you think we on *American Me* or something? Fuck wrong with you?"

"Don't make me put that knife in your ass then, baby boy. I mean that shit," Gunz said as he walked out the door.

"Nigga, fuck you!" I shouted at the door and went back to sleep.

Najee thinks a nigga playing with his ass. I'm all the way street and that's the way it is. Money over bitches, straight like that. If a nigga falls in love, I'm not against that, but there's a time and a place for all that shit. Right now, is not the time. I drove down Bowen Road and hit Sheridan. From there I hit MLK Avenue. In minutes, I was pulling into the parking lot of the Horace and Dickie's Fish Market. They had the best fried fish I ever tasted. I walked into the crowded carryout and waited my turn to place my order.

When I finally got to the counter I said, "Gimme the six-piece Whiting fillet on wheat bread, a side order of Macaroni and cheese, twelve chicken wings, a boat of fries and a large lemonade and iced tea mixed."

While I was waiting for my food, I decided to call home in Newark and check on things. I was so engrossed in my call that I never paid attention to the three cops that walked into the spot. By the time I looked up and saw them, the people were calling my number. I went to the counter to get my food. In my hast, I dropped a few coins as I tried to balance both bags of food in my arms.

One of the cops closest to me bend down and picked up the coins. "Here you go, buddy," the cop said.

We locked eyes momentarily as I said, "Thanks."

I thought I saw a hint of recognition pass through the cops' eyes, but that wasn't possible. So, I kept it moving out of the store. I got to the parking lot and opened the door to the used Ford Expedition that we had just copped. I put the food in the passenger seat. I looked over my shoulder and saw that the cop was still looking in my direction. I got a little nervous and it showed. I went to put the key in the ignition after closing the driver's side door, but I fumbled, and the key fell on the floor. As I reached down to pick up the keys, I heard a knock on the window. I raised up and looked out the window. It was the cop that was just inside the store. Knowing I hadn't done anything, I calmed myself and rolled the window down.

"What's the problem officer?"

"Sir, can you please step out of the vehicle?"

Instinctively I looked to my right and saw that the truck was now surrounded by the other cops. They each had their weapons drawn. I didn't know what was going on, but I did know that I was outmanned and outgunned.

"Sir, keep your hands where I can see them, and please step out of the vehicle! Don't make me ask you again! Do it now, sir!"

I thought about the handgun in my waist and the Calico machine gun in the back of the truck. I couldn't forget the fact that it was the one I had just used in the pool hall killing. Damn! I fucked up. For a brief moment, I thought about holding court right there in the parking lot. But that thought quickly faded as I realized whatever they found on me would be the result of an illegal search and seizure.

I put my hands up and stepped out of the truck. I looked around and saw a crowd that had started to gather. I thought about Najee and Tye in the apartment up the street and wished that I could reach them. The cell phone on my hip vibrated and vibrated, but I couldn't answer while handcuffed.

Ring! Ring! Ring!

The sound of the phone woke me out of my sleep. I grabbed the phone off the floor and answered it. The caller ID told me that the caller was George.

"Ger, what the deal, son?"

"Najee, y'all hot, slim."

217

"What the fuck you talking about, son? Who hot?" I exploded into the phone.

"Naw, slim. Not that kinda hot. Hot as in ten people is onto y'all."

I woke up completely and said, "What people? Them people on too who?"

"Turn on the TV slim and see what people I'm talking about." I crossed the room in a flash and clicked on the TV. "What channel?"

"Fox News, Channel 5."

I put the TV on channel 5 and sat back down.

"Two men that may be connected to a siting of murders in the District. DC Police are asking for information into the whereabouts of this man. Gerald Minnis is thirty-one-years old, six feet tall, and about two-hundred pounds. He may be going by the nickname Gunz. He is to be considered armed and extremely dangerous. DC Police are also asking for the public's help in locating Kareemah El-Amin. Kareemah El-Amin, also known as Angel, is five-feet-three and one-hundred and thirty pounds. If anyone has any information about either one of these people, please contact DC Police at 202-724-5645. Again that number is 202-724-5645. If you are just tuning in."

I couldn't believe my eyes or ears, was I still asleep and having a bad dream?

"Najee? Najee?"

I put my phone up to my ear. "I'm here."

"Slim y'all can't stay in DC another day."

Then it hit me, I looked around the living room. I pushed open the door I expected to see Gunz lying across the bed, but he wasn't there.

I called his name, "Gunz!" I checked the bathroom and the balcony. No luck.

Tye woke up out of his sleep. "Najee, what's the deal fam? Why you shouting like that, fam?"

"Did Gunz ever come back from the store?" I asked frantically.

Wearing a puzzled look on his face, Tye replied, "I have no clue, fam. What store did you go to?"

I ignored Tye and ran outside to see if the truck and Gunz were outside. When I got outside and saw that the truck and Guns were I became afraid. I went back inside and picked up my cell phone. I called Gunz on the cell his answering machine picked up. I called back again and again but he never picked up.

"What am I being charged with officer?" I asked one of the cops once we reached the police station.

"I don't know, buddy. We were told to bring you in for questioning your picture has been all over the TV since this morning. Someone will come and talk to you shortly. You'll probably be charged with the gun we got off of you, though. I don't know." The cop locked me in a cage and walked away.

What the fuck was he talking about? He said my picture had been on TV since this morning. How could that be? What the hell is going on? I Waited hours for someone to come and process me or question me but nobody came. I was vexed.

Then a pretty, light-skinned policewoman came and blocked my cage door.

"Minnis your ride's here."

"My ride? What ride," I said totally befuddled.

"Marshalls."

The pretty lady cop led me through a labyrinth of cubicles until I reached a side door. Sitting at a desk, filling out paperwork, was a young, looking woman with blonde hair. She was clad in blue are slacks and a dark blue T-shirt. She also wore a blue windbreaker jacket that had US Marshall emblazoned across it. She reminded me of Heather Locklear. The white lady Marshall put her own cuffs on me and locked them. Then she led me outside to an awaiting vehicle.

Where is she talking to me?

Once I was in the backseat and my seat belt was fastened, we hit the road. I wasn't in DC long, but I'd been there long enough to know that we were leaving the city.

"Marshal, where are we going?" I shot through the glass but received no reply.

The city of DC got farther and farther behind me. Alarms went off in my head and I knew that I was in trouble, deep trouble.

An hour late, I saw the Lady Marshal pull a cell phone and speak into it softly. I tried, but I couldn't make out what she was saying. A few minutes later, the Crown Victoria turned down a dirt road and kept going. Then it abruptly stopped.

"Ayo, Marshal. What the fuck is going on? Where the fuck am I?"

The bitch never responded. She got out of her car and leaned on the hood. About ten minutes after that, two cars pulled off the dirt road and stopped a few feet away from the car I was in. One of them was a new model Lexus and the second one was a Mercedes Benz Maybach. I watched as several men got out of both cars. My blood began to run cold as my heart momentarily stopped. None of the men looked all that meaning that wasn't what stopped my heart. It was the fact that each man approaching the vehicle I was in was Hispanic. The door to the car was snatched open and I was force-fully pulled from the backseat.

A tall, well-dressed Hispanic man stepped to the front of the crowd and said, "Gerald Minnis, right? Or should I call you Gunz?"

I never responded, but from the looks of things, the man knew me and I knew exactly who he was. A second later he confirmed what I already knew.

"Allow me to introduce myself. My name is Carlos. Carlos Trinidad."

Right then, at that moment, I knew I was about to die. This nigga looks just like Najee.

Chapter 39

Naimah El-Amin

"Umi, when am I gonna see my mommy again?"

I stared into the eyes of my grandchild. "You just saw her. Aniyah. She face-timed you, didn't she?

"Yes, she did but it's not the same. I wanna really see her. I miss her every day."

"I know, baby. I miss her, too. Insha Allah, she'll stop by to see us soon. Now go to sleep. Did you say your prayers?"

"No, I forgot 'em."

"Think real hard."

"Bismillah hir Rahman nir Raheem—Alhamdulillahi rabbil alameen—"

I listened to my granddaughter say her prayers, the love I felt for her was undeniable. "That's good, baby. Sleep tight and don't let the bedbugs bite."

Watching her laugh reminded me so much of the child that I lost. Thoughts of my daughter that was raped and killed always threatened to make me cry, so I put those thoughts out of my mind and focused on the one living child that I had left, Angel. I called her cell phone one more time but still got her voicemail. Then I texted her. //: *Call me.*

I called the phone at her house and still received no answer.

Angel where are you? Was she already in police custody? I made some phone calls but got zero information that was helpful to me. What had she done this time? That girl was a handful and a half. The streets had her mind and refused to let go. Every time I try to talk to her, she tells me nothing is going and that she's chilling. My mind flashed back to the news broadcast I had seen earlier asking for the public's help in locating Kareemah El-Amin.

"*Kareemah El-Amin also known as Angel is five-feet-three and one-hundred and thirty pounds.*"

I walked out of Aniyah's bedroom and went back downstairs. I needed a cup of coffee to calm my rattled nerves. Angel's name coming out on the news took me back. I remembered all the news broadcasts that said she was the female version of Playful Edmonds being that she was the youngest and the first female to take over D.C. drug trade. They depicted my baby as all sorts of things back then. They even had me believing that she was responsible for the deaths of over thirty people.

I heard the coffee machine beep and went to it. I poured myself a steaming hot cup of Taster's Choice, sipped it, and exhaled. It was good. I took my cup to the dining room table and sat down. It felt good to finally relax after being on my feet all day. Taking care of a nine-year-old is a job within itself, but I enjoyed it. Aniyah brought me satisfaction and joy that couldn't be replaced so I never complained even when times got rough.

No matter what I did or thought about, my thought always came back to Angel. Even though I haven't spoken to her in a few days, something inside me tells me she's okay. Call it a mother's intuition. But I still needed to hear her voice. I picked up the phone and Facetimed her. Then I called. When the voicemail kicked in I decided t to leave a message.

Beep! Beep!

"Assalamu Alaikum. Give me a ca—" A knock on my door stopped me. "Who is it?"

I hung up the phone and went to answer my door. I peeked through the peephole and saw two police officers. Here we go again. "Yes?"

"Ma'am we need to speak to you," the female officer said. "It's in regards to your daughter."

Thinking that something might be wrong with Angel, I quickly unlocked the door and snatched it open.

"What's wrong with my daughter?"

I stared into the face of the officers at my door. Something was all wrong, I could feel it. The female officer looked awfully young and the male officer had a tattoo on his neck.

"Ma'am can we step inside the house and talk?" this was from the male officer.

222

I stepped back and let them in my house. I locked the door behind me and then turn to say something, but my words got caught in my throat. In the light, it was easy to see that the uniform that the officer wear said, *Security*.

"What were you saying?"

The female sensed my concentration and saw me read the insignia on their uniforms. Before I could say another word she pulled a gun and point it at me.

"I need you to call your daughter and get her here," the female said. "Who else is in the house?"

"My granddaughter that's it," I said meekly. "What daughter are you talking about?"

"Don't waste my time, Mrs. El-Amin. I know exactly who you are and who your daughter is. You only have one daughter. The other one is dead. I don't wanna hurt you. All I want is Angel. If you give her to me by calling her and telling her to come here, I'll spare your life. If not, I swear on my mother's grave I'm gonna kill you. You decided."

The decision that she 'posed wasn't a hard one to make. I had always asked myself would I give my life to save one of my children. I never answered the question in my mind because I never thought I'd be faced with decisions like that to make. But there is was and here I was. I thought about Aniyah asleep upstairs and my eyes watered. I had failed us, I failed my daughter Adirah. I failed Angel and I failed my granddaughter, too. My life was over, and I knew it. I swallowed the lump in my throat and embraced it. Tears openly fell from eyes and I made no move to wipe them. My decision was made.

"I am a humble servant of Allah the most-high. If you kill me, I will be granted paradise. As a Muslima, I have lived my whole life waiting to return to Allah. I would never give up the life of my daughter to save my own. Do what you gotta do, Masha 'Allah'

Time seemed to move in slow motion, as I watched the female standing in front of me raise the gun.

"Have it your way," she said.

I first saw a flash of light and then nothing.

Anthony Fields

Chapter 40

Angel

By the time I got home, I was exhausted. After riding around all day trying to find somebody that knew how to get in touch with Carlos, I finally did. I remembered that Marvin told me one day a while ago that my homie Pretty B was hooked up with the Trinidad Organization. I went around the Circle looking for Marvin but couldn't find him. I rode up and down my old street hoping that I spotted his gold GMC Yukon Denali.

I turned down Hillside Road and saw a brand-new Mercedes 600 SL double-parked. I couldn't get around it because the street was too small. I blew my horn repeatedly until finally, the driver came out of one the tenements. I had to do a double-take but I was sure that the driver of the Benz was Pretty B gone were his long dreads and glasses. The man I saw had a low-cut fade with waves and the brightest hazel eyes I had ever seen.

I rolled my window down and called out to him, "Hey Pretty B? What's up?"

"Who that?"

"Angel."

"Angel? Little Muslim Angel?"

I got out of the car and kicked it with him for a while. I got a number for Carlos out of him and promised to hook up with him later. Then I came home. I decided to wait until tomorrow to call Carlos since it was kind of late. I'll call first thing in the morning.

I saw my cell phone lying on the coffee table and picked it up. As soon as I turned it on, the voicemail indicator popped on. Checking my messages was the last on my list of things to do, but I did it anyway

"You have twenty-three messages."

I hit the button to play the messages and silently prayed that one of the messages was from Najee.

Everybody and their mother had called me. One person even said that I was on TV. What was she smoking? The very last message was from my mother. I instantly felt bad about not calling her and checking in. I saw that she had attempted to facetime me. I knew she was worried about me. Plus, she probably wanted to tell me something about Aniyah. I looked at my watch. It was almost 11:30 p.m. then I saw the text message my mother had sent. *//: Call me.* It read.

I listened to my mother's message, then I listened to it again. Something she said didn't sit well with me.

I played the message again for the third time—

"Assalamu alaikum. Give me a call—Who is it?

I listened to the message a fourth time and then checked the time of the message, it came in at exactly 10:40 p.m. That was fifty minutes ago. Why had my mother said, *"Who is it?"* Who would've been at her door at that time of night? There had to somebody at the door and it scared her because she never got the chance to finish the message. I called my mother's house and waited for her to pick up. She never did. Now, one thing I know about my mother, she is a light sleeper. If she heard the phone, she would answer it. I kept calling and calling but my mother never picked up.

Something is wrong.

I grabbed my keys and ran to my car. I took the capital Beltway and got to Branch Avenue in ten minutes. It took me an additional ten minutes to pull up to my mother's front door. I jumped out of the car and left it running.

I ran up to the front door and bang on it. "Ma-Ma-a-a-a-a-a!"

I stood there near tears for a minute before my brain kicked in and I ran back to the BMW and pulled my keys of the ignition. My heart rate soared as I ran back to the door and opened it. I didn't make made it three feet before I saw her. I stopped dead in my tracks and stared at the body on the floor. Tears instantly flooded my eyes as the realization of what I was seeing set in. I walked up to my mother's body and saw the two, neat little holes in her forehead. Every limb on my body cried out in pain. I didn't know I was screaming. My mind needed to send me that signal. I dropped down to the floor and grabbed my mother. I gathered her up into my arms and cried. I rocked her slowly back and forth until it dawned on me that my daughter was in the house

"Aniyah!" I hollered as I laid my mother down and ascended the steps two at a time. I ran straight to her room hoping that she was still alive. I pushed open the door and turned on the light. Again, my breath got caught in my throat. I stopped in the spot where I stood and looked around the room. Her bed was empty.

"Aniyah, baby it's Mommy! Where are you, baby? Aniyah?"

I searched the whole upstairs and came up empty-handed. Where could she be? Who killed my mother?

The first person that came to mind was Carlos. Carlos had come to my mother's house and killed her. He took my daughter. An uncontrollable rage welled up inside of me. I was about to run downstairs and search for my daughter until I saw it. It was there right in my face, as plain as day but I never paid it any mind. On the end of Aniyah's dresser was a piece of paper. I walk over to the mirror and stared at what seemed to be a letter. I snatched it off the mirror and read it.

Dear Angel,

How does it feel to come home and find your mother dead! Not too good, huh? Well, now you know how I felt. I thought by killing your mother, we'd be even, but then I remembered that you killed my father, too. You were always one up on me, but not today. You killed my father and my mother. I killed your mother and took your daughter. Now we're even.

Honesty

I must've read that letter a hundred times before I realized that it was real. How did I slip and blunder so seriously? Didn't I know the law?

"Crush your enemies totally. Never stop halfway through total annihilation of them, lest they recover and come back for you!"

I let myself be blinded by arrogance, overconfidence, and love. The one person that I forgot all about never forgot about me and she came back for me.

To Be Continued...
ANGEL 3
Coming Soon

Submission Guideline

Submit the first three chapters of your completed manuscript to ldpsubmissions@gmail.com, subject line: Your book's title. The manuscript must be in a .doc file and sent as an attachment. Document should be in Times New Roman, double spaced and in size 12 font. Also, provide your synopsis and full contact information. If sending multiple submissions, they must each be in a separate email.

Have a story but no way to send it electronically? You can still submit to LDP/Ca$h Presents. Send in the first three chapters, written or typed, of your completed manuscript to:

LDP: Submissions Dept
Po Box 944
Stockbridge, Ga 30281

DO NOT send original manuscript. Must be a duplicate.

Provide your synopsis and a cover letter containing your full contact information.

Thanks for considering LDP and Ca$h Presents.

Coming Soon from Lock Down Publications/Ca$h Presents

BOW DOWN TO MY GANGSTA

By **Ca$h**

TORN BETWEEN TWO

By **Coffee**

THE STREETS STAINED MY SOUL **II**

By **Marcellus Allen**

BLOOD OF A BOSS **VI**

SHADOWS OF THE GAME II

By **Askari**

LOYAL TO THE GAME **IV**

By **T.J. & Jelissa**

A DOPEBOY'S PRAYER **II**

By **Eddie "Wolf" Lee**

IF LOVING YOU IS WRONG… **III**

By **Jelissa**

TRUE SAVAGE **VII**

MIDNIGHT CARTEL III

DOPE BOY MAGIC IV

CITY OF KINGZ II

By **Chris Green**

BLAST FOR ME **III**

A SAVAGE DOPEBOY III

CUTTHROAT MAFIA II

By **Ghost**

Angel 2

A HUSTLER'S DECEIT III
KILL ZONE **II**
BAE BELONGS TO ME III
A DOPE BOY'S QUEEN II
By **Aryanna**
COKE KINGS V
KING OF THE TRAP II
By **T.J. Edwards**
GORILLAZ IN THE BAY V
De'Kari
THE STREETS ARE CALLING II
Duquie Wilson
KINGPIN KILLAZ IV
STREET KINGS III
PAID IN BLOOD III
CARTEL KILLAZ IV
DOPE GODS II
Hood Rich
SINS OF A HUSTLA II
ASAD
KINGZ OF THE GAME V
Playa Ray
SLAUGHTER GANG IV
RUTHLESS HEART IV
By Willie Slaughter
THE HEART OF A SAVAGE III
By Jibril Williams

FUK SHYT II

By Blakk Diamond

FEAR MY GANGSTA 5

THE REALEST KILLAS

By Tranay Adams

TRAP GOD II

By Troublesome

YAYO IV

A SHOOTER'S AMBITION III

By S. Allen

GHOST MOB

Stilloan Robinson

KINGPIN DREAMS III

By Paper Boi Rari

CREAM

By Yolanda Moore

SON OF A DOPE FIEND II

By Renta

FOREVER GANGSTA II

GLOCKS ON SATIN SHEETS III

By Adrian Dulan

LOYALTY AIN'T PROMISED II

By Keith Williams

THE PRICE YOU PAY FOR LOVE II

DOPE GIRL MAGIC III

By Destiny Skai

CONFESSIONS OF A GANGSTA II

By Nicholas Lock

I'M NOTHING WITHOUT HIS LOVE II

By Monet Dragun

CAUGHT UP IN THE LIFE III

By Robert Baptiste

LIFE OF A SAVAGE IV

A GANGSTA'S QUR'AN II

By **Romell Tukes**

QUIET MONEY III

THUG LIFE II

By **Trai'Quan**

THE STREETS MADE ME III

By **Larry D. Wright**

THE ULTIMATE SACRIFICE VI

IF YOU CROSS ME ONCE II

ANGEL III

By **Anthony Fields**

THE LIFE OF A HOOD STAR

By Ca$h & Rashia Wilson

Available Now

RESTRAINING ORDER **I & II**

By **CA$H & Coffee**

LOVE KNOWS NO BOUNDARIES **I II & III**
By **Coffee**
RAISED AS A GOON I, II, III & IV
BRED BY THE SLUMS I, II, III
BLAST FOR ME I & II
ROTTEN TO THE CORE I II III
A BRONX TALE I, II, III
DUFFEL BAG CARTEL I II III IV
HEARTLESS GOON I II III IV
A SAVAGE DOPEBOY I II
HEARTLESS GOON I II III
DRUG LORDS I II III
CUTTHROAT MAFIA
By **Ghost**
LAY IT DOWN **I & II**
LAST OF A DYING BREED
BLOOD STAINS OF A SHOTTA I & II III
By **Jamaica**
LOYAL TO THE GAME I II III
LIFE OF SIN I, II III
By **TJ & Jelissa**
BLOODY COMMAS I & II
SKI MASK CARTEL I II & III
KING OF NEW YORK I II,III IV V
RISE TO POWER I II III
COKE KINGS I II III IV
BORN HEARTLESS I II III IV

KING OF THE TRAP

By **T.J. Edwards**

IF LOVING HIM IS WRONG…I & II

LOVE ME EVEN WHEN IT HURTS I II III

By **Jelissa**

WHEN THE STREETS CLAP BACK I & II III

THE HEART OF A SAVAGE I II

By **Jibril Williams**

A DISTINGUISHED THUG STOLE MY HEART I II & III

LOVE SHOULDN'T HURT I II III IV

RENEGADE BOYS I II III IV

PAID IN KARMA I II III

By **Meesha**

A GANGSTER'S CODE I &, II III

A GANGSTER'S SYN I II III

THE SAVAGE LIFE I II III

CHAINED TO THE STREETS I II III

By J-Blunt

PUSH IT TO THE LIMIT

By **Bre' Hayes**

BLOOD OF A BOSS **I, II, III, IV, V**

SHADOWS OF THE GAME

By **Askari**

THE STREETS BLEED MURDER **I, II & III**

THE HEART OF A GANGSTA I II& III

By **Jerry Jackson**

CUM FOR ME I II III IV V

Anthony Fields

An **LDP Erotica Collaboration**
BRIDE OF A HUSTLA **I II & II**
THE FETTI GIRLS **I, II& III**
CORRUPTED BY A GANGSTA I, II III, IV
BLINDED BY HIS LOVE
THE PRICE YOU PAY FOR LOVE
DOPE GIRL MAGIC I II
By **Destiny Skai**
WHEN A GOOD GIRL GOES BAD
By **Adrienne**
THE COST OF LOYALTY I II III
By Kweli
A GANGSTER'S REVENGE **I II III & IV**
THE BOSS MAN'S DAUGHTERS I II III IV V
A SAVAGE LOVE **I & II**
BAE BELONGS TO ME I II
A HUSTLER'S DECEIT I, II, III
WHAT BAD BITCHES DO I, II, III
SOUL OF A MONSTER I II III
KILL ZONE
A DOPE BOY'S QUEEN
By **Aryanna**
A KINGPIN'S AMBITON
A KINGPIN'S AMBITION **II**
I MURDER FOR THE DOUGH
By **Ambitious**
TRUE SAVAGE I II III IV V VI

236

DOPE BOY MAGIC I, II, III

MIDNIGHT CARTEL I II

CITY OF KINGZ

By **Chris Green**

A DOPEBOY'S PRAYER

By **Eddie "Wolf" Lee**

THE KING CARTEL **I, II & III**

By **Frank Gresham**

THESE NIGGAS AIN'T LOYAL **I, II & III**

By **Nikki Tee**

GANGSTA SHYT **I II &III**

By **CATO**

THE ULTIMATE BETRAYAL

By **Phoenix**

BOSS'N UP **I , II & III**

By **Royal Nicole**

I LOVE YOU TO DEATH

By Destiny J

I RIDE FOR MY HITTA

I STILL RIDE FOR MY HITTA

By **Misty Holt**

LOVE & CHASIN' PAPER

By **Qay Crockett**

TO DIE IN VAIN

SINS OF A HUSTLA

By **ASAD**

BROOKLYN HUSTLAZ

By **Boogsy Morina**

BROOKLYN ON LOCK I & II

By **Sonovia**

GANGSTA CITY

By **Teddy Duke**

A DRUG KING AND HIS DIAMOND I & II III

A DOPEMAN'S RICHES

HER MAN, MINE'S TOO I, II

CASH MONEY HO'S

By **Nicole Goosby**

TRAPHOUSE KING **I II & III**

KINGPIN KILLAZ I II III

STREET KINGS I II

PAID IN BLOOD **I II**

CARTEL KILLAZ I II III

DOPE GODS

By **Hood Rich**

LIPSTICK KILLAH **I, II, III**

CRIME OF PASSION I II & III

By **Mimi**

STEADY MOBBN' **I, II, III**

THE STREETS STAINED MY SOUL

By **Marcellus Allen**

WHO SHOT YA **I, II, III**

SON OF A DOPE FIEND

Renta

GORILLAZ IN THE BAY **I II III IV**

Angel 2

TEARS OF A GANGSTA I II

DE'KARI

TRIGGADALE I II III

Elijah R. Freeman

GOD BLESS THE TRAPPERS I, II, III

THESE SCANDALOUS STREETS I, II, III

FEAR MY GANGSTA I, II, III IV

THESE STREETS DON'T LOVE NOBODY I, II

BURY ME A G I, II, III, IV, V

A GANGSTA'S EMPIRE I, II, III, IV

THE DOPEMAN'S BODYGAURD I II

Tranay Adams

THE STREETS ARE CALLING

Duquie Wilson

MARRIED TO A BOSS... I II III

By Destiny Skai & Chris Green

KINGZ OF THE GAME I II III IV

Playa Ray

SLAUGHTER GANG I II III

RUTHLESS HEART I II III

By Willie Slaughter

FUK SHYT

By Blakk Diamond

DON'T F#CK WITH MY HEART I II

By Linnea

ADDICTED TO THE DRAMA I II III

By Jamila

Anthony Fields

YAYO I II III

A SHOOTER'S AMBITION I II

By S. Allen

TRAP GOD

By Troublesome

FOREVER GANGSTA

GLOCKS ON SATIN SHEETS I II

By Adrian Dulan

TOE TAGZ I II III

By Ah'Million

KINGPIN DREAMS I II

By Paper Boi Rari

CONFESSIONS OF A GANGSTA

By Nicholas Lock

I'M NOTHING WITHOUT HIS LOVE

By Monet Dragun

CAUGHT UP IN THE LIFE I II

By Robert Baptiste

NEW TO THE GAME I II III

By **Malik D. Rice**

LIFE OF A SAVAGE I II III

A GANGSTA'S QUR'AN

By **Romell Tukes**

LOYALTY AIN'T PROMISED

By Keith Williams

QUIET MONEY I II

THUG LIFE

240

Angel 2

By **Trai'Quan**

THE STREETS MADE ME I II

By **Larry D. Wright**

THE ULTIMATE SACRIFICE I, II, III, IV, V

KHADIFI

IF YOU CROSS ME ONCE

ANGEL I II

By **Anthony Fields**

THE LIFE OF A HOOD STAR

By **Ca$h & Rashia Wilson**

BOOKS BY LDP'S CEO, CA$H

TRUST IN NO MAN

TRUST IN NO MAN 2

TRUST IN NO MAN 3

BONDED BY BLOOD

SHORTY GOT A THUG

THUGS CRY

THUGS CRY 2

THUGS CRY 3

TRUST NO BITCH

TRUST NO BITCH 2

TRUST NO BITCH 3

TIL MY CASKET DROPS

RESTRAINING ORDER

RESTRAINING ORDER 2

IN LOVE WITH A CONVICT

LIFE OF A HOOD STAR

Coming Soon

BONDED BY BLOOD 2

BOW DOWN TO MY GANGSTA

Angel 2

CPSIA information can be obtained
at www.ICGtesting.com
Printed in the USA
LVHW022323131222
735147LV00003B/244

9 781952 936326